About the Author

Rory Forsyth is a British novelist born in Edinburgh. Rory specialises in fiction with an interest in both World Wars, the wilderness of Scotland, the history of London and the Golden Age of Piracy. In his novels, he writes on themes of love, the natural world, the complexity of families and the importance of place. Rory resides in London, a place which provides a base of inspiration for much of his writing.

A War of Secrets

Rory Forsyth

A War of Secrets

Olympia Publishers
London

www.olympiapublishers.com
OLYMPIA PAPERBACK EDITION

A CIP catalogue record for this title is
available from the British Library.

ISBN: 978-1-83543-152-8

This is a work of fiction.
Names, characters, places and incidents originate from the writer's
imagination. Any resemblance to actual persons, living or dead, is
purely coincidental.

First Published in 2025

Olympia Publishers
Tallis House
2 Tallis Street
London
EC4Y 0AB

Printed in Great Britain

Dedication

For William and Hugo

Acknowledgements

Thank you to my mother Fiona for so much, and to my late father for taking me to the battlefields when I was a boy. Alex Wilson for the Punchbowl chats, Tom Misselbrook for the NYC base, Alex Lowry for standing tall, Toby Cripps for drawings in Saint Rémy, Will Davies for listening and Tom Sleigh for understanding. Thanks to the Western Front Way team, Richard Mayon-White and all our contacts on the continent. Anthony Seldon for saying I should write this story and Andrew Derrick for the endless support. A special thank you to Amanda and Peter Carpenter, one of the main reasons I picked up a pen. Lastly, to Kim Steffen for getting me to persevere.

Part 1

Runner, Gunner, Rider, Prisoner

"No man is so foolish as to desire war more than peace: for in peace sons bury their fathers, but in war fathers bury their sons." – Herodotus

Prologue

Present Day, Arras

For over a century, this story remained buried in Europe, and as I was drawn into its centre, I met the man I fell in love with. The secrets that had haunted both our families for over a century were uncovered close to my home in France, on the banks of the River Scarpe by Arras, during a summer punctuated by great thunderstorms.

Our story concluded in a time of peace, but it was forged in the crucible of two World Wars. I thought I knew about war, about our family's role, and about the legacies left from living through such times, but I did not.

In conflict, as in love, the very best of us can come to light, but so too can the very worst. On the battlefields of France all those years ago, as the mask of a united Europe slipped again, that duality was played out not once, but twice.

There were scars left so deep that a century was needed for resolution, and for me alone to break one hundred years of grief. To survive war, and indeed love, some are bold and brave, others foolish and cruel and the figure at the centre of the secret, William, was all of these.

I understand why William did what he did in those woods. However, given what happened, how fate played its part and how he was judged, can a whole life be defined by a moment? Should he have been damned as he was? What does doing the right thing mean when the world is at war?

The story of the Bremners begins in the spring of 1917 with Jolyon Bremner, but even after 1945, when the world found peace, that family did not and neither did mine.

I used to pity them until I knew the truth and uncovered the mystery. Now I admire them, and I feel them with me when I walk along the river Scarpe amongst the rocks and the trees with the birds in the sky above.

This secret that haunted us for so long did lead me to the man I still love, and to me, that was a price worth paying.

Amélie Mulot

Chapter 1

April 1917, Arras
Runner

Behind Jolyon's sluggish expression was fear; all the youngest recruits tried to keep their terror secret, even from themselves. The perched Solomon stared down at the mud caked around his boots and banged his heels together. 'Within the hour,' he said.

Jolyon swallowed and heard a pop in his throat, his fingers rubbing the lighter Evelyn had given him in his pocket; the men would be assembling soon. He had been at this forward outpost on the frontline for three days now, judgement was close.

He had tried to rest, but between the constant chatter of nervous voices and machine guns ticking through the night, he hadn't done much but doze fitfully. All these noises were new to him, and his dreams had been full of unknown faces and tangled wire. He knew fate had already dealt its hand, all that remained now was to turn over the cards.

'Catch any sleep?' Solomon said through winding cigarette smoke, looking up at Jolyon. Solomon was always one of the first awake writing in his small black journal tied with fraying butcher's twine.

Jolyon let his head fold back against the damp parapet and shook his head.

Solomon popped the diary back into his breast pocket, 'How are those legs feeling? You've got some distance to do.'

Solomon was as close to a friend as Jolyon had in this place, but he had been told that forging strong bonds was foolish. He admired him though; he looked up to all those who had been sharpened in so many ways by the fight.

'I think I'm ready,' Jolyon said before standing, his sodden canvas sheet falling away from his shoulders. Running a hand across his jaw, he rolled his neck left and right looking up at the pinking dawn. Somewhere down the trench, a bagpiper was tuning up for the offensive, the notes hovering over them. Over the top of the trench by about half a mile to the west, he could see dense woodland, still strikingly untouched by shellfire and it looked curious in this barren landscape, and he wanted to go there and be away from all this, to be away from the fray.

A bird flew up from deep in the woodland and he watched the pigeon, the chalky wings clapping together, its tiny head looking down on these scars in the land. Jolyon was envious of how easily it escaped this place, unencumbered by wire, mud, and metal. In an easy arc, it sailed away south back towards the bulk of the British forces carried on the building breeze. From above, he and the rest of them must have looked like nothing more than indistinguishable dots.

'Do you think they will forgive us?' Solomon said, taking a pinch of grizzle from his pouch.

Jolyon looked at the grubby face in confusion. 'Who?'

'The ones that come after us.'

Jolyon felt a deep sadness and began wringing his hands roughly together to warm them. 'I don't know.'

'What about our families?'

'I don't know,' Jolyon said quietly and turned away.

Within the hour, Private Jolyon Bremner was to be at real

war, and until now he had thought boredom was the overriding worst feeling in this place. Evelyn, his wife, always worried about the food, the cold, the mud, whether her letters were arriving, and his spirits, whatever that meant. Would he live to tell her the truth?

Until he went over the top, he would not be a proper soldier, but he had heard the stories of what happened out there. The Somme was fresh in his comrades' minds and had shattered any suggestion that tactics mattered, only luck counted. There had been nothing left of so many of them they had said, 'just bits and bobs.'

The oldest ones seemed to enjoy telling the new recruits this the most and they gushed about the endless rattle from the machine guns on the inclines, punching holes in khaki chests. They spoke about it like it was easier now, but the Somme was only last year, and nothing had changed as far as Jolyon could see.

He checked his pockets, secured any loose ones tight and put his helmet in his nook so his ledge wasn't taken. With a brusque wave at Solomon, he made his way along the trench to find some food; he could smell bacon. Rare as that was compared to gruel and biscuits, bacon was a treat and that meant they were going over the top.

A soldier was shouting in his sleep, so Jolyon looked away, blowing on his fingertips.

'Morning runner,' said another heap of clothes and bones, though his eyes did not really look at Jolyon, but through him and somewhere into the distance.

He knew neither of these men, but he knew their commanding officer Leatherbrook. These men had been on bagging duty, and the walls of their trench, Stonehill, were now well secured and he said so cheerfully to the men strewn around, but no one looked up. One of them was asleep standing up, his head leaning against the parapet, his rifle swaying to-and-fro off its shoulder strap.

Jolyon passed a gaunt man who was manically sharpening his bayonet on a large, rounded pebble taken from the wall of the trench. He wondered if he should be doing the same; he had been told to keep busy as according to the veterans, the unbusy ones were the first to meet it.

The pink dawn that had surrounded the eight-foot-deep encampment was turning blue, and most men were still unmoving. Even if they were awake, Jolyon knew they kept their eyes closed hoping the scene that awaited them had transformed. Just a few hundred yards away on the other side of the gap the enemy would be waking up too; Jolyon wondered if they felt the same, if they missed loved ones like he did.

He was part of a large machine, with millions of cogs, and he hadn't signed up to shirk despite it all feeling a little pointless now he was here. His older brother Tom, killed at Loos, had been brave in the dispatch he had read, and Evelyn knew why he had come; his parents knew too which mattered to him a great deal, but he hadn't written to them yet.

In late 1915 when he had first tried to enlist after scores of men were wiped out at Mons, then the second crop, including his brother, obliterated by gas at Loos, the months had dragged by. Time had moved a lot faster since he had been sent to the front.

It hadn't taken long for him to be told his calling after his superiors had seen his speed. Since a boy, he had been fast but being tall meant that until he was a teenager, his limbs had hindered him. He had built his speed running up and down the cobbles of Belgrave Mews in Edinburgh, trying to outrun the trains hammering along behind the rows of terraced houses and cobbled streets.

'Like a damn fox,' had barked one of the drill sergeants who watched him on a rotation of the assault course at Aldershot. He was fast and kept very low to the ground, close to cover, no more than inches above the barbed wire peppering the assault course.

'You might be a message runner one day boy.'

'Yes, sir,' was the only answer he had ever given at Aldershot.

That had been that, and his role was assigned but he didn't mind, it could have been worse. The stretcher bearers had the worst draw, a priest had told him on the crossing over that he had read more last rights to those with red crosses strapped round their biceps than anyone else.

'At least they can carry themselves up to God on their own stretchers,' a private had joked, but no one had laughed.

When running, Jolyon's mind was occupied and that at least made him feel freer of this place, and if he was going to die, he would die moving.

Since reaching France, there were moments when he wasn't sure where the supposed camaraderie at the front was that they spoke of back in Britain. He remembered the recruiting posters with men cheerily placed around a cooking stove, ruddy complexions, all smiling and writing letters in neat and tidy trenches awash with cans of food drawn in neat brushstrokes. He had written letters over here but none of the rest had materialised. Being a runner was seen as cowardly by some soldiers as you didn't run towards the bullets but parallel to them and at first, he was called out by the others, why should a pup not have to join in the forward advance?

On his first day in the reserve lines, he had come back to his nook and found it full of white chicken feathers and they had blown about his feet as the men along the trench spat at his feet and shoved him roughly between their uniformed gauntlets.

'Quick, quick, the coffee's boiling over,' a mocking soldier had squealed in a high-pitched voice, pretending to run on the spot. He had then passed a folded piece of paper which was relayed at speed and with great hilarity until it reached Jolyon and inside was the heart of the chicken.

Over the weeks though, as more and more message runners were killed, their scorn had softened as he approached the frontline, edging closer to it trench by trench, truck by truck. He repeated to himself like a prayer that he was stoic in his last thoughts before attempting sleep. His father had told him when he waved him off at Waverley that stoicism was the greatest trait of the Scottish, and he would do well to remember that.

He was informed with zeal by the older soldiers that the Germans had worked out the value of runners and now singled them out through their rifles. They knew runners carried information and information always won wars. He was a target for anyone inclined to see him through eyes or scope, and a sniper had killed his predecessor Clarke stone dead.

Jolyon had heard that Clarke had been a lucky runner, something of a charm to the men. Luck on the front was more valued than cigarettes and the other men missed him as a talisman. When men from the regiment had returned to the reserve lines after a skirmish looking discombobulated and carrying what was left of Clarke, Jolyon had been burdened with a promotion. A mine had exploded right in front of Clarke, and they somehow blamed Jolyon for this, warning him he would never be Clarke, which Jolyon of course knew as that wasn't his name.

During the heat and confusion of the explosions, stumbling forward and alight, apparently Clarke had been lacerated with machine gun's bullets from a nest on the ridge, spinning to the ground like a sycamore seed.

When someone pointed out Clarke's new replacement, a Sergeant's eyes widened, and he fastened his teeth over his bottom lip. He grabbed Jolyon's lapels, smashing him against the wall of the trench. 'A sniper shot him in the bloody face when he lay there. He was dead anyway!'

Jolyon was dumbfounded. 'I… I don't—'

The sergeant's spit landed on Jolyon's lips as he raged, 'There was nothing left of his face. His head looked like a rose in bloom.'

Jolyon apologised; his shoulders being slammed against the trench wall until Solomon had pulled the sergeant off him and rammed a bottle of rum into his hand which pacified him, and the sergeant dragged himself off mumbling.

Solomon had then walked Jolyon forwards three nights before, tapping out a rhythm on his rifle butt, showed him his nook and now it was just an hour away.

'Bacon up,' shouted the cook and Jolyon stepped forward, the first in line. The canteen next to the commander's post was surprisingly immaculate given the mud. The cook had been with the regiment since the start but because of his poor sight was not allowed to fight. Jolyon thought he was as brave as any of them, with only his pots, spoons, and buckets.

He took his bacon and stuffed it between two oatcakes from his breast pocket, the wrapper now flimsy and faded. He perched on a wooden step leading towards the enemy which had been freshly painted with white letters to the side of it, 'Next stop, Leicester Square'.

Jolyon watched Solomon who had finished his diary scribbles and was heaving himself towards the canteen. Jolyon often wondered what he wrote but his words were likely one of his only escapes, so he let him have his private armistice with his thoughts.

Solomon held up a hand towards the cook in greeting, he had gotten thinner. He had ink spots between his thumb and forefinger from his writings, some had smeared onto his jacket cuff beneath the row of faded buttons.

Jolyon checked his watch between bites of bacon and oatcake, the fat making his lips wet and only then did he realise how hungry he was. A fight had broken out from behind the cook's tent with jostling and pushing about portions and shouts of 'Swindler.' Men could handle a lot on the front, but not unfairness.

He savoured the fatty rind and then took a pull of water from his canteen. Despite the temptation to eat it all, he put a third of the bacon and oatcake back in his pocket hot against his chest, then cooling over his heart.

Fits and starts of activity followed, the countdown had begun, and the smell of silicone oil was thick in the air, which covered up the stench from a battalion of Royal Scots men in ankle deep water with no escape to a privy.

'Back to our posts son,' Said Solomon.

'We only move along the trench to eat or shit.' Jolyon pointed out.

Solomon laughed. 'I hadn't thought of it like that.'

'They're that way, son,' Solomon said to a recruit readying himself against the wrong wall of the trench, his teeth bared, and cheeks smeared with leftover charcoal from a stove.

Cigarettes were handed round, rations of drink swallowed down gratefully; Solomon always shared the last of his sweet rum in his flask. Nobody at home would understand the mood, there was a grim inevitability about the whole thing and a refusal to meet anyone's eyes. The spirit of all being in this together Jolyon had read about in the papers was not the case, everyone out here was an island. Even the most junior like Jolyon knew they had no control over the outcome, so thoughts scattered from memories of home right up to that morning in a blur, refusing to say goodbye outright but saying farewell to loved ones just in case.

The sense of order would not last long, not once those German guns opened up with that high-pitched whistling. Solomon had warned him that the idea of tactics went to hell, Jolyon was there to deliver messages and run, that was all.

During the briefing no one had spoken, no one had even smoked, they just stared at the map which could have been anywhere in France or Belgium. Trying to be steadfast, Jolyon imagined they looked from above like a drawn bow and arrow, the bowstring the reserve, the front line being the bow and the Royal Scots the tip of the arrow facing forward. In truth though, if he was honest, he knew this was futile, but he forced that away before it overwhelmed him.

Last-second rumours spread through camp that the Germans were retreating, and it was over, last hopes burned bright, the lies seemed more believable.

Solomon tutted aside to Jolyon pointing over no-man's-land, that few hundred yards that looked easy to cross right now. 'They always have a plan.'

If it didn't look easy, it probably wasn't, and nothing about the enemy had been soft so far. Plans to attack were made by men at desks, but soldiers here just ran forward.

'It looks further than it is,' Major Leatherbrook had said the night before. 'Smash the first line and they will run. Speed is everything. If we pause, we are done.'

Jolyon remained still and silent; whatever was said by Leatherbrook, they could be bloody certain it would not turn out like that. After those first few moments of calm, even if they stretched their minds to breaking point about how bad it would be, still it would be worse.

After the briefing, Major Leatherbrook had beckoned towards Jolyon and Seaton, the other runner, handing them a flare gun, a map and three flares of different colours.

'Green flare,' Leatherbrook said after inhaling on a cigarette and hawking a cough. 'Means we have had success and broken the line and will push on until dark and secure positions. Yellow says we need more support from the Canadians, and the third, red, says to abandon position and retreat. When you see the flag from your hideout, fire the corresponding flare from the high ground. We are way out of communication lines range, so the Canadians and the men must see the flare.'

The weight of the task pressed down on Jolyon, and he gripped his cigarette case hard in his pocket, running his finger over the thistle engraved on its outer silver layer.

Leatherbrook went on, 'If we get hammered, we retreat. We are in the centre on this and if we don't break through, well...' and his voice trailed off.

Jolyon looked at the map on the desk, moving a tankard

under the candlelight. His eyes assessed the height markers on the hillocks, the gun emplacements and knew it didn't really make a bit of difference, there was no cover, just holes and mud and hope.

He traced a line with his finger on the map and found where he would aim for, his firing spot and to get there he would bolt towards the untouched wood he had seen and await the raising of the flags. That first minute was crucial, the head start was everything.

Jolyon watched Leatherbrook's lip curl, his moustache stretching tight over his creased face, behind the eyes was a hint of pity. Jolyon took the package of supplies silently, the flares chalky in his hand.

What had been a light blue sky had been replaced with streaks of yellow and the sound of far-off metal chaffing on metal. Behind him, he heard some men assembling for prayer, but he didn't join them. The God he had known left this place a long time ago.

Talk was quieter now as artillery smoke began to drift over their position. There were distant clanks of iron as guns were loaded and aimed then the rolling barrages began in a series of belting growls from a mile behind, the whistle of howitzers leaving trails of smoke behind them in the sky like brushstrokes on canvas. The ground shook violently and he had to put a hand to his mouth thinking he was going to vomit, his mouth filling with the taste of the bacon and oatcake but he swallowed it back down.

He reached out his palm in front of him, steadied it and pressed it into the cold and damp mud of the Stonehill trench, the noise was intolerable. Their outpost shuddered with fury as the repeated booms of the shells hit the German lines, he felt his ears fizzing. Immersing himself almost fully into the wet soil, he was amongst its embrace and thought of home. He bowed his head until his face lay flat on the mud, breathing deeply, smelling dank earth, and feeling the flares dig into his hip pocket.

Instinct made him want to run, or to hide, but he battered it away as a shell screamed overhead and thudded into the enemy lines with a delayed crack that sucked the air from above him. The noise was infinite, his hearing now not working properly, men's mouths moving around him but no sound registering. A white flash glinted off the bayonets of the assembled men, now neatly in lines, as the rapidity of fire reached a thunder.

Dread mounted in his throat and a low whinny of terror escaped his lungs, seconds counted down; this was so real he could taste it in his spit. Some faces would see home again, others only the embrace of the lost, anything he might want to do in life would be decided soon, he had never had children, and that upset him acutely.

Solomon put a hand on Jolyon's back, a tender touch but enough to snap him out of his trance. The sign reading 'Leicester Square' was covered in mud from heel flicks and one man leaned against it vomiting, another was pulling at his hair leaving spots of blood pricked on his scalp.

Calls to jump-off positions rang along the forward trench with short blasts on whistles, sergeants unclasped their pistols, ready to shoot any men deciding they did not have the fight in them that day but that never happened, they always went forward.

'Battle stations' ran along the trench from the sergeants and a surge of khaki walked up onto the fire step, inches below the lip of the trench.

'Scots. Ready.'

Bolts cocked along the line, a unison of bullets sliding into chambers. Some men screamed a last word to a god who had long ago lost interest but every single one of them wished for it to be quick.

'Scots. Advance.'

One last smack of a shell hitting the enemy lines sending mud and flame towering up into the sky. One last thought of Edinburgh, and one last thought of Evelyn as they began rising from the trench as one.

Chapter 2

April 1917, Arras
Gunner

'Again,' Otto murmured.

'So soon,' Kummer replied.

Staring across the gap between the armies, Otto's eyes narrowed through his binoculars. The fine layer of mist that had marched in that morning obscured the detail of the enemy and the British looked like spectres, shapeless and floating about their routines. Occasionally he could make out the peak of a helmet or the barrel of a rifle held vertically to the sky.

'Again, again,' Kummer drawled through the butt of a cigarette, most of his features obscured by smoke apart from his eyebrows.

They knew the British were preparing to attack, the entire German army knew the drill by now. Artillery had increased but that barely registered it was so constant, other warnings though flagged that trouble was coming and echoes of past actions had tattooed themselves onto Otto, he had seen it all before after one thousand and twenty-two days of active service.

The grind and repetition made the finer details of home start to fade, and his daughter Alice's voice had slipped away, and he could only just about picture his wife Sofia's smile. One distinct memory remained, picnicking on the banks of the Glan in Rehborn but it was foolish to picture it clearly in case his veneer slipped, it might tip him past a point of no return. When the swell of his heart drew him towards her, he refused to look towards home. He busied himself with giving orders or rolled a cigarette with the flimsy Eckstein paper that always tasted slightly of liquorice. He had not smoked before he left, now these white sticks were an essential part of his routine and about the only source of consistent joy he could find here.

'They are making a play of it,' Captain Otto Zweck had said along the trench line to his men on the morning of the attack.

As was his custom, he told them one by one with a cupped hand around the back of their necks and they nodded. Otto knew some would live, some would die, and they knew that too. Grubby, tired, and brave faces then went about their duties like spiders spinning webs in spring preparing for the assault, bracing for the strike.

The sport of all this had been played out by now but despite not knowing the day, and sometimes not even the month, he knew it was 1917. He had not seen the boulevards of home with the hanging baskets of forget-me-nots, or the main square circled with blossoming apple trees, in three years. He had refused leave every time, but he did wonder what was left away from the front and whether he felt like he did because he hadn't ever been back.

Bending to tighten his boots in the morning light, his knuckles grazed along the muddy floor of the trench; it was drier with the new floorboards in place. His medals pinched his chest as he straightened, they were a source of pride but all he had to show for his service. The bright discs and black cross hardly seemed enough given what he had endured, though he kissed them before lights out and would pass them onto Sofia one day, or she would be sent them. Even in the warmest days of summer like this morning, with wildflower scents carried on the breeze and a heat to the air, there was a chill that inflated from within him.

Sipping on coffee from a chipped mug, Otto was alone in his thoughts which was rare. At the very start of all this, it had felt like the wind was with them but the ordeal of the months that became years had gotten so predictable it was both draining and damaging.

When he had first crossed the frontier at Triers their boots were not even worn, their orders exciting. Feet were still marching not dragging, and bellies were full not empty. He had bellowed the words of Im Hausam Meer boisterously then.

'Let me be with her tonight in the house by the sea,
It's dark in the room and the night is so long,
Time flows so slowly and yet passes so quickly,
Perhaps the narrow, winding corridor leads,
In the dunes, above the cliff, it's getting light.'

It would be over soon they had chorused, but he no longer whistled that tune. The naivety made Otto sick, and he had thrown away his faded photos from home and refused to celebrate Christmas or New Year, a private act of defiance that nobody else seemed to notice. Underestimation by his people had proved costly but it was a general's prerogative to do this, a soldier's dilemma to always solve.

He wanted Sofia carnally, but not just to make love, though he thought of that unique warmth often. It was after, being held in her embrace, intertwined in clean bedding knowing morning would come without thick mustard gas layered up between splintered birch trees and the shouts of 'Gas, gas' lurching him

30

awake.

Alice too, how old was she now? Seven, eight? Running through meadows pinpricked with daisies and clovers surrounded by life. In his nightmares, she was running away from a man she did not know, a father she did not trust, as no child could trust someone who had not been there. A dark part of him did not want to make it home at all, not if Alice saw through him and how often he seemed to slip into these ghastly trances.

Chewing on a crust, his coffee now cold, he stared through the wire coils, today he had no choice but to fight again. There was no glory left that he could sense, just a will to survive and outlast the gathering groups opposite waiting for the whistle blasts.

'Up, up, up,' he growled at a sentry who was dozing.

It was absurd what the British were up to, preparing to attack in plain sight with the sun up and glaring. They would be up and over within an hour; his cold rifle barrel would be hot to the touch with the spent and smoking casings amassed at his feet. Then a day or two later it would be their turn. And for what? Appearances? Was it just something to do? Nobody was winning this thing in this place, certainly not at this point in the line. Here was a mesh of wire, guns and sleeping quarters so deep he knew even the big boy shells from across the stretch couldn't injure them when they popped.

Shouts from across the gap made his stomach tighten, he looked across for Kummer who was prepping grenades on a ledge under the trench lip. Kummer was a friend from the start, but he and Otto didn't count his kills anymore like they used to at the beginning of all this over a sweet peach schnapps.

'Calm along the line,' Otto said. They had to pick their

targets carefully and concisely and shoot to wound to attract the relief parties.

The British had gone quiet the night before their attack, they always did. Otto knew they were preparing for battle as they were having hot food, cook-ups blazed along the enemy trench lip. The smell of frying meat drifted over the black gap between them with a hint of parsnip in the broth. He pictured Sophia's suckling pig they always had on Christmas Eve, and he could smell the honey melting into the skin, the sticky meat tearing away between his fingers, fat running down his chin.

Otto and Kummer stuck their heels into the edge of the wooden rafters facing up the hill and lay back on the rolling trench wall with stretched canvas on. If he found a good spot some of the clips would have come away meaning he could lie flat, the gentle curve of the trench supporting all his weight as he looked at the stars and chain-smoked.

They spoke of what they would eat first when they returned. Kummer always wanted fried chicken. 'Great platefuls,' he would say excitedly, spittle forming in the corner of his mouth. They joked about what they would say to their wives' parents who had doubted them before the war but not now they were German officers returning victorious with black ribbons tied round blunted bayonets for the endless street parties.

Then they would try to sleep, still hungry. 'Pointless,' Otto whispered as his eyes flickered shut as the wick of the candle on the wooden table of their bunkroom fizzled out.

Now it was morning, and the dawn, a beautiful pink one, stretched overhead. A rumble from behind the British lines made binoculars snap up against eyes along the line.

'Down, down, down,' Otto barked.

The first shell hit behind their trench line, the two-second delay and then a thump and flash of spinning metal and stinking smoke. Earth was thrown up in the air, then dumped down like heavy rain on tunics and helmets, small stones pinging off with light dings.

Otto moved calmly into the redoubts knowing they were safe as eggs in a box down here, shrapnel above was falling like petals on a river. The British thought their hits were causing havoc, no doubt imagining Germans writhing and screaming, clutching their own innards back inside them with slippery hands.

The earth shook for a few minutes more, the lamps swinging from the wooden boarded ceilings, each dropping fragments of sawdust that floated down in the fragmented light. Otto finished a cigarette and stubbed it out against his boot heel, noticing the polish had worn off already from last night, it did not do well to look scruffy in front of the men. He saw a brass button missing from his tunic, he must have snagged it on the way down.

'Stations,' he said, and there was a thundering of boots as men went back to their positions. As the shells dwindled out the smoke began clearing and there was a vile stink, bodies from past conflicts had been thrown up by the shelling. Fragments of comrades were catapulted into the sky along with their makeshift wooden crosses with entire lives shortened to a few numbers and letters; age, date of death and rank. Along the barbed wire, all around the trench hung bits of bodies of long-buried men.

Otto checked his watch and knew they had three minutes, the British did not take long to arrange themselves into those neat little lines, final preparations would be underway on the other side.

Kummer laid out his friend's mat, and Otto went to his knees. He had forgotten the words inscribed on the stone altar of his hometown, but he thought of good words. His eyes were shut tightly, tiredness nagging in his twitching lids, and he stayed like that until he heard the first faint whistle from the other side. Making his way to the fire step, Otto brushed his shoulders from ash and debris, and he stepped into the light. His immaculate men all gave a sharp nod and he nodded back and raised a gesturing hand for them to take their places.

Otto ran his palm against the soft wooden butt of his rifle and leaned forward onto the trench parapet, through his sights he could see the tops of bayonets glinting in the sun.

There were three short blasts of a whistle that carried over the chasm, then the figures started approaching, an outline of a face, then shoulders, torsos, and targets. They walked slowly at first, unsure why no one from his side was firing and he could make out their shadows in the thick smoke, they looked like ghosts.

Otto ran his tongue along his bottom lip, it was cracked and dry. Quietly he released the safety catch as the sunlight threw javelins of light down through the smoke. He could start to make out exact faces, hair colour, cap badges and features and still it was silent, not a German moved.

The British, feeling freedom and air in their lungs were now starting to run towards them, galloping boots ate up the ground, occasionally he heard a yelp of laughter, a cheer of hope. He could hear the clank of webbing, see the creases on the faces of the Scotsmen and closer they came, all of them now beginning to smile thinking they had made it.

Otto took a deep breath, steadied himself one last time and with a whisper to Kummer and his men said softly, 'Prepare to fire on my signal.'

Chapter 3

May 1940, Arras
Rider

The river Scarpe and the dense woods along its banks settled William, he breathed in deeply and let his body unlock sinew by sinew. The trees, rocks and rivers that surrounded him had no concept of the war that had engulfed the whole world, nature still ran its course, nature persevered.

The torrents of rain that had fallen in the past few days and slowed the British retreat, had quelled. Now it looked to William as before, the water gently flowing with two small eddies either side of the grey stone bridge that was to be blown before they left Arras. He could see a group of engineers at either end of the bridge unloading supplies and spools of wire, they worked without noise, possibly without hope that this one act would make a difference.

The rains had taken away the corpses that had been lodged in debris downstream towards the centre of the city, where the British headquarters for the Dunkirk retreat was based in the Grande Place Hotel.

Forward Command was overseeing the evacuation of troops and was now stationed in the basement of the hotel having moved from the cathedral. William had been there when a Stuka bomb had clipped the guttering and punctured the stained-glass window sending coloured glass down onto the maps and desks like confetti. They had watched the bomb waiting for it to detonate and end it all, but it was a dud and it just lay there surrounded by the glass staring at them reminding them what a close-run thing war was.

Five miles from the cathedral altar, in the woods of Athies forest, William Bremner sat under a large oak tree writing in his diary, away from the noise and the rumours of salvation. The ancient, riddled bark pressed into his webbing like an embrace, these woods were impenetrable and ancient, and they hid thoughts, stories, and secrets not even a world war could touch. Deep down within him he too had a secret, and he could only whisper it here in his jottings.

He put his pencil back in his top pocket and closed the diary, unable to write much but names of comrades and places he had been, even the faces of the recently dead he couldn't describe, they all rolled into a single head in pain above a khaki collar. His breathing was rhythmic, and it felt better to be silent, to be still. With eyes closed, he rolled a cigarette between his fingers with practised hands and made a mental note he needed more tobacco and would need to find something to trade. Mayon-White was an excellent forager and a capable soldier, he had saved William more than once and he always seemed to have the three principle things soldiers on the run wanted; liquor, cigarettes and gallows humour.

There were not many of the originals from basic training left, most of the faces had perished or changed into versions of what they had been when they stepped foot on the Continent. His unit had undergone a brutal rotation, and he had been here since the start in 1939. William and the rest had been told their efforts to hold up the enemy would earn them possible medals which only a few of them cared about anymore, they had also been told they would be relieved, but no relief had come. When Poland was dusted and the enemy pushed back West it was only a matter of time, and time was almost up.

A voice rang out very close, 'Do you think it's because we are off?'

William jumped as John Cronk sat down next to him with a clang of metal off his canteen tied around his waist. His brother Hugh was a few paces back and he kicked at a clump of grass which sent a puff of dandelion seeds into the air. William checked his diary was hidden with a hand, he had sat for hours sometimes looking at the pages wondering how he might describe what he was witnessing, and how he had ended up in the one place he swore he would never come.

Cronk's face looked tired but cheerful.

'What a shitshow,' he tried to say jovially.

'Total screw up,' Hugh chimed in, sitting next to his brother, then lying out flat on the grass.

Even the Cronks, jokers in their section, had been diminished of spirit in recent days. The relentless running and hiding, only punctuated by brief moments for rest took its toll. Bullets moved faster than people so despite their exhaustion, they would rather keep moving but it was all starting to feel a little inevitable.

'Still, least it's not raining,' Hugh said with his eyes closed.

They were retreating towards Dunkirk, and if William got off that beach, he was never coming back no matter what anyone thought of him. His father had lied, there was nothing glorious about any of this, most of these men would be tried for murder if they weren't at war. He had done his bit, honoured his family's wishes, it was up to someone else to finish this thing. The Cronks laughed their way through war, but nothing at all had seemed funny for so long now to William.

The sun had been beating down relentlessly all day, there was not a breath of wind and the whole world seemed to shimmer in haze. There was a glinting above the surface of the Scarpe and a jet-black cormorant glided just above the surface, honking as it went by. William and the Cronks section had been permitted to bathe here, just outside the city walls before breakfast, the usual fare of biscuits and an egg if they could barter any from civilians camped by the walls who had come from the East. Poles in the main, most wearing an expression to William that the British soldiers had no idea what was coming for them. The men were told to check the kit and have two hours rest, which had been met with furrowed brows throughout the section.

'Bollocks to that,' John Cronk had said loudly when given the orders, his brother giving a 'Here, here' after.

Changes in their routine slowed their retreat.

'Will,' John said with a smile, jabbing him in the arm, 'Are we resting because we are moving again?'

'I guess so,' said William bringing himself back from his thoughts and handing John the cigarette from his fingers. Eyes closing again he removed another tab from the crumpled pack in his breast pocket to stick between his lips.

Hugh, despite still lying flat piped up, 'What about me?'

'Roll your own cigarettes,' his brother said and kicked at him in the grass.

William had both tobacco and straights, straights he saved for special occasions or when he considered he might die, he was smoking more straights these days. Occasionally, the officers claimed in the morning they could stand and fight, but by afternoon they would be running again.

Their orders changed daily, sometimes even hourly as the great retreat to Dunkirk limped and stumbled on. The news had spread disbelievingly, and they had laughed when they were first told they were heading home and wouldn't stand and fight, how naïve they had been.

Men chorused, 'What will we say when we get back?'

'That you would have died out here,' an officer spat.

'My father stood against them,' William had said.

'Same country, different threat,' Cronk had said.

Those comments had gone on until they realised quickly, they were not going home as victors or even soldiers but retreating as the defeated. They may as well have sent civilians. The further they ran towards home, the more William felt obtuse about how they could have thought it would be over so soon or they even stood a chance, made worse by the shelled-out landing crafts on the roadside. With a grim plod, they passed the bodies of women and children scattered at intervals on the lanes, horrifying sights that would not leave him no matter how much he drunk. At first, they had buried them, then they nodded at them, now they just stepped over them and had been since Douai. An expedition this had been, but a force it was not.

He remembered his father and his father's friends swearing it would not happen again, but the promise of lasting peace and a united Europe was a bloody sham. Jolyon, his father, had taken him to see the battlefields when he was a little boy, he could still remember it. Even then seeing the headstones he had marvelled at both the number and the waste.

Growing up, his feelings towards the army had dulled, and he did not want to do something just because his father had but the pressure had been acute and evergreen. Jolyon had worn him down with veiled threats about community shame and the pride of the nation. William said he would not fight at first when war broke out, but the devastation in his father's face had made him come, that look that a son could not give a father all he had ever wanted of him. That was the only reason, some outdated code and now his father was not here to face the consequences, he was. William was the one staring at the blank eyes of children as young as three lying dead in ditches with hands reaching out on their long walk towards the sea.

However this war ended, William knew millions more would die, and sitting here, trussed up in green, he was only adding to the obsession of those who dressed up national pride in spent bullet casings. They had been ordered over here to save the world, now they were being called back having failed.

John Cronk and some of the men had grumbled about the British mettle, their sticking power as soldiers.

'I'll die, but not with my back turned,' said a soldier whose ancestors had apparently been at Waterloo, like that mattered.

William wondered what would those men from the last war say about their costume uniforms? Some of them even said they would have preferred to have been in the last war, but William had grown up on the stories from his father and sitting here by the riverbank smoking and warmed by the sun he did not share that view.

Their unit was part of the half a million men left in mainland France and they couldn't see the sea yet, so it was only a matter of time and either they reached the beaches, or the Germans cut them off.

'Light?' John said reaching forward with his zippo.

William sucked in the cigarette gratefully, watching the smoke curl up into the branches above. Summer was almost here, the dry grass hailing this season of bud and sap. He and the Cronks sat there silently smoking, the time it took to smoke a tab about as long a silence until someone had to speak before the conversation turned to retreat.

'You heard the chatter from Raynes?' Cronk said, extinguishing the cigarette on his boot and putting the butt in his pocket.

William looked at Cronk sardonically, chatter was everywhere, and he had learnt since joining the army the vast majority of it was nonsense.

William leaned his head back against the trunk. 'Raynes moaning about retreat?'

'Execution,' Cronk muttered staring straight ahead.

William opened his eyes, gnashing down on the inside of his lip tasting the end of the cigarette in his gums. 'Execution? Who?'

'The enemy. A few of them were found behind the lines by the camp. German scouts I think, they made a hell of a racket by the perimeter. One of them couldn't stop talking like he wanted to be caught. There's a whole group of them. One of them is senior enough to have caused a flutter at headquarters. Huge bloke, great big rack of medals tucked in his jacket. Orders are to... well...'

William stayed quiet, there was a rushing in his ears, and he clenched his fists into the stubbled grass around the base of the tree. Executing prisoners was surely not an order, how could it be? Rogue soldiers looking for revenge, possibly drunk even in the day as a lot of them seemed to be now.

To William, to anyone surely, executing prisoners was murder. That small but precious flame of duty, of any kind of moral code was being extinguished all over Europe. It crossed a line. Most of the violence felt out of reach, but so close to where he now sat, he could not abide by execution, he felt less soldier now, more terrorist. Their section blamed everyone but their own capabilities, they couldn't accept that the grey-uniformed hardened men were better than them at fighting. The men who had just been captured were the living embodiment of all that was wrong with their lives right now and they would be made an example of for a pound of flesh.

'Why murder them?' William said bluntly.

Cronk looked at him quizzically. 'Murder them? Come on, Will. Look where we are, we are surrounded. We are here to hold them up long enough for someone to come up with a bloody plan which they won't. We'll never stop them. May as well take as many as we can with us.'

'Still,' William said and let his voice drift away, saying more was dangerous. You did not argue with orders, and you did not show sympathy.

At basic training, they had tried to convince them they were honourable soldiers, sergeants ranting away about the pride of the uniform, their place in history. What tosh, they would not win a war this way. The papers at home talked of the German maniacs, but what did it mean if they acted the same way shooting prisoners with their arms bound?

William thought of his nearly crippled father who had lived and fought in this place, and he blamed the overblown war stories for why he was here. Jolyon had been stationed only a mile or two from where William currently sat at Feuchy. He wondered if his father had seen this tree, this river, this place, had he asked himself these questions about morality? His father by all accounts had been good in war but did being good at war only mean being good at killing?

Did they shoot people at will back then? His father had said there were high spots, had always spoken of the community of brothers and how belief in the left- and right-hand man of you could penetrate any defence.

That war, the first one, with promises about it being the last of its kind, was only twenty-three years ago but nothing could be recognised here. William knew that his father would not agree with execution, and he felt something like validation for the feelings he had harboured for so long before he had made the grave mistake of coming here.

William and the Cronks stood; it was time for their briefing. As they walked along the riverbank back to camp, William turned one last time and looked at the bridge, river and a farmhouse peeking through the trees along the Scarpe.

'This execution, where is it happening?' William asked John, slotting into stride with the gravel crunching softly under their boots.

'In the woods.'

'These woods?'

'Yes. Doubt they will even bury them, won't be here long enough for the stink before we move off.'

'Right. When is it?'

John grinned. 'Now. During the briefing. Don't want to alert everyone to it, there are still those who think we can shake hands with these people. Men were picked at random to do it, there were plenty volunteers, mind.'

'I volunteered,' said Hugh from behind them. 'Didn't get carded though.'

William looked ahead at the patched-up canvas tent with soldiers gathering at the front of it, waiting to go in for another briefing which would be pointless. How many of the men in there knew what was about to happen? How many agreed?

'Look,' Will said sharply to John. 'I am going to catch you up in there, save me a seat.'

'Got a date?'

'Need to take a leak.'

'Okay,' John said, not thinking anything else of it and slowing so his brother could catch up.

Something from deep within William had found its voice, and he might have a way to make it heard at last. A chance to change course, if only once out here, drew him closer like an old friend.

Killing, he had found, was remarkably unplanned out here, courage came in spurts and moments of rash action. No one should die arms bound, blindfolded and on their knees in a far-off wood in France. That was not the way any human should die and if he could save them, maybe that would be the bravest thing he could do in all this. Maybe it wasn't a sentence for the men to be killed, but a chance for him to do war differently.

William skirted around the men gathering at the tent just as a wispy cloud crossed the sun, and for a moment William found half his body in shade, half in sunlight. He held out a hand in front of him, the glare on his scabbed knuckles and the fingers that had pulled triggers were steady.

The chatter of the men by the tent had died away and there was a grunt from behind him as he heard their commanding officer begin the briefing. He turned, as if his body knew it should go to the tent, but his eyes met the distant bridge and the very top of the oak tree and the farmhouse beyond.

His eyes scanned the deserted camp as the briefing went on

with the tapping of a wooden stick on a map. 'The enemy…' but William shut it out.

Brew stoves still spluttered, and boxes of ammunition lay half-filled around him, the forthcoming decision weighed heavy with reminders of his code and creed all around. He was about to retreat in his thoughts, when from behind the last poncho he saw a black shadow flicker and he made out a nose and a thick neck bucking as the animal stirred, there was a bay horse tied up to a post.

Her thick mane had been recently brushed and it fell lazily to the side of its neck, she was the property of the commanding officer. He liked it for status and because he was a hero of the First World War, he told those who still listened to his war stories nightly. He said he wanted to keep up the morale a horse brought to the men and William remembered being castigated when he pointed out they were not as fast or as bulletproof as tanks.

'We must never retreat without order,' he heard from the CO in the tent, carried on the ever-rising wind, a storm was coming in fast.

Was he running from a fight, from shame or was he desperate to do a good deed? He had always taken the hard way but had had never cheated or lied. A good man, his father had called him but a rash one who could never settle. Perhaps that was why Jolyon had forced him to join, as some kind of enforced structure. Some birds though are never meant to be caged.

One foot began to follow another, treading lightly so as not to spook the bay horse, the long reed grass pulling at William's boots. The horse whipped its head up, and its big hazel eyes took in the figure approaching. In the centre of its forehead was a white diamond, so distinct amongst the brown it looked like it had been branded on. William could smell the sweat of the horse and the scent of glycerine, the tack recently cleaned down and polished. The clouds above were amassing in ranks, beginning to steal the light from the bright morning.

The horse stepped forward a pace and then back and William was unsure what the punishment would be for this. As an idea became a deed, he was starting to weigh up the consequences of acting. Brave or a coward? The briefing was ending, men were beginning to fidget, and he could hear cigarette packets being readied and unstripped, that thin layer of foil being pulled away.

William bent down and snatched up a handful of the long grass and approached the horse with one palm open, the other offering the grass. William stroked the horse along its nose which flickered under his touch, the whiskers pricking his palm.

He heard the men in the tent begin to stand. In a single movement, he put a boot in the stirrup, grabbed the loose mane, flicked the rope off the post and flung himself onto the horse. The first few spots of rain began to fall, a light drumming on the ammo boxes.

William looked up at all the faces pouring out of the tent and fingers pointing at him. Rain made everyone look the same, just outlines of men, but as the canvas tent door flapped open and the commanding officer emerged, hands on hips, his pudgy features screwed up.

'Bremner,' he hollered.

William made out the Cronks who mouthed something, but he kicked the flanks of the horse and it jolted forward with a skip and flicked its back legs high in the air.

'Go on, son,' a soldier shouted.

'Next stop, Berlin,' another chorused.

They did not know his destination thought, they would have shot him if they had.

Hooves were churning against the gale and the rain, and his eyelids narrowed as the storm battered him and he could taste his last cigarette from the riverbank in his teeth and tongue. The horse hurdled a mess table on the edge of the camp, knocking off a jerry can with its back hooves sending it clattering to the ground spilling black two-stroke oil in great gulps onto the grass.

One more yell of 'Bremner. You're dead,' then the storm and the hooves swallowed the noise of men.

On the pathway by the river, the horse gained speed towards the wood, and he urged it on with his bootheels, his face unmoving, his baggy British uniform soaked through and indistinguishable in colour. He was just a deserter atop a horse now, his oaths shattered.

Its hooves banged heavy on the path leading into the woods, branches snapping under its weight as they were swallowed by the thick green. Raindrops like marbles pinged off broad leaves like bullets, the canopy above singing under the storm like drumbeats.

William only looked ahead as he was thrown into the shade. He had no idea where he was headed but galloped on over roots and trunks deeper and deeper into Athies forest.

Chapter 4

May 1940, Arras
Prisoner

Guy Schwarzbär growled a command to hush, loud enough for all his troopers to hear him. The old bear had been snared, the rope was chaffing into his wrists and stumbling blindfolded knowing that having been captured, they would all be shot.

Rough hands shoved his shoulder and he stumbled over a tree root, the man pushing him had to reach upwards to keep Guy straight. He knew they were in deep woods, the sounds of the laughing men who prodded them echoed off branches and trunks. Through his blindfold he could only make out changes in light and when it got consistently brighter through the material, he guessed this would be the spot. The blindfold annoyed him more than anything, he hated the thought of going blindly to his grave.

One of his troops, Aidan he guessed, had been shot already for struggling and dumped some way back, he never liked the man anyway. What a pitiful way to die, crying to men whose minds were made up, this was war. Did the dead trooper think telling them he had children would help? Aidan had always talked of home too much.

Guy was a soldier of the Wehrmacht and would meet death with an understanding smile, that had been the contract since the start. He had a family too, but he had buried sentimentality and memories of them deep down. Being caught and nearing his execution gave him these moments to reflect which he despised. As he said to his troopers who followed his every move and word, 'Sentimentality is the way of the man at peace, not the soldier at war.' He did not make that statement to be superior to his men, he said it to keep them alive.

His family would be in grave danger with him dead as his dislike of the new creed at home was well-known, but his rank had protected them up to this point. Guy always wondered, secretly of course, whether he and his fellow veteran Wehrmacht officers should have done more about the rise of the Nazis and their tendencies. They did not know the consequences of war these men, only its instigation. The plan was violence and it had worked. His sons would be forced to join the SS and would die over here, and that he reflected would have killed him in a different sense.

'On your knees,' the British voice sounded out in the clearing.

Guy understood English as did most of his troop, not that any of the British ever assumed that. They had been caught creeping up to the encampment, it has been soldierly chatter of women, woes, and drink from the British. They were there to scout out the threat their armour faced, very little as it had turned out. They were almost clear and heading back when someone in his group had been spotted but he knew it wasn't him, perhaps it was Muller, lumbering about always talking of his belly. They had been surrounded, bound and had now been marched to their death.

'On your knees, you big bastard,' the voice sounded again, closer this time.

A boot lashed at the back of his calf and his knees gave way. He would obey for the moment unless a chance presented itself, but that was unlikely. The Black Bear felt the long grass surround his knees, a meadow for a grave. A black bear was on the flag of Berlin, his home, and his reputation had earned him the moniker. He was silent most of the time, but when he spoke it was with a quiet authority and this being his second war, everybody listened.

The British soldier kicked him again under his ribs, but as the boot struck, Guy remained unmoving and kept his chest upright, his chin high. The smell of cigarette smoke was strong, as was the summer grass. It reminded him of the Tiergarten in early May, where he used to walk with his sons and tell them stories from the trenches. They would buy toffee apples, the caramel making their lips stick together, as he listened to their hopes of becoming soldiers one day, their optimism the kind only people who had not been at war could harbour.

A breeze was swelling making the branches chatter, and once again he told himself that whilst nobody wanted to die, there were worse places. One of his troops had been shot in the gut a few weeks back and it had taken him seven hours to die, a pitiful and weak way to be extinguished. He could hear his men drop down onto knees next to him one by one, a neat little line of them. A rifle cocked and quickly a shot rang out, echoing around the clearing. A second later he heard the slump of a body and the rifle cock again.

One of the British soldiers said in a hurried whisper, 'Well go on then…'

'No, I want to make these Nazis wait, hear them beg me one by one.'

'Wait,' Guy said abruptly which stopped everything.

There was a pause, the German soldier speaking fluent English had made them check, then the sound of boots moving closer.

'What?' said one of their captors.

'Nazi pig,' spat another.

This man sounded drunk; he had slurred the insult.

From behind the blindfold Guy said, 'I am no Nazi.'

From far away in the woods Guy heard shouting and he could have sworn he heard a name, something like Brenner.

The British soldier cut the silence. 'What was it you were muttering?'

Guy replied, 'I do not want to die being called a Nazi. Understand?'

'You all are,' one of the soldiers said.

'No, we are not,' Guy said coolly and made a move to rise hearing the British executioners take a step back. The Black Bear kept his temper in check though, he refused to die by starting a fight he couldn't win just yet, his mind, strong as it was, knew that sacrificing himself extinguished the very last hope of an unlikely salvation.

'At least give me a soldier's death, let me see the man who is to kill me, let me see the sky one more time.'

A brief silence followed and then he could hear whispers between the executioners.

'Fine, I don't mind looking you in the eye.'

Guy assumed this was their leader but if that was by rank or just willingness to pull the trigger, he wasn't sure.

The blindfold was torn off, Guy blinked quickly to take in the scene. In front of his eyes at point-blank range was the muzzle of the rifle, the man behind it was scruffy and drinking from a bottle, he was dirty, unshaven, and looked strained.

There were three of them, one tall and skinny, disinterested and very drunk. Another was tiny, almost wizened and had a

51

dreadful scar running down his cheek and smelt terribly of sweat and was chewing at his nails intently. The third, their leader, and holding the gun had a madness and lust in his eye, Guy did not trust.

'What's that?' the leader said, flicking at Guy's jacket pocket with the barrel.

Guy looked down. 'A bear.'

The skinny soldier sneered, 'A bear?'

Guy nodded.

'Why?' the skinny one added, leaning down for a closer look and blowing cigarette smoke into Guy's face. The metal fighting bear hung there from his pocket, it glinted in the sunlight through the trees and made a faint ting as it blew against his pocket button.

'No matter,' Guy said.

'Matters to me,' the leader said as he cocked the rifle like he was itching to pull the trigger.

'Okay,' Guy said soothingly. 'I am called the Black Bear. Soldiers call me it. I did not choose it.'

'He's famous,' drawled the scarred little soldier from behind them, hopping from foot to foot.

Guy shrugged as if he was not right or wrong in his assumption.

'Bears still die if they are shot in the head,' the leader said. Guy knew the leader was not enjoying this chatter, it was making him pause and hesitation lost more lives than it saved. This was now not just a lump of flesh but a person with a story, maybe a family, he was well known too which would make him wonder if he wouldn't be better off being questioned and not shot in the woods.

Guy looked around, trying not to think of his sons but

finding it harder as the seconds of his life ran out. The dead man who had fallen forward, his arms bound up behind his back, had gone rigid. Between the blades of grass, he could make out a streak of blood running from the temple, under his helmet, round the eye socket and dripping off his chin.

The leader was uneasy. 'So, you want to die looking at me?'

'I don't want to look at you, I wanted to see the sky.'

The man's lip curled in frustration. 'Won't be any sky where you are going.'

'Maybe, maybe not. But you will never know what I see,' Guy said, craning his blonde head to take in the blue canvas above streaming with sunlight and a black buzzard high above them circling.

'Get on with it,' the skinny one said. 'All this talk...'

'You fucking do it then. You shoot this bear.'

'Not my orders,' added the small soldier backing off.

'Well, shut up then.'

There was a splutter from the skinny soldier but nothing more as he pulled on the bottle again.

Guy took a final look around and lowered his head inch by inch, waiting for the bullet, he shook his shoulders and was ready.

Nothing happened, the leader was trying to light a cigarette, the gun resting in the crook of his arm, making him wait.

'Bears and all this crap. What kind of a man wears a fucking badge to war?'

'It was made by my sons,' Guy said quietly.

The skinny man's face dropped, his expression pained, and he stepped up to the leader. 'Mate, should we be doing...?'

The leader turned around and pushed the rifle into the skinny one's gut. 'Shut up. It's my job. You see what these bastards do when they get hold of us? They skinned one of us and strung him up to a tree. They left him there for days, crows ate his eyes.'

The leader snatched the bottle off the skinny one, the small one was looking between them, wobbling on his feet.

Guy was looking past the British and thought he saw something moving fast through the trees. It wasn't armour, he would have heard it. Sunlight glimmered off something in the distance, a badge of some sort and Guy felt something masquerading as hope. Perhaps it was another scout team, or a dispatch rider with an order from the rear. He remained stock still on his knees and watched the gaps between the trees. The British leader finished his cigarette, taking a long drag and squared the gun at last, as if remembering why they were all there.

Another blaze of brown was heading towards the clearing, directly at them, it would not bypass this scene but was here because of it. None of the British had noticed, the spectacle of having live Germans on their knees had dulled them along with the hard liquor.

Guy watched closely, the mesh of leaves and spears of sunlight between branches making it hard to see but between two thick tree trunks, he then saw it clearly, a bay horse with a white diamond on its forehead heading for the clearing. The horse was bolting through the trees, hurdling all in its path, froth around the corners of its bridle. Its eyes were set on the line of British executioners, its browband dripping in sweat. The rider urged the horse on, kicking its quarters hard and whipping its flank with an open palm.

The leader pressed the cold steel against Guy's forehead.

'Any last words?'

'Just one or two,' Guy said.

'You are a talker.'

Guy nodded towards the horse, looking beyond the executioner. 'What is that?'

Atop of the horse was not a German soldier as Guy had hoped, but a young British boy who couldn't have been much older than his sons at home.

The British execution party swung round but in the second it took to register the horse, it had burst into the clearing, its mane thrashing wildly about, the boy's knuckles tightly gripping the reins. The horse arched up, its front legs rising off the grass then began to churn as the hooves reconnected with the ground.

The horse went straight at them, the British soldiers covered their faces as horse and rider rode straight into two of the men, knocking them flat, the little one was badly hurt as a crack came from his leg which had folded underneath him and he screamed. The skinny drunk one fell over and did not move, his head hit the ground with a dull thump. The horse stopped still in the clearing, rattled its lips, the boy atop said nothing.

The British leader stumbled away but fell, turning as he did with his rifle. He began to shoot at the kneeling men of Guy's troop and Guy screamed at his men to get out of there.

'Run,' he shouted, the word punctuated at the beginning and end by shots from the rifle.

Two of the troopers twisted downwards stone dead as the British soldier recovered his aim. Blood from one of the troopers' heads sprayed straight up and spattered across the lush grass and the flank of the horse. The Brit was shooting wildly, scrabbling his legs backwards, trying to reload. Guy rolled forward as a bullet missed him by inches, the volley of air whistling as it went over him.

The horse wheeled round again, rearing up to its full height once again. The young boy had a streak of blood running down his cheek from a whipping branch, and one word came to mind for Guy; determined. The last troopers separated, leaving the British soldier still on his back with targets to choose from. The rifle shook in his hands and Guy watched the barrel skipping up and down with the recoil. He fired randomly as his troopers approached the edge of the woodland. Ludo made it to cover, Brett did not as he tumbled forward, his upper body smashing into a tree trunk which made his helmet roll off and bounce amongst the roots of the oak.

Guy was on the move, the bear emblem jangling against his chest. As he was about to run in the opposite direction, he felt the horse's hind bump him and it made him stumble. He looked up as the boy looked down on him, his uniform soaked through with rain from the storm that had departed just as soon as it had arrived. For a second that seemed to last much longer they looked at each other, wondering what would happen next given their creeds.

Leaning down from the saddle, the boy pulled out a knife and Guy watched the boy slash at the rope binding his wrists. Guy yanked his hands apart, splitting the remaining strands.

'Get up,' the boy said.

Hands grasped at Guy's jacket, the boy's grip strong, and Guy scrabbled his feet against the flank of the beast until he was sitting behind the boy in the saddle.

The boy kicked the flanks of the horse and it burst forward with a jolt towards the woods, away from the flaccid bodies and bullets which were still ringing around the clearing. Guy had to hold onto the boy's waist, feeling himself almost bumped off the back of the horse with every stride as they gathered pace. Guy looked back at the last of the executioners, his face drawn in a grimace of hatred as the escape. The British soldier fired twice more, the first bullet causing the bark of a branch just above them to explode in sap and splinter.

As the second shot hit, Guy grunted but said no more, he knew the feeling by now, but it was only a flesh wound.

As the horse picked its way thicker into the forest, Guy realised how close to death he had come, and how unlikely this rescue was. He was right not to have sacrificed himself in a struggle whilst blindfolded, there was always hope no matter how slim. The Black Bear had seen more than one war but had never seen something like this, something so irregular. The pride of being a German officer in the highest class determined to kill the enemy at all costs dulled and the duty he had sworn a life to on his dagger seemed less black and white. In that moment of being rescued, the long-held beliefs that all the enemy should die without reason was questioned.

They were soon surrounded by dense wood, the boy slowing the horse to a trot, it was exhausted. The thick trees were impenetrable, not even the sun could fight its way through from above leaving the whole scene cast in shadow. It smelt strongly of wild garlic and a chorus of crickets began to announce their passing with a clicking of their wings. It was damp in here and quiet but not peaceful. It felt like the woods were watching them.

The boy looked over his shoulder at Guy, he had a purpose about him, a sternness that he thought only possible of people from his own land, the boy's drawn features held courage.

'There's a farmhouse through these trees,' the boy said quietly.

'How do you know?'

'A map I saw. At camp, before…'

'Do these people know you?'

'No. We have no choice. People will come looking for me.'

'As will mine,' Guy added. 'They are close. I was expecting them here already.'

The boy gestured towards the farmhouse. 'All we can do is ask and hope.'

Guy nodded.

'I'm Guy Schwarzbär. Look…' But his words drifted as the pain in his calf started to throb. He wanted to say something grand, something worthy of his high rank, to show his gratitude and to show he understood that the boy had saved his life, but nothing would come.

'I'm William,' the boy said and looked up as the woods began to thin out.

With a tap into the flank of the bay horse, they trotted on towards the white brick farmhouse nestled amongst the dense trees, the sun fading over its red-tiled roof.

Guy was confused and not purposeful for the first time in years. He was being led, but he did not mind. They were boxed in here though and that was a problem. The Germans would be coming as well as the British so maybe they should turn around, bid farewell to each other and be done with it and take their chances alone. He was hurt though, and the thought of a rest pulled at him, coming so close to execution had pushed even him. Perhaps too he mused he wanted to know more about the strange boy on the horse.

'Look.' The boy's head bowed but he said no more.

Guy, unsure why, put a hand on his shoulder.

'I just couldn't… I just…' But again he went quiet.

'I understand.'

'That's good,' the boy added quickly, as if he needed reassurance.

'I have seen a lot. But that… that was…'

The boy nodded.

'I feel tired,' Guy said quietly, not sure why he said that as it showed weakness.

This selfless deed of the boy took more courage than a killing one, perhaps not in the eyes of the army and the war, but in terms of being a human being, Guy knew it. It had made him stop and think, the hesitation he despised in his men had settled on him like a fine morning dew.

The men were bound now, not by blood but by deed. And that, thought Guy as the horse came to a stop and they both nearly fell off it with exhaustion, was perhaps what mattered most of all.

Chapter 5

Runner

Jolyon gagged with the stench of dead men and beasts in the air, his sleeve over his mouth did nothing, the stink easily penetrated the fabric. Parts of horses and bits of corpses were tangled together amongst the labyrinth of barbed wire in front of the lip of the trench. He didn't feel like he had expected to, he felt nothing really, his body moved mechanically onwards. The acrid smell of smoke left over from the howitzers was lifting and daggers of sunlight poured through from above exposing them.

'Steady,' a man in a gasmask to his left whispered, pushing him forward.

Jolyon crouched down as he moved forward, moving from shadow to sun to shadow as he picked his way forward with the Scots, flare gun gripped in his hand. Hillocks of earth with parts of corpses sticking out and mud-banks had formed across the landscape; the enemy could be lurking behind any number of them. Covering his eyes with his forearm against the glare, he jumped back when he passed a mound, and a German had his rifle raised at him. The man was dead though, suspended there by his coat on the wire in firing stance until he rotted away under the elements. A writhing mass of tails whipped about the dead man's boots. The rats worked from the feet up except the eyeballs and lips which were prized and went first, the mouth with all the teeth exposed was still open in a shout.

'Hold the line,' someone shouted who seemed far away.

'As one,' another said, his voice eerily clear after the shelling and Jolyon had been braced for all the noise in all the world out here.

One man was babbling and went to turn but was prodded forward by his mates with gentle hands, there was no safety backwards. Their own artillery hadn't landed on them when they waited in the trench as Jolyon had been promised it would by those at the front who took pure joy in frightening already terrified men. The veterans said being vapourised by a shell, even your own, was preferred to being winged by a rogue shot and left to bleed out in no-man's-land. After the battle, despite the promises of officers, men were left out here until some kind of temporary armistice was called by the raising of flags indicating the bearers were on the move. Jolyon could picture that slow death in all its horror but tried to bat it away as he passed the poor bastard in front of him hanging there, a shifting of black fur and pink tails writhing around the man's calf muscles.

To be left out here in this landscape surrounded by ghosts would be hell, he had to keep moving. Jolyon had gone to sleep two nights before hearing the chorus of cries after an offensive, he had lain awake hearing the wailing from the chasm between the armies. They got softly weaker until they succumbed, maybe it was the hanging man he had heard before the rats took his lips.

Another few steps forward through the wire fortresses, the land flattening out the further they got from their own line and away from where the mass of the German artillery was focused. There were bits of uniforms caught in the razor-sharp coils, green and grey strands intertwined, sagging and stuck. He was now exposed in the gaps amongst the craters and the gentle undulations levelled out, he caught first sight of the enemy trench. The ground was all so monotone that the distance was hard to gauge, it was like a vast blanket of mulch had been pulled over the landscape and the Scots. The endless brown sludge made him check his senses as his feet stepped over the flat mud which pulled at his boots, and he had to ensure he was walking forward and not standing still.

By this stage, he had been told he would be running between positions if not dead already, but there was nothing to run towards or away from. He looked back to his trench and saw men streaming through the gap in the wire cut by engineers, they wore the same expression of surprise that the first wave had not been obliterated. Jolyon had been one of the first through the gap, hundreds of them joined him quickly, edging forward with apprehension. It was silent from the enemy trench, nothing moved, only his line of comrades moving forward starting to look side to side at each other.

'Move on,' a corporal said through gritted teeth, unable to still the disquiet in his tone. 'And hold the bloody line.'

A soldier said, 'From what?'

The corporal just pointed a leather-covered finger at the enemy trench.

Had the enemy retreated as rumoured? A momentary skip of Jolyon's heart wondered if it was all over, at least for today. But why? They had the better ground, the higher ground, slowly Jolyon felt the gentle undulation begin to take his feet forward. Could he return home knowing he had almost fought a battle and made it through? Could he call himself a soldier?

Renewed, Jolyon and the men of the Scots without speaking went from walking cautiously to churning their legs in the mud, the furthest and fastest they had moved in days. The release of adrenaline hammered into all of them, the sheer audacity of still being alive struck hard. They picked up their sodden boots over potholes filled with oozing black water and sunken helmets and pressed on.

'Come on lads,' Jolyon called, a new voice of courage found out here in the middle, it was nothing like what they had said it would be like.

Another one yelled, 'You owe me a brick of tabs, Brody, I bloody told you, didn't I?'

Jolyon was running behind a couple of boys younger than him now sprinting towards the enemy lines. They looked identical, definitely brothers, and their arms and legs ticked along in tandem, their breathing perfectly in time. Their shadows were synchronised in the sunlight and he wondered if they felt as he did as the enemy lines came closer. What was it, relief? Or was it just too easy? That creep of unease would not be shifted but they would have fired by now if they were there.

They were approaching the German line fast now, the towering mesh of wire looming like the arches of great cathedrals over them casting spliced light down onto the mud. Jolyon saw the dappled light on the faces of the two brothers approaching, both looking up at these alien sights having never gotten this far.

The mighty Hindenburg Line was much further back, this wasn't it, it couldn't be. This was the old front line, it bore the scars of nearly four years of being lived in. So they had retreated back leaving this place to be taken by the Scots. Would they have left food? The savoured pork and beans. Jolyon's mind was on sharing a can with Solomon. He had been promised he would die at the end of the tale, within the first minutes.

The wire towered over Jolyon, they were within a minute of dropping down into the enemy trench. It was obscenely big, otherworldly in scale and out of place where everything else here was so temporary. The enemy trenches had been unmoved for four years, they had built them to outlast anything thrown at them, which they had.

Jolyon dropped to a knee, ramming binoculars against his eyes, cupping his elbow with his other hand to keep them steady. He took a few seconds to focus and scanned the torn ground and lip of the enemy trench covered in faded canvas and fine netting that kept the stones and soil in place. He had to squint as men charged past him, some beginning to cheer in the final run up.

Between the kilted legs of the Scots rumbling onwards he thought he saw a small black circle pointed directly at him from the enemy trench, but looking again, it was gone. It was almost invisible between the sprinting men, the melee, his shaking and the bright sun beating down. That black eye had met his though, a tiny pinprick of warning that had vanished. As he panned left and right, he saw another through the lenses, more black circles opening their eyes towards them, towards his regiment.

'Down,' Jolyon shouted, but simultaneously a shot rang out. A single crack which made a thousand men change their minds within a second of what this day would bring.

'Down,' Jolyon shouted again; the men were too bloody slow or didn't want to hear him. It was like a drumbeat in his ears rising in intensity, great crashes in his head of panic. Now he saw the tops of helmets begin to rise slowly from behind the German parapet, the spikes of the pickelhaube's becoming innumerable. The Scots had all slowed looking for the source of the rogue shots, some were within but metres of the enemy. All of them were gaping about and pointing as the wind blew over the front and cleared the last of the smoke from the big guns, then they saw everything.

Another crack echoed over the space between the two lines of men and a nameless man who was kneeling next to Jolyon slipped into him and made him tumble down into a shell hole. His webbing buckle caught Jolyon in the bridge of the nose and made him grimace, quickly followed by the sensation of cold water filling his boots. He felt hot blood seep from his face and wiped it away with his sleeve, the man was still leaning against him.

'Get up,' Jolyon yelled to the man, his voice echoing around the crater he was now in, bouncing back at him off the mud. A horror was dawning on the men's faces he could see above, and some began to throw themselves down, others started running harder at the enemy.

'Get up,' he said again to the fallen man, the man was dead though, Jolyon spying the small hole above his right eyebrow with a single trickle of blood meandering down to the corner of his mouth, the blood mixed with the dirt on his face. Jolyon tried to wipe it away but every time he did the red hole wept more. Drops ran down the chin and dropped with quiet pops onto Jolyon's forearm. The man's head was snapped back onto Jolyon's shoulder and his mouth lay open, he could see his yellow teeth and flaccid tongue, pimpled with white blotches.

Jolyon moved enough to let the body tilt back over his shoulder face first. It slid into the stagnant puddle in the shell crater with a gentle plop of putrid water engulfing the man, only the heels of his boots and the back of his helmet could be seen.

Another crack rang out, then a few more and men started to duck as the bullets passed over them and that sickening noise of metal hitting soft flesh began to pepper the air. The men at the very front started shouting retreat but were drowned out by blasting whistles and the Corporals screaming, 'Forward.'

A running man in green tumbled forward and Jolyon wondered if he had dived for cover, but he did not get up. Jolyon watched from the edge of the crater; another man went down. The Scot soldier was hunched forward on all fours, his face impaled on a barbed wire pole making him stay forever falling, his head slamming into it and the rod piercing his skull. His hands twitched violently until the rifle slipped from his grip, the finger still stuck in the trigger guard.

'Move,' Jolyon yelled, urging men forward as the dreaded sound of a machine gun from a bunker at the end of the trench opened up, the persistent spatter making the mud around the crater lip pop up in tiny bursts. A tiny black slit in the bunker was alive with yellow light, the outline of two curved helmets behind it twisting side to side raking the Scots.

Another burst from the opposite end of the trench, short, sharp and accurate. Bullets came inwards from both sides, squeezing the khaki wall, trimming its edges. Men began folding, that awful sound of the death moan rising from left and right, screaming for people they would never see again.

The entire enemy line ruptured into life; the noise impenetrable as the full force of the Germans was upon them hitting each of them with both the force of fire and knowing they were trapped. It felt to Jolyon like all the hardware ever invented by man was in the one spot at this one time.

Jolyon rolled a wounded man in front of him, who kept calling for Sophie, roughly he jammed a shoulder into the dirt to keep down and hidden. A high-pitched whistling had started but unlike any he had heard before, air above him was thrown back and forth as the rounds cut through it, causing pockets to pop and buzz all around him and his human shield.

The Germans had waited until it was too late to turn back, waited until they had lined them up, they could not go back, they could not go forward, and they could not hide for long.

Parts of soldiers were being torn off by grenades and roughly tossed far away from what remained of the man. Jolyon saw one man look down at his own blotched chest, a look of utter confusion about what had happened to him before he slumped onto his knees. Panic was spreading, the desperation quickly becoming inaction which only added to the chaos.

Jolyon, for the briefest moment, just wanted to cower down there forever. Maybe he should raise himself up on his knees until one of the thousands of German bullets being disbursed found its mark on his forehead. Or did he run towards them with arms in the air yelling like some of the others now were, done with this place and knowing it was hopeless.

These thoughts were a carousel of speed, colour, and noise. No rational thought had space, only instinct to survive or choose to die. He pressed his face against the back of the dead man, now being torn into by bullets again which made it shake and quiver like it was still living.

He sucked in air and smoke, and the rank smell of the man's khaki breeches pressed into his mouth. One of the dead man's hands flopped over Jolyon having been severed by bullets and he felt the sickly cold against his own warm flesh.

From deep inside, a place he had not been before, some forgotten duty fought back against the terror. It came from a primal place and hollered that he would not die yet, it forced him up from a sickening pit and the shell hole as still more men dropped around him. Bullets zinged into the dead man on repeat, the body starting to crumble into pieces as the head rolled away bobbling into the crater.

The enemy reloaded, a few brief seconds of quiet, only broken by the re-cocking of bolts and magazines, the screaming voices of the wounded Scots and the lone piper briefly heard. Then like a set of ocean waves, the one behind was bigger, the intensity of firing increased.

Jolyon watched as a man's skull collapsed in on its torso like it was on a spring, the body carried on running for a few paces until his legs gave way. From the black hole where his head had been the bright white bone of his jawline protruded from his neck, the teeth still attached, a stark white against the red.

Jolyon rolled into another shell hole and whilst on his back a man jumped clear over him, one leg buckling as a bullet tore through his kneecap. He stumbled on, firing his rifle at the wall of Germans before landing in the mud with a soft bump like a barge striking a jetty. Rolling again, Jolyon found himself flat behind a ridge of mud, felt the flare gun in his pocket and was reminded of his task.

'Stop,' he yelled. 'Stop running.' He held his palms open towards his own trench.

Amongst the roaring of the killing machines, next to him, a young boy was shouting for his mummy over and over, a huge part of his ribcage torn off by a stick hand grenade. He was half sitting up, his legs straight out in front of him, his back against the ridge. Jolyon looked down on him, aimed with the boy's rifle he had snatched, and when the boy looked skywards, he shot him through the head.

The smoke from the enemy guns had reached the men running at them which added to the melee. His hand was now aching from gripping the flare gun so tightly, but his legs were desperate to be free. He saw his route amongst the debris and peered up, covering the side of his face with a hand knowing that would do nothing to help but it felt comforting. In one movement, he pounced up, running along the trench line, adjacent to the mouths of the guns and ducked as he ran, bullets firing past him, he heard them clipping off metal barbed wire poles surrounding him.

He sucked air hard into his lungs as they began to burn from the exertion, weaving through the land now littered with the wounded, one man stretched out a hand in desperation to grab his ankle, but he kicked it away.

Ahead was a compression in the land of mud, bodies, and the burnt-out shell of a tank left over from their last big push. It had been blown in half some days back and the Scots had zeroed their rifles on it the preceding morning. The barrel of the tank was bent at a right angle, and over the top of it, he could make out the woodland beyond.

Out here, away from the main thrust of the advance through the centre, it felt that bit quieter. His mouth was dry and rasping, his canteen had come off in the crater. He ran onwards towards the tank, but just as he thought he had found some respite, the sound changed again; the machine guns were raking back towards him having finished their curved arcs. Behind him, he heard the wallop of bullets hitting men again, seconds and they would be on him, riddling his body, sending his uniform back to Evelyn and his parents in a burlap parcel.

The tank loomed large in front of him, its metal edges ringing with the impact of bullets and spinning shrapnel from grenades. Its massive hull of rust was almost there, within metres. He leapt up over a sandbag wall and a bullet caught his bootheel, skimming the sole of his foot. Rotating with the impact, he landed as bullets tore into the structure of the tank above him, fresh dents and holes painted the side as bullets ricocheted all around him. He rolled and slammed his back against the tank letting out a scream so loud he could make it out above the noise. The machine guns moved back the other way again and he vomited, the bacon of earlier sliding through his fingers and making them syrupy.

Pressed against the tank, Jolyon looked towards his trench line as figures still fell, all along the line, there seemed no order to what anyone was doing. Some of the Scots who had made it to the German positions were held up in the wire tearing at it to escape, maiming themselves, great chunks of skin coming loose before being picked off by sharpshooters.

He waited for his signal to fire the flare as the rest fought forward, he had to remember his one task at hand. Jolyon's eyes started to stream with the smoke as gas grenades exploded in front of the German lines, some of the Scots were throwing them as cover despite knowing it would suffocate them. He could see the heavy square boxes exploding in dust clouds above the Germans, his own men writhing in agony as the particles found their lungs. A dense yellow haze sat there unmoving that only showed the flashes of barrels through it.

As he raised himself up a few inches to take in the length of his trench, a sniper's bullet zipped into the tank. It made a dull thwack against the metal leaving a clean smoking hole in the shell. Someone was watching him closely and amongst the pandemonium, this felt personal which grated him, it felt too selective for what he had witnessed.

'Please,' he screamed towards his trench. 'Get that flag up,' he begged to the air.

He saw a movement where his dugout had been, his binoculars were fogged with the gas in his eyes. Through the bodies flailing about he made out the movement of a flag, they had a pulley and post in place, but he couldn't see the dugout, just a space of blackened smoke where it used to be.

He watched the end of his trench knowing his moment was almost here, then he saw a familiar figure, Solomon was clambering onto the top of the remains of the dugout. He sunk to a knee, briefly, like he was praying, then looked directly at Jolyon. He was shouting but Jolyon heard nothing, just the garbled mouth forming shapes in the distance. Solomon crouched there, as if readying himself and then he stood, showing his full front to the German lines, drawing the flag upwards above his head and waved it furiously.

It was red, they had failed. 'Abandon positions and retreat.' Leatherbrook's words stung.

Solomon seemed to buckle; the sodden red flag wrapped itself round his body, Jolyon watched as he was hit in the hip by a bullet. Jolyon shouted towards him, his only friend out here, his binoculars slipped as he waved his arms, but he saw the silhouetted figure of Solomon struck again and fold backwards over the billet, wrapped in the flag. His hand had gone to his chest where he kept his journal tied with fraying butchers' twine.

Another sniper's bullet pinged off the hull of the tank which snapped Jolyon back to his task, he would mourn if he was still alive in the coming days. The wind gusted from the direction of the wood making the yellow clouds of gas swirl in slow rotations upwards out of the tank allowing him to see. He primed his flare gun and looked at it in his hand, he had the signal, and more men would die without it.

For his men he would stand in plain sight, the flare had to

arch over the German lines so it was soon. He hoped the survivors would turn about and skid and slide their way back to the trench, no more need die in this slaughter. With a final look, his back pressed against rusty metal he saw the edge of the woodland he had dreamed of being in earlier, it was like it called to him.

He clambered up the side of the tank, the whole panorama before him. Hundreds of bodies lay writhing, the ground looked like it was covered in green and red snakes. Trinkets were being clutched all over the field, dying words being spoken aloud to nothing but the sun and the wind.

Jolyon pulled the trigger on the flare gun and a resounding crack filled the belly of the tank. A red rocket erupted from the barrel leaving smoke trails in its wake, a white plume arching over the German line. He was surrounded by a red haze from the flare which made everything look like sunset, it was like he was inside the embers of a fire.

He watched the rocket go up into the blue sky and explode in crimson, and then for the briefest moment, almost too small to register, he felt a sharp stab somewhere near his shoulder.

He felt himself falling backwards through the red cloud and he had a funny taste in his mouth of metal. The last thing he saw was the rusty floor of the tank coming up to greet his face, but his eyes were closing already. Then everything went quiet, and everything for the first time in days went still.

Chapter 6

Gunner

Torrents of rain washed over the battlefield in great sheets soaking everything but clearing nothing, it was so thick it looked to Otto like a thousand coiled ropes suspended from the clouds. When the attack had fizzled out and the British finally stopped running at them, great storm clouds had begun to collide in the heavens. There was an electricity of an oncoming downpour in the air, which felt odd for Otto as these moments after intense action were usually dead flat.

'My god...' he said quietly.

There was no debrief yet, no quarter for reflection, that might or might not come later. His men just stared at the space in front of them, hot rifles in their hands.

The kaleidoscope of blood, tumbling khaki and muzzle flashes were replaced with monotone grey when the drizzle turned to rain and little was discernible, just outlines of bodies now shadows amongst mounds of bubbling mud. The whimpering of the wounded was fading, the sound of drumming rain off wires and machine gun positions was metronomic, like a steady heartbeat. The final thrashes of broken bodies succumbed to the rivers that ran between the craters of no-man's-land, water submerged their beaten corpses, went into their mouths and down into their lungs.

Otto was still hunched over the top of the trench, the barrel of his rifle smoking with water accumulating in the rivet on the front of the scope, and gently pulling his face back, he removed his aching finger from the trigger. He looked along the trench, his men were all still tucked in place resolutely, an unbroken line. He could only make out shoulders and helmets which looked like black molehills along the fire step.

'Kummer... Kummer,' he called.

His man stepped up next to him. 'Sir?'

'Tell the men to move to watch mode, half go down and get out of this.'

Kummer nodded and began moving along the trench tapping every second man on the shoulder. Those touched gratefully put their rifles skyward, emptied chambers, stepped back, and scuttled towards the warmth and whisky waiting for them below in the dugouts.

Before each soldier disappeared below, each one looked at their commander Otto and gave a sharp nod making rain tip off their helmet rims onto the front of their tunics. Otto half smiled at each exhausted man, a nod for victory, but mainly for being relieved.

He looked hazily across the grey landscape in front of him and sighed, the air rattling over his teeth. Beneath his feet was a small mound of spent magazines and bullet casings, he could feel the edges of the casings chafing against his shin through his soaking uniform.

From his pocket, he took out a flask and drunk the mix of peach brandy and water feeling it warm his throat. He considered lighting a cigarette but the rain would destroy it and he hated the thought of such waste. He had fought for a long time in this place, this was his third trench summer, but that had been worse than most he could remember.

'God's sake,' he said again, the rain hammering his helmet.

Would those faces appear in his nightmares to tap him on the shoulder and level blame? He had been close enough to make out their eye colour, hear their last words. Was no one on their side watching the bloody thing? Could no one just say enough? The flare of retreat seemed to take an age to be fired, he would have turned back a long time before the Scots did. That had been slaughter of the most indelible kind on him and a hint of something like guilt made him pull on the flask until it was almost empty. After intense action the lapping fatigue soon returned, he was saturated and smelling of damp with just a hint of purple powder discharge along the arm.

It could have been minutes, maybe hours since it had ended. He scanned the horizon through his scope and between the sheets of rain could make out the remains of a brewed-up tank with its barrel bent but its outline clear against the tempest. He looked harder, seeing its shape phase in and out through the rain as his nagging tiredness fizzed his eyeballs and he considered again the cigarette even if only for one puff.

Slumped across the side of the tank he could see a man lying still, his hand gripped around the handle of a flare gun. The man had fallen awkwardly with his face looking straight at Otto, it was unpleasant to be stared at by the dead. He looked back at the man's face, unmoving and ghostly white against the brown, black and grey of the tank and the mud. The lips were a thin line with no expression on the contours and he could have been sleeping.

Another one not going back, another one left out in the rain for the rats and the soil to take him under. Maybe his Scots men would remember him and mark his passing with a simple wooden cross, at the very least a song to him. He had heard those laments cross the gap between them on flat nights, groups of men in chorus together. Or maybe with so many dead today they wouldn't, and this man would just go down as missing.

'A bad day it had been,' they would say, just as they did on his side and then they would return possessions to families with a curt letter and if lucky a memory or two from another soldier thrown in to soften the blow. This was the way of it, he had written reams of those letters himself to families in Cologne, Düsseldorf, Munich, Aachen, Potsdam and the rest.

He felt himself dozing off again, and twice he lurched himself awake with a jolt from his legs. A hand on his shoulder made him snap away from his slumber with a jump, but he knew the touch.

'Sir,' Kummer said.

Otto nodded, still looking out over the front, like it was all he would ever see again. Images had started to replay, exact moments in time punctuated with the racket of the guns pelting bullets towards the fracturing green line.

'Go and get some food, there's something hot for you.'

For some inexplicable reason, Otto wanted to stay as if turning his back on the scene would crystallise it and he felt a wave of great sadness rise in him. It would be their turn next, possibly tomorrow, although it was a Sunday, but certainly by the day after. The tear that rolled down his creased face was masked by the rain still hammering away from the skies.

Kummer bumped his again, this time with a friendly shoulder. 'Sir, it does no good to dwell on these things.'

'I want to go out there,' Otto said dreamily.

'Sir?'

'I want to know what they were looking at.'

'Sir, some rest first. Some food.'

Otto could hear the concern in his friend's voice.

'Yes, yes,' Otto said but that thought had settled.

Kummer nudged him again, this time it annoyed Otto.

He would crawl out there to the middle of all this that night, between the lines and look back on his own men whilst they slept. He wanted to see exactly what the man in the tank had seen, what had been his last vista. It felt like they had met before, somewhere, but that wasn't possible.

Otto slunk backwards off the lip of the trench, turning about towards the dugout, so wet every miniscule movement made him colder. He looked up at the sky, the storm showing no signs of abating. Rain streamed off the bridge of his nose and brows, and he opened his mouth wide, feeling the drops prickle his tongue.

His self-appointed mission to go out there and see the man in the tank would have to wait, Kummer was right, he was fraying and needed to eat and close his eyes.

Underneath the battlefield was a different world and Otto was hit with a roasting heat that embraced him, pulling him towards it, and there was a stale atmosphere of men's ablutions, liquor, and cigarette smoke. Picking out troopers was difficult, just outlines of forms with glints of teeth or eyes in the light from the burners. The table in the centre of the dugout was crowded with half-naked men, their uniforms hanging limply around their waists.

Helmets and guns were strewn at random as if they were for another time, a different place. They were drinking from short glasses and playing with battered cards, arguing over each hand as the cards were turned over and inspected. One man knocked over a bottle to much shouting, another man raising a fist to strike. On realising it was empty they all laughed raucously and slammed each other on the backs and began singing in jumbled gurgled prose, Otto did not know the tune.

The underground layer was spacious, the size of a large crater from the battlefield above, they had taken plenty of British trenches and they had nothing like this. The British seemed happy to sit in their own shit and eat from tins in the rain which made their willingness to keep running towards them even more baffling.

Against the sooty back wall, men dozed or slept, a bottle close to lips or to hand. One man faced the wall, curled up in a ball and Otto could see his shoulders shaking and heaving. He was in the minority thought, for they had won so the celebration always followed; Otto was not going to stop them and he was not sure he even could.

'Sir,' said an orderly, handing Otto a glass full to the brim with what smelt like rum. They mixed them all together now, whatever spirits were available were tipped into a jug and passed around, his men had taken to calling it Firebrand.

Otto nodded in thanks and let his long coat slip off his shoulders, the weight of the rain made it wind its way down his back like a serpent. He hung it on one of the pegs by the door along with his rifle, helmet, and webbing. A puddle of droplets started forming underneath, and he found himself nodding in time with the drips. He opened his throat and drank the fiery liquid down in one, it was refilled at once by another trooper. He took a seat at a corner table where no games were played, but three men debated the day that had passed them.

'Just so many...' one man said, his eyes already red and wet with drink.

'So many,' the other said, a flash across his face of

something like shame until he pretended to scratch his temple and hid his eyes behind the folded hand clutching a quivering cigarette end.

'And where were the planes? The mighty planes of England,' roared another. He slammed his hand down on the table sending a glass skidding that teetered on the edge of the table that just held. The man then proceeded to raise his arms parallel to his shoulders and ran around the table making put-put noises like an engine.

'Broooomm,' he yelled as he ran round the table faster and faster. 'Sorry, boys, no support today.' He cheered as he then feigned a British soldier being riddled with bullets. The three men fell over each other in laughter, splintering a chair under their weight until they all collapsed onto the floor. Hands reached up like crabs scuttling on a shoreline until they found their half-full glasses from where they lay, these they rammed together with a toast.

Otto finished another glass and yawned widely making his ears pop and blocked out the din for a second. In front of him was a plate of thick white bread and butter but as he reached a hand towards it, the whiteness reminded him of the face of the man in the tank. He dropped his hand and played with a lighter in his pocket as the men at the card table started up another song from home.

Otto did not know where to look, liquor had dulled him to the point of inaction. He had no desire to review the day like the men at this table, and he did not want to enter a game of cards, officers did not mix well with men. When they had begun this thing they had separate quarters, officers dining well under candlelight to the thumps and bumps from the next-door billets where the men would drink and fight. Now, though they were all together, sharing glasses, crapping in the same buckets, and sleeping on top of each other before passing out.

'Kummer,' Otto drawled, looking around as the din on the voices reached a pitch of constant rumbling like the shells that were always somewhere overhead. Someone was holding court, telling a story he thought he knew the end of, but it felt far away.

'Kummer,' Otto pleaded.

Kummer though was still up top, busy as he always was, he wanted him here next to him. He cared deeply for Kummer and at times when he lay awake with the artillery shells popping overhead he wondered if more than he should, he had never met anyone like him. Sometimes he watched him for hours move along the trench, so light of foot and always with a smile on his face no matter the obstacles that lay ahead.

Another glass-full disappeared down his gullet and Otto Zweck, for the first time in months felt the first swell of drunkenness. The room was unbearably stuffy, and he felt sweat dripping from the middle of his back down to his buttocks making them itch furiously. He was offered a bent cigarette but declined, the thought of inhaling anything right now but cool air made him nauseous.

He had to get out of here, it was just too bizarre. Men who an hour before had reloaded until spent were now at play and they played rough, slapping each other round the jowls with open hands in jest, but that would soon turn sour as one landed just a bit too hard on a fractured collective patience. It was like the whole hot dugout was in cahoots, but Otto hadn't been told the joke.

He steadied himself with a hand on the table getting up slowly, as he did the glass that had been on the edge of the table toppled off and smashed. For a moment he wanted to go to the back wall and crawl up next to the shaking man and hold him, they could embrace in mangled sleep and soothe each other and leave the others to drink and drown.

Stumbling towards the gaping mouth of the dugout, he retched aloud. Otto turned quickly away from the men, grabbing his webbing and coat from the peg and fell forwards through the opening onto his knees and into the fresh air, the rain having passed and replaced with a flat light of dark blue before sunset. The storm clouds rolled on to the east, off to batter another horizon and another regiment.

Kummer was there in flash by his side. 'Sir?'

Otto waved him away with a hand, taking in great gulps of air. He wiped saliva away from his lips, squeezed his hands into his webbing and let his head loll backwards on its pivot. He stayed like that on his knees facing up at the sky, eyes closed for a full minute. His breathing returned to its normal rhythm, and he felt the waves of sickness pass through him as he regained some of himself.

Kummer put an arm around Otto, the burden of command weighed heavy and after three years of this, most shoulders were worn out.

Otto whispered an apology, but Kummer waved it off with one of his dazzling smiles that illuminated his whole face, the shape of his grin traced his helmet strap.

'It's just...' Otto began.

'Please, sir...' Kummer whispered, and both men, in the absence of words still knew exactly what the other one was thinking.

Otto took a pull from the canteen offered, gulping hungrily making his eyes close again and, in that moment, he thought again of the man in the tank.

The bright red disc of the sun began to lift from behind the clouds of the storm turning everything dark orange. The craters and piles of bodies buzzing with flies in no-man's-land bathed in tangerine looked less shocking than the flat grey of before.

Otto picked up his binoculars to check on the man in the tank hoping his staring face had magically disappeared. Kummer was off again to tend to more needy and grateful souls along the line.

He checked again and had to rub his eyes, he must have been exhausted, his mind playing tricks. Otto was not mistaken though, the man in the tank was gone.

Chapter 7

Rider

The implications of his actions had begun to flutter like a ragged sail in a storm. The hulking man behind him and the horse were breathing heavily as a constant reminder of the deed which he would never be forgotten for.

William was not tired exactly though his eyelids were heavy, more in deep thought chewing his bottom lip as the horse came into a flat patch of sunlit grass by the river. It came to a stop in front of the small, red-roofed farmhouse off the banks of the River Scarpe, perfectly hidden by the forest all around. The house looked well lived in, and William felt the tug of home, he had not seen his own home in so long, and he had hated leaving it. He had refused the traditional farewell given to others by loving parents at the station, he had left one morning before they woke.

The horse ambled towards a water trough in front of the house where it bowed its head and took long spluttering pulls over its whiskers.

He let the reins go slack, feeling the skin chaffed and bitten into by the hard leather. His hands were trembling, pinking from the strain and he cracked his knuckles with force sliding his teeth over his bottom lip and pinching his face up.

The entire episode had felt over very quickly, and flashbacks of images caught in time hit him with staccato repetitions, each one pulling him further forward towards understanding he had made a grave mistake. Scenes whirred at random from the British soldiers falling over under the horse, dead Germans littering the clearing and the bullets missing their heads.

William spoke half over his shoulder, 'Did you know them?'

'Very well,' the German said.

William nodded slowly, the only sound the lapping at the trough by the horse.

By his hand alone, he had saved the man behind him. If all the prisoners were dead, including Guy, the upcoming recriminations would have been utterly in vain. Where the rest of the prisoners who had survived were now, he didn't know, but he could not go back and look for them. Two he saw make the edge of the woods, running awkwardly in their thick grey coats with their arms trussed up.

William asked hopefully, 'A few made it?'

'Some, yes,' the German said, the words rumbling together in a low growl. 'That means my people will come here sooner though.'

Would he be shot when he was caught? And by which army? Patrols would be searching for him already; the siren of insubordination would be ringing loudly at camp. This act of mercy was likely to end not in glory, but in death. Any joy he had felt was now gone as the adrenaline drained from him, replaced with a hollow nagging of question upon question about why he had acted so impetuously.

He slid down off the horse, the sweat from the beast dampening his inner thigh and pulling at his trousers which he noticed were stained with blood though he didn't know whose.

Guy looked uncomfortable on the horse, almost irritated like he had an itch in the middle of his back he could not reach. When their eyes met, the German's eyes flicked down involuntarily towards his legs still astride the horse and William saw the dark red patch spreading from the back of his calf.

As the men's eyes met again, they took each other in fully, William measured the German now clambering off the horse. He raised a hand in refusal of help when William had seen he was wounded, the other hand clasped around the saddle, the fingers leaving streaks of blood and sweat on the leather.

In silence they watched each other, keeping their distance, not quite circling one another in the clearing but almost. William passed him a metal bucket from the trough which he took with thanks and drank deeply, tipping the bucket up so the water ran over his wide features and down onto his broad shoulders, staining the grey jacket to a dark black.

Standing next to each other, William saw he was at least a foot shorter than Guy. His chest was twice as broad as his own and an emblem hung from the pocket he could not quite make out. His blonde hair was the kind that always went almost white in summer, his skin already bronzed and hard. Thick lines spread like branches from the corners of his eyes, meeting with a scar over his eyebrow that ran round to under his hairline. If he had to guess he would say Guy was about forty, old for the front.

'Is it bad?' William said, flicking a wave at the man's legs.

Guy shook his head firmly. 'No.'

Another long silence passed between them, both went to speak but said nothing or thought better of it. The heat of the day began to creep and made William's uniform feel sticky on his skin. It must have been about midday, the base camp and bathing in the river felt like he had been watching someone else do it in another life.

Guy offered the water pail back having refilled it. 'I feel my injuries may have been a little worse if you had not arrived, eh?'

William grinned slightly, the effort at humour was appreciated. The man's English was almost perfect and behind the hardened face he sensed a calm worldliness, he was like a season of weather, relentless and unstoppable. He didn't speak to William like a soldier, not even like a friend but something else. When he smiled, he showed no teeth, just a tight line of lips. The corners of his eyes folded down slightly giving him a pained look that knew joy out here was rare, like he had seen all aspects of war.

William had been raised to look for qualities in people, no matter how hidden. His father had been very sure to teach him that, a father who in adulthood had made an ironclad rule of only ever spending time with good people. Then that man, the man he had learned all he could from and looked up to all his life, had sent him to war.

William noticed the emblem again hanging from Guy's pocket.

'What's that?'

Guy looked down, and William saw sadness cross his face making the scar on his temple more pronounced. His hand rubbed the emblem gingerly. 'From my boys. They call me the Black Bear, in my army that is.'

'A bear?'

'Yes, a fighting bear,' Guy said before shaking his head of the last water droplets from the pail.

Guy had sat down with his back against the water trough, his movements laboured, yanking off one of his boots and rolling up the trouser leg of his uniform. He revealed the syrupy red patch on his skin where the bullet had clipped him.

'A scratch,' he said, slapping his kneecap with an open palm.

He carefully washed it with water and wrapped it in a bandage from his inside pocket.

William lit a cigarette and watched the man at work from the shade, the first 'real' German soldier he had met. He seemed almost business-like, unthreatening in a sense as he was so engaged with the task at hand. What had he expected? Should they be wrestling in the long grass until one of them squeezed the life out of the other? He would have lost that struggle. What William had done in the clearing seemed to have stalled them both for the moment from their sworn duties. They were in flux, but it was temporary, and William could be certain Guy was thinking the exact same thing. If one made a move, so would the other.

When the hulking man leant forward to check his patching up, William saw the Iron Cross slip from between his open shirt neck and bump against his bent knee. It sat almost in line with the bear emblem, both facing each other.

Guy saw him spot it, and looked down, holding it between his fingers. He turned it in the light, the silver edges glinting in the sun, the centre jet-black.

'For bravery,' he said, tucking it away again and fastening a button behind a red ribbon.

'In this war?' William asked.

'The last. My one for this war I was awarded I do not wear.'

William thought he knew why. 'Because of...?'

Guy cleared his throat and smiled grimly, looking beyond William at the hazing edge of the woods now a dark line against the bright square in front of the farmhouse.

'Because bravery in the last war was decent, it was honest. In this one bravery can be given for many things in my home, not all of them brave. Some think to be brave just means to kill.'

'In my country, you have to die to get a good medal.'

'No medals for death are good,' Guy said sharply.

William nodded and went back to his silence; their skirmish in conversation had failed.

Whatever this man was, he was not what William had expected. The man had two Iron Crosses; how many soldiers were there in the ranks of the entire German army with two?

Distracting himself with anything but the consequences of who he had saved, William set about tying the horse sturdily and wiping down the sweat from the flanks, giving the horse a stroke along the breadth of its nose. The horse had drunk its fill and had moved to chew the long grass accumulated around the edges of the stone trough. William removed the saddle, washed it in the trough, and laid it out in the sun to dry.

The house, despite being old and fraying at the edges was sturdy, William imagined it had not known war. It looked old enough to have been in the last war though, it was tired but not tatty.

'I had better check if anyone is here,' William said.

Guy nodded. 'I will watch for us.'

William turned, a momentary wave of unease at turning his back on the enemy. All his training, all he had read and been told about the Germans, and he was turning about, unarmed, leaving his one method of escape from this place tied up to the trough.

He assured himself that if this soldier from the other side was going to do something sinister, he would have done it already. Those hands could have crushed his neck to splinters when he sat behind him on the horse.

William walked past a row of lavender bushes towards the house and butterflies exploded up and around him. One brushed his face so lightly with a wing, and so close to his eyelids, he closed them tight.

William felt uneasy as his eyes flicked across the treeline, the peaceful farmhouse was out of place given the brutal events of the morning. It reminded William of something from the last war his father had told him about, a farmhouse at the end of the trenches deep in the woods where the German executions happened. Most buildings had been flattened back then, but that house it was rumoured had stood through it all. Legend had it that both sides made a pact to leave it be, it was a potent reminder for them all back then that whilst they said they were fighting for their country, truly they were fighting for their homes.

The house was set back from the river, the gently eddying water a satisfactory soundtrack. The woods they had ridden from were the only way to get here, the bright square of lush flat green grass was man tendered so someone lived here. Up behind the house, the land rose sharply on three sides, banks of thick trees circling the house like a curved hand. It was a safe place to be if you lived here, but a bad place to be if you were on the run, one way in meant one way out.

A willow tree on the bank obscured some of the farmhouse, its branches loosely jigging which sounded like a repeated hushing. It had all its shutters bolted except one that hung ajar. A step led up to the front door, the cast iron knocker in the face of a lion. Above the door was a balcony which formed a porch over the entrance and there were two diagonal wooden supports holding it in place. From one hung a watering can, and from the other, a faded Marseilles frayed at the edges by the wind.

Over where Guy sat was an outbuilding that looked like a good place to hide if they had to move quickly, the door would give way easily enough under their boots. Both men were unarmed though, they stood little chance if the owner of the house had a weapon. Something about this whole place made William stare harder at it and take in every detail like he had seen it somewhere before.

Ambling along the bank, William began whistling and kicked a stone into the water which made a hidden duck quack in annoyance. Looking back up at the farmhouse and shading his eyes with his hand, the one shutter on the top floor that had been a fraction open closed with the faintest click. He went down on his haunches, looking at the window and listened intently, somebody else was here and had been watching them.

Guy came around the corner of the farmhouse from the barn, he had heard it too.

William got up from his crouch and raised both hands openly towards the house in surrender knowing this was futile given his uniform.

'Hello?' William called out, his voice echoing around the open space.

No sound came back, just the flutter of the willow branches.

'We mean no harm. Is someone there?'

His head was pressed against the door, his face close to the lion's head. He heard faint footsteps coming down the stairs, soft steps like they were unsure, and each step was being debated before being taken.

Guy walked up next to William, looked down on him briefly and then stood to attention, his heels snapping together.

The fading timber door opened with a slow creak, light flooding into the hallway of the farmhouse, a cracked black and white umbrella stand glinting. William had to move his eyes lower than he had been expecting as standing there in the doorway, was a little blonde girl of about five years old.

She tilted her head questioningly, taking in the strange sight in front of her. Freckles were rampant across her nose and cheeks, and the girl just stared back at him.

A flash of fear crossed her face, momentarily, and then it changed to an embarrassed smile. She looked behind her into the shaded house to call out but seemed to remember something and tucked her hands behind her back, the head bowing showing a faded pink Alice band. William smiled widely and waved, and she blushed, a light pinking drawing up from her neck to her cheeks.

'Hello,' said William in French, the girl's face registering a language she knew.

'We are friends,' Guy added.

The girl paused, one foot hovering forward into the light beyond the front doorstep, her bare foot and tanned ankle in the sun. She retracted her foot, looked a little sad and went to close the door on them. Just then, the horse neighed from round the corner and her face lit up. She skipped forward between the soldiers, her hair caught in the sunlight, her blue overall creasing as she ran forward. She careered right, her legs churning through the grass until she was standing in front of the bay horse looking up at its form.

The girl emitted a squeak of delight and then looked back at the men as if to check what she was doing was allowed. She was bouncing up and down on the spot, her hand reaching towards the horses' massive flanks, desperate to stroke them. Guy stepped forward and plucked a handful of long grass from the edge of the trough. He walked round to the head of the horse and held out the grass to the animal so that it bent slowly and started chomping and licking his hand in thanks, he motioned to the girl to get some grass which she did.

The horse bucked its head and flicked its ears, but William cooed gently to it calming it, stroking the white diamond. He held his hand flat and motioned feeding the horse which the girl copied. When the horse began to nibble, and the whiskers brushed her skin she giggled, and for the first time, William saw Guy smile.

As the girl busied herself with feeding the horse and William held the reigns, Guy whispered aside, 'Where are her parents?'

William shook his head but kept smiling so as not to alarm the girl.

William watched with curiosity the ease at which Guy had scooped the girl up onto the horse. William had held her hand like he would have a bird's egg, believing her so delicate and fragile she could snap at any moment.

Guy had swung her onto his shoulders so she could pat the top of the horse before it went for its doze. As a final act of excitement, she had bounced on the horse, her feet kicking on the horse's flanks.

Guy had searched through his jacket, making a big show of laying everything out on the grass for the curious little girl to inspect. When she had gotten to the bear emblem, she had fingered it in her hands making it march up her forearm, then held it up to Guy and William.

'I don't like this,' Guy said to William away from the girl.

William shrugged, what else could they do?

The girl was now by the river hitting stinging nettles with a stick and with his eyes closed, William breathed in deeply, his long breaths akin to those ones in Arras by the Scarpe that morning. He had stripped down to his vest and felt the heat tingle on his skin.

He was uncertain whether he should be running further away from his seekers. Dozing in the sun like a dog when half the British army would be looking for him and Guy seemed idiotic, but a pervading sense of nonchalance had blanketed him. He was trapped here but for some reason had accepted his fate.

William watched the girl play gloomily as the realisation dawned on him, he was going to die, the Germans were heading this way too, Guy had said so.

Taking one of his cigarettes, Guy said, 'You did what you felt you had to do.'

'Look what I brought here,' William said forlornly pointing at the girl.

Guy listened as William said he wanted to return from war to prove to his father he had done it but would never come back. William's felt queasy about the talk of home and in one movement he had gotten up and walked down to the girl by the river.

William and the girl were walking back towards Guy, the hot sun beating down. William had slung his jacket over his shoulders and turned the collar up so his shadow made a funny shape in the grass. She tried to skip away from his shadow, the scary outline, jumping in great leapfrogs but William moved to keep her in the shade pretending to roar like a monster with his arms outstretched.

William waved at Guy, shouting to him, 'Her name is Lucy.'

'Hello, Lucy,' Guy shouted, at which she grinned back and pretended to hide behind her hands.

'Says she wants to get us some milk and bread,' William said with a smile.

William and the girl were seconds away when William saw

Guy's face change. If it hadn't been for the glare, he might have seen it earlier, that might have helped. For a second, he thought it might be the British who had found him already. An awful premonition seeped into him and despite having his eyes open, he saw it clearly like a warning. He imagined he was dying, badly wounded and in chains on a ship.

William went to turn and saw a small man appear from the woods, running past the riverbank. He threw down a rabbit with its neck broken which bounced on the hard ground, then he dropped to a knee with a shotgun raised.

Guy scrabbled to his feet and William heard him shout, 'No!'

A boom shattered the calm of the tranquil scene, starlings flying up from branches surrounding the house. The rolling sound spiralled around the farmhouse and William clutched at his back. His white vest showed splatters of blood along the sides, the small circles growing. He dropped to his knees slowly as the little girl Lucy began to scream.

Ahead, Guy went to move forward but he heard the shotgun cock from where he now lay. Tears streamed down Lucy's face as she ran back to the man's side, he was shorter than both soldiers and had a thick beard, his teeth gritted, Guy kept his hands raised. Slowly the man prowled towards William, now lying still on the ground.

The man put a foot on William's back, pressing down which made him squeal pitifully.

The man levelled the shotgun at Guy, ready to pull the trigger. In the corner of his mouth hung a toothpick and he rolled it with his tongue over his lips. Lucy though was pulling on his jacket, straining against the dark blue sleeves with dried sweat at the cuffs. The darkly tanned face of the man looked down at the girl, his eyes narrowing.

'Daddy,' she said desperately, fresh tears rolling down her cheeks. 'They are friends.'

The Frenchman would not stop pressing on William's back with the sole of his boot. William had not been wounded in war until now, so he had no idea if this was life-threatening. Did they all feel like this? He felt calm, almost puzzled but the pain came in waves and was not constant. He had broken his arm when he was young, but that had been acute. This was not sharp, but his whole torso throbbed like it was slowly emptying with each pump of his heart.

As he wasn't dead yet, he was sure his thick coat draped over his shoulders which had used to entertain the girl in the shadow game had stopped most of the blast. Some had gotten through though and he was certain he could feel pellets burrowing into his skin further every time he breathed.

In panic, the Frenchman must have fired immediately when he saw them, too far away with a shotgun to be lethal. It felt dreamlike as the hot sun beat down on him and he lay there in the stubbled grass and just wanted to sleep.

What kept him awake was what would happen next, his options were narrow. If the man shot Guy dead next, he would roll, grab the Frenchman's leg, and try to pull him over. He would cup his hands just above the kneecap and yank downwards until something gave way. He would then either take the shotgun and run into the woods or lay it at the feet of the father and daughter and hope they provided shelter.

If the man did not shoot Guy, they had a chance. A small one, but he knew that in war freak occurrences did happen. William had been told by his father, that people never did quite what you expected or acted how they would in peacetime. William's father had spoken of being rescued by strangers, he seemed to know that war brought out the very worst in man, but amongst those endless nightmarish and violent deeds, his father said moments of mercy shone brightly.

The girl was still yelping next to her father, pleading in rapid French to spare the soldiers. The Frenchman seemed to take an age to decide, all the while William remained cocked and ready to spring up if he pulled the trigger on Guy. He had found purchase with one foot, bent into the dry grass and his arm by his side was clenched and taught.

Something seemed to break the trance of the rabid father who was trying to silence his daughter with his free hand in rapid French. With a curse, he lowered the gun and took his foot off William's back.

He spoke to William who looked puzzled, he only knew basic French. This frustrated the father as he cursed again and clenched the butt of the gun so hard his knuckles went white. His tanned skin wrinkled around his gaunt cheeks, and his small black eyes narrowed. He ran a hand through his grey beard, twisting the end of it with his fingers in thought.

Guy, on his haunches, said, 'I speak French.'

'Good,' the father said. 'You need to speak now. Immediately. What the hell is going on?'

Guy motioned to William. 'May I check his wounds?'

The father looked at the huge German in front of him on his knees, and then at Lucy putting a hand on her shoulder and bending low to her ear. 'Go and get warm water and cloths. And get the metal tin in the kitchen. Bring it now.'

William had no idea what was happening, he just lay there

watching words that made no sense be exchanged between the other three from where he lay.

Guy nodded once in thanks at whatever the Frenchman had said to him.

William watched Lucy, sprinting off towards the farmhouse as instructed, her bare feet thudding like paws on the dry grass. The Frenchman looked down again on William and spoke in broken English, 'Can you move?'

'Yes,' William said, sitting up and feeling this fresh heat of being wounded creep up his back, the skin felt taught as if already trying to knit back together and a wave of nausea caught in his throat.

'Before I do anything. Who the hell are you?'

Guy regaled the story of the halted execution in rapid French, gesturing towards William as he did.

The father stood listening intently to Guy, the shotgun lazily slumped in the crook of his arm as he chewed thoughtfully on his toothpick. The little girl returned standing between them, her arms laden. She looked down on William and smiled, jumping into his shadow like before, he smiled back which made him wince. The girl had his jacket under her arm and, now worried, covered William in it, despite it being so hot.

'Roll over,' the father said bluntly.

William did as he was told, lifting his vest and he felt the man kneel next to him. He could smell the powder from the spent cartridge on him and the blood of the rabbit he had been carrying was smeared down his wrist which looked unnaturally bright.

The Frenchman searched through the box and then dunked a cloth into the warm water. 'I don't need to tell you not to try anything do I?'

William looked at Guy who said over his head. 'No.'

William swore as the hot salted water ran down his sides, Guy put a hand on his shoulder and pressed down with his thumb. He watched the pink water drip onto the grass and disappear between cracks in the mud. The Frenchman was firm but practised, and William wondered why a man and his daughter would stay in a place like this with all going on around them. Perhaps they had no choice, a home was a hard place to leave, he of all people knew that.

The father opened a small canvas bag tied with an old shoelace from the tin which had a faded red cross emblazoned on it. In his hand, he unfurled the material and held a pouch of white powder. 'This is from the last war, but it should still work. It's acriflavine, all your boys used it in the First War.'

William looked worried but Guy translated close to his ear. William shrugged and let his body go flaccid, he was totally in the hands of his carers now.

'I know it,' said Guy. 'We have Pervitin.'

'I got this off a British soldier a long time ago. It works well on animals just as well as men, you are lucky I kept it.'

Liberally he sprinkled the powder across William's back which made him let out a shout as the antiseptic began to work. William felt Guy put the other hand on his shoulder, pinning him still.

The Frenchman repacked the medical tin carefully. 'We do this again tonight.'

'Ok,' Guy said.

'Thank you,' William said quietly.

'My daughter is everything to me,' the father began as William stood, helped by Guy who was wrapping a dressing around his ribs and talking to the father.

The Frenchman put an arm around his daughter, pulling her close. 'We have seen so much war. If she had not said you had played with her and the horse, it might have gone differently. You are a father?'

Guy translated for him; William just shook his head slowly.

'She knows nothing but war, she is not old enough to remember before this. To see a horse will be a treat that will last her months. It will feature in all the stories I make up for her at bedtime. Your people have come back here, you said you would not. I can make you better, but you are not welcome here.'

'I understand,' Guy said as William stayed silent.

'And what about him?' the father said, pointing at William. 'He has broken the code by saving you. Men will come looking for him, I do not want that. They will tear my house down if they must, my daughter will be in danger.'

'She will,' Guy said bluntly, knowing only too well the bearded old man was right.

'You cannot stay long.'

'I understand,' Guy said putting an arm round William.

'First, we need to eat. Maybe I will be rewarded if I save you. God has been quiet of late.'

As he walked off Guy repeated what the Frenchman had said.

William had been told since he was young that fate and luck were the gods of the soldier, not prayer and hope.

Chapter 8

Prisoner

The father and Lucy went into the house, leaving Guy to help William to the door. He had watched William throughout, seen how he kept lowering his head, and reddened when Guy had translated, that they were not welcome for long because of his actions.

Guy and William checked the horse and then ambled off, side by side up behind the farmhouse to gain some height so they could weigh up their options.

Guy knew William was trying to be brave, but the occasional gasp gave him away. The trees closed around them both in a tight embrace, blocking the sight of the house and left just the two of them and the woods. It was dark in these woods, the trunks, branches, and brambles thick and awash with a hundred hues of green. Not even the crickets followed them here and the only sound was the crunching of dried leaves under their boots.

'Keep going,' Guy said.

William made a noise that sounded like a hiss.

'You can't stay here.'

'Where will we go?' William said as they were almost at the summit of the hill, both men out of breath. William was clearly in agony, but he pressed on with the help of Guy's shoulder to lean on, he wanted to reach the summit.

'Where will you go more like,' Guy said with a sad shake of

his head.

'What do you mean?' William said, turning away from him.

'My people are coming. The soldiers are close, we were on this bearing towards Paris, its why I was caught. We were scouting. I knew our operation plans before I was captured. If anything, I am surprised they are not here already.'

'Are you not meant to be chasing us all the way home?' William asked.

'We can do both,' Guy said bluntly, and he could see William think about this, these British really had no idea what was coming for them.

Guy softened his tone. 'By morning an even graver threat could be here than your own men. I can wait for my army, hide somewhere, and tell them the truth about what happened. I am known in the Wehrmacht. You...' he trailed off.

William sighed and for just a moment Guy thought the boy would break.

Guy gave him a last shove forward as their feet found clear space on top of the hill, the brambles receding at last from tugging at their ankles. William's pace had slowed as the words of Guy settled on him like mist of a winter's morning and the wound began to tell.

Guy put a hand on his arm. 'You saved my life, but I cannot do the same for you. The British will be looking for you and if they see me, they will not wait for words like our friend down there at the house did.'

'But—'

'But nothing, they will shoot me the first chance they get. If I get back to my people though, if I can do anything, I will.

The boy looked forlorn. 'Please don't, not for me.'

'Call it fairness. Today has been strange.'

Guy watched William look out across the vista, all they could see was a blanket of green below the tops of the trees all around them, thick forest stretched out for miles.

A thin trickle of smoke lazily curled upwards from the chimney of the farmhouse below. Aside from their breathing, it was the only sign of life in this place. Up here the air smelt sweeter, the sun not so hot. A breeze wrapped itself around them both and on it came the fear of marching boots and thumping hooves coming for them, it was only a matter of time.

Guy had dodged death that morning, so it felt easier, like borrowed time. William, though, was in a trap. He could not escape to either side without being killed or worse be taken as a prisoner. He was done for, and Guy knew it and so did the old Frenchman, but both had waited for this inescapable bleakness to find its way to William of its own accord.

Guy had spent a while looking over the trees as William sat next to him on a rock on top of the hill throwing pebbles which bounced and rolled down the side.

Pointing, he showed William where the Germans would come from, the exact route they would break their way through the forest. William marked where the British camp had been in relation to the farmhouse.

They were exactly in the middle of the two armies, both armies were on the move, one looking for William personally, one searching for any British or French survivors before they could retreat to the sea, and neither would abate.

At that moment, Guy thought, on that hilltop by the River Scarpe, they were truly in the tinder box of war, the moment before the match was struck. So often he was in the fray before he realised. This collision course was set though, it was rare such things were predetermined. The old Frenchman had been right, not only were these two men unwelcome, but by staying here they had put his family in grave danger.

Lucy was swinging her legs so hard in excitement the table was moving, juddering against the cold stone floor of the farmhouse.

'Patience, Lucy,' the father said with his back to her. 'It won't be long'.

Guy was quiet, he could not shake the grim feelings from on top of the hill, it was now only hours away.

William looked even worse than he did, a whiteness had engulfed him and refused to leave his countenance. He looked tired and weary, too weary for a boy of his age. It was like he had seen all the sights of war twice over and only lived to keep the horrors alive. Guy had seen that look before, more so in the First War. A look of utter emptiness when the pressures on the mind and the futility of continuing drowned the soul from within. The eyes still blinked, and the lungs still moved up and down, but there was no spirit left.

The father placed the worn blue steaming pot in the middle of them, the girl letting out a squeak. The rabbit he had shot earlier had been skinned and boiled with a handful of vegetables the Frenchman had to hand, some swede, a carrot and celery. There was even some black pepper which he had ground carefully in a pestle and mortar. This he served with warm flatbreads and a jug of wine, the faded pattern on the jug showing a French soldier on a horse from the first war.

Lucy served up with a broad metal spoon, and she bent and sniffed deeply with every portion, this was her job as she had informed the soldiers and she did it with great care and thought.

She eyed up all the plates, checked they were fair and shared out what was left spoon by spoon until the metal scraped the bottom. Finally, letting the spoon rest, she opened her hands to her father who squeezed them tenderly.

The father made them say grace, each man doing so in his own language. It felt the right thing to do, and Guy said it with more force than he usually would.

The plates were steaming, and the smell intoxicated them all. Just before they ate, the father raised a small glass of wine in the air. 'We must do what we can for the common man.'

Guy raised his glass, quickly translated for William who then stuck his shaking hand in the middle, a dribble of wine running over the back of his wrist. Last to join was Lucy who raised her glass of water theatrically and then very deliberately clinked each of their glasses with a smile.

They began to eat, slowly and purposefully, chewing in silence. The rabbit was tender and slippery, Guy's teeth savouring its muscled hind and the swede dissolving in his mouth covering his gums. Talk was minimal, and Lucy who finished first started to hum a nursery rhyme and everyone else just listened, silently watching. Guy checked on William who looked in a trance.

Guy thought about the words the father had said, William had saved him, and this Frenchman in turn had shown kindness to them. Would Guy be able to return the favour?

His time as a notorious soldier was ending, he didn't want to fight for the Nazis. He did though want William to know he understood what had been given for him on that bright hot day by the Scarpe.

'What you did was brave,' Guy said abruptly to William.

William said nothing but the Frenchman nodded and added, 'Murder, no?'

Guy nodded, knowing these things happened more frequently now. 'Of sorts, yes.'

'Is there no code?'

'Not anymore,' Guy added finally.

Guy lay awake on his back in the outbuilding, the crickets quietened as the darkness began to swallow the farmhouse, and even the ragged branches of the willow seemed still at last. The horse slumbered by the trough, its tail flicking occasionally and the peace of the place had brought disquiet like only pitch darkness can.

Guy knew the Germans were on the move towards them. Very soon, the rumble of track and grind of wheel would begin clattering through the trees. One of the men from the failed execution would have made it back to his own soldiers and would have talked.

On the other side of the forest, he knew the British would have interrogated locals and there was only one place William and he could have gone.

As Guy's eyes closed for a few hours before first light, he knew both armies would be committed. Within hours they would meet in the forest on the banks of the Scarpe with the farmhouse in the middle.

Guy had pleaded to be able to return the favours shown to him that day. He had demanded one last shot to prove his mettle, and he had a grave feeling that chance would come soon.

Chapter 9

Runner

A dripping was the first thing his fractured mind registered, a repeated rhythm that sounded like boots marching towards him. It was sensing the steady plop of raindrops on his helmet that told his body he wasn't dead; they made a metallic dink as they landed on the rim that repeated somewhere distant and over and over in his brain. The droplets worked their way over the skin and trickled down the inside of his uniform, involuntarily his whole body spasmed with the cold.

The pain, searing and hot like a poker was pressing against him, blistering the layers as it wedged deeper and deeper into his clavicle. His whole heartbeat was coming from his shoulder, the thumping pulse radiating from where the gritty red hole was under the frayed khaki.

A rising and a soaring back to consciousness, he could see something like light above him and then the final few seconds as the brain and body ignited in survival, the match caught gas and flared as Jolyon Bremner opened his eyes.

He went to shout but no words came, just a pitiful moan of agony, he repeated, 'No,' in slurs. The discombobulation was monstrous, his recent memories disintegrated, his head rolled on the neck in ever-widening circles, air forcing its way over his lips.

He thought the abandoned tank above him was moving

towards him and he was about to be crushed. Trying to roll over brought with it a fresh bout of agony that coursed through him, making him wretch yellow bile into the dirt. With dribble spilling from his lips, he closed his eyes again and lay shivering, waiting to be run over, his teeth chattering.

When nothing happened, he looked again at the bullet-marked tank which brought back the faintest memory of his run for cover.

'Please,' he said thickly ducking as if bullets were still flying all around him, his hand grasped at the mud and squeezed until it shot out through the gaps between his fingers.

It was a tremendous weight to bear, knowing he was dying, and if the mud could have opened then and there, he would have gladly succumbed and been sucked into the soil.

From what he thought was his grave, he looked at the rusty holes in the tank, the almost perfect alignment of them. No one was shooting, no one was screaming and nobody else was here, night was coming, and he was aware of dew's fingers creeping over him from underneath. The sky above had cleared, though the tail end of the rainstorm clung onto the metal edges of the tank in drips.

'Solomon,' he whispered over cracked lips.

A jolt of memory reminded him of his protector getting catapulted over the back of the dugout with a bullet in his gut, the hand clasped over his diary.

Memories of the attack jabbed like fists but the actual moment he had been shot was foggy. He explored his limbs, starting with moving each finger and toe in turn and tried to master the pain in his shoulder, but every breath brought a crushing on his ribs. He looked down his own body and craning his neck he could make out the hole above his lung where the bullet must have entered, he hadn't heard the shot that put him down.

Jolyon reached into his webbing, fumbling with a field dressing and drank from a puddle scooping water into his mouth, coughing as he did and all the while his vision steadily cleared as the daze began to lessen. The pressure of the dressing helped a little as the silence all around continued, just his fingers working at the white gauze and a low whistle of the wind through the bullet holes in the tank.

He wished he had told Evelyn the truth about how bad it was over here. He also wished he had told his parents; would it have made them prouder?

As he pulled at the edges of the bandage his thoughts would not leave home. He wasn't sure if telling Evelyn he loved her one last time would soften her grief, knowing she would always be his last thought. He had no children, no one to outlive him and he would die leaving his wife all alone, he would die out here with nothing.

Jolyon was in danger of drowning in panic, and he did not know how to master it, no one had bothered to tell him about this bit. He began to take in his sheltered world from his prostrate position talking aloud.

'Wire,'

'Barrel,'

'Hole,'

'Soldier,'

'Canteen,'

'Raindrop,'

'Me.'

He was lying half over the edge of the tank, and from where he lay, he could see the edges of a massive coil of barbed wire that looked like a curled fist.

'Get up,' he said softly, and as calmly as he could muster.

Inch by inch, and by digging his palms hard down he pulled himself into a sitting position, all the while the throbbing in his shoulder becoming more targeted.

'Get up,' he pleaded again, this time looking skyward. His fingers found and clutched the sharp metal edge of the tank. He felt the rusty metal tear through his palm, but this was his best chance and he battered away this fresh pain to somewhere else, sticky blood running between his fingers.

'Move now,' he had heard men die out in no-man's-land, those that lay and just hoped for help succumbed quickly, there would be no stretcher bearers coming for him today.

Sitting on the edge of the tank, he supported one arm with the other, cradling it close to his chest which helped. Huge craters, recently topped up with rain stretched ahead. Splinters of trees stuck up at odd angles, not even their deep roots could protect them, and it looked unnatural to see the underside of them.

There was a dense layer of mist over everything, and ghastly mounds of freshly broken bodies lay in heaps on top of each other, most with their eyes still open, occasionally he thought he saw a hand flicker. Men were indistinguishable from one another, just a mass of the dead.

The British trench was deserted, no lookouts peered out, no cook-ups, no orders being given. The German trench line looked just as before, untroubled, unbroken, and massive in comparison with thin trails of smoke rising at intervals on their lines from their dugouts. Pockets of artificial light from underground lairs pooled over the lip of their trench and the machine gun posts sat there unmanned with the barrels still pointing forward.

His entire ribcage squeezed in frustration, and he looked down at the wound. The upper half of his jacket was soaked in blood, he almost toppled backwards, seeing his own body so smashed was horrible.

Jolyon was going to start crawling for home, back to whatever was left of his regiment, he would slide amongst the bodies towards his comrades. Then a movement caught his eye, German soldiers, maybe four or five, were rising from their trench into the field of battle. From the trench lights, he could see their shadows stretch out to double their size, elongating and surging forward. They didn't bother having their rifles out in front, just casually slung over their shoulders, one eating a bread roll roughly, tearing chunks off between chatter.

One by one they checked the British bodies, occasionally giving one a jab with a bayonet, looking for prisoners. For a moment the pain in his shoulder subsided as the far worse proposition of capture beat down on his mind. His hand scrabbled like a trapped spider under a glass amongst the mud looking for a rifle to end it himself.

'Over there,' a shout went up from a soldier in dark grey.

Jolyon looked from the tank as the scout was pointing directly towards him. He could not make out his face, the collar of his jacket was pulled high so only his eyes showed. All four German soldiers turned his way, one scanning with binoculars.

Jolyon rolled over so his face was pressed against the mud on the floor of the tank, then, inch by inch he began to crawl out of the tank, its bulk obscuring him from the searchers.

A few metres from the tank the mud got thicker, heavier and he tasted the dirt and felt the warm water of the rain in the rivulets as his neck sagged and his open mouth closed around the soil. He was lying next to a heap of other bodies and the smell was revolting. He slid sideways, nestling himself into their corpses and tried to lay flat amongst them.

Just before his eyes closed again, he looked up to check his bearings and the edge of the wood he had seen from his trenches was nearby. In amongst nature, if he could get there, he could hide.

The voices of the Germans were getting closer, and he was sure he would be seen and shot. His tongue felt enormous in his mouth, and he tried to quell the panting the wound was causing him to emit. The voices seemed to be on top of him, surrounding him and with a final heave he landed on the other side of the pile of bodies, now only his legs could be seen. His front half was facing down, his elbows dug into the ribcage of a dead Scotsman which collapsed in on itself, so his jacket sleeves were sunk into the man's entrails.

One of the German scouts reached the tank, banging his butt on the metal which made a loud din.

'Where did he go?' They were so close he heard the strike of a match.

Jolyon sank deeper into the dead bodies, breathing as softly as he could and laid dead still.

Maybe another bullet he wouldn't hear would carry him away, but he heard a different and unsettling noise, he heard laughter.

He assumed it was the Germans, laughing at the scale of their victory, maybe laughing at the hopelessness of him sucking in earth before they killed him.

The laughter cut the air again and it was manic, a high-pitched giggling that sounded close. From his lying position, he saw boots, British boots coming from the wood straight ahead, a solitary pair sprinting towards him.

'Stop,' the Germans were shouting.

Jolyon saw the man's face briefly, it was Major Leatherbrook, stripped naked save for his boots running through the battlefield with a stick in his arms like a spear. His eyes were almost entirely white and rolled back, his face stretched into a permanent mask of laughing, the tongue lolling around like it had been severed at the source. He had gone utterly and completely mad.

Jolyon readjusted himself slightly to ease the crippling pain pressing down on his elbows was causing, knowing the Germans would be looking at Leatherbrook. He had seen this before behind the lines when the slaughter and the noise got so much it tipped the scales of sanity, the saturation of so much death had drowned Leatherbrook from within. Jolyon had watched men babbling on stretchers being taken away from the front, another thing he hadn't told Evelyn about. At home, they called it shellshock, out here the soldiers feared it more than bullets.

Leatherbrook had reached overload, and this latest slaughter had thrown him headlong into the spiral of lunacy from where there was no coming back.

He was now hooting like an owl between laughs, spittle shooting from his open mouth in globules. His lips were bleeding heavily from where he had almost chewed them off, he was gnashing at his own face with his bright white teeth. He scratched at his face with the stick he carried causing deep cuts in the skin that started leaking blood onto his chest and down over his ribcage. Leatherbrook continued his laughing, and he looked lost as he started to run in tighter and tighter circles around a shell-hole.

'End him,' he heard from one of the German soldiers behind him.

The shot rang out and Leatherbrook folded forward into a deep crater, only his boots, legs and buttocks sticking up in the air. The stick was left flicking and pulsing in his hand as his nerves twitched and fizzled out.

Jolyon just lay there, his mouth open and blackened with mud, the Germans' voices faded, they had seen enough.

Jolyon eventually reached the edge of the wood, pulling himself along on tree roots and stumbling upright when he could. Inch by inch he was distancing himself from the enemy as the darkness of evening embraced him. The Leatherbrook episode had momentarily lessened the pain in his shoulder, but it came roaring back as he slithered. His strength was not infinite, and he knew if he did not find shelter soon, he would die.

'Help me,' he said aloud, knowing that whilst he had escaped capture, he had dragged himself further from his lines. He was totally alone now, without anything but the tattered uniform on his back which was starting to feel very heavy.

It smelt thick with damp in here, the long grass curled all around his frail body as he crawled onwards, it was like gentle hands gently arching over him pulling him downwards into the dew. The trees around were silent, not even the wind could get in here, not even the shells had troubled this place yet. The war seemed a long way away, but his survival was at its height of battle.

Hunger and thirst were starting to dominate over pain, and he wondered if he was bleeding out as a calmness of acceptance settled on his spirit, a dreadful feeling of admission and that he was close to the end.

If he was going to die, he was going to die standing so with a hand on a branch that left a bloody print on its silver bark, he righted himself. Leaning against the tree, one shoulder folded over in agony, up ahead he saw a change in the wood. The trees were thinning, and the land started to roll down.

Lurching forward using branches to cling to, the sound of running water filled his ears, a wide river gently flowed below him, and the surface was still in the evening light. The moon was reflected perfectly in its glossy sheen, and he licked his lips with thirst.

On the other side of the banks was a farmhouse with a faded red roof, its lawn leading down to the edge of the river where a willow ran its branches over the surface. Jolyon rubbed his eyes with his hand, so tired he could just close his eyes here standing against the tree and sleep. The house looked like somewhere he had known for years but was not sure why and in the front window behind shutters, he could see a dull orange light.

Eyes hazing, looking up wearily he saw a fox on the opposite side of the bank staring straight at him, its red fur glimmered and its small, pointed face was cocked to one side.

'Like a damn fox,' they had told him at basic training.

Jolyon looked up at the sky as if wanting any further signs, but only briefly. A breeze ruffled the willow opposite and a jab of pain reminded him to act so he let go of the branch and fell face forward. Part of him had no strength left to care, part of him regretted it instantly. Down towards the river he rolled, with the grass, moon and the fox spinning as he tumbled, down towards the Scarpe his limp body swung, until he hit the water with a crash.

He remembered drinking a few mouthfuls before the water

engulfed him whole, he had been so thirsty, but the water was too much, filling every inch of him. It was so cold it woke him up long enough to realise he would drown. Spluttering, he tried to swim but his arm refused to work, and the saturated webbing yanked him under. His legs couldn't find the bottom and he saw the fox one last time on the banks high above watching down on him, it had not moved, the black eyes just searched into him.

He bobbed up for the last time and saw the fox skip off the front lawn of the farmhouse and the whole scene was suddenly bathed in orange light. As his head went under, he thought he saw a figure through the churning water, there might have been a face in the light.

Then all went quiet as he sunk to the bottom of the River Scarpe, his body bumping the bed of the river amongst the sand, rocks, and reeds. The water closed over him, and Jolyon opened his mouth letting water come crashing in.

Chapter 10

Gunner

'Where was he found?'

Kummer jerked his head towards a hillock behind the trench line, obscured from the line of sight of the frontline men, and most importantly, the officers. The British artillery had created these mounds all over the reserve lines, making hundreds of elevations and depressions in the landscape that rose and sunk innumerably.

'Did he run?'

'No,' Kummer replied. 'He knew the jig was up.'

Otto folded his hands together, tapping the two index fingers together in a beat getting steadily faster as his mind worked.

'Enders you say?'

Kummer nodded.

'Shame, seemed a good man.'

Kummer sneered. 'No good men do that in battle'.

'I mean before, of course,' Otto said, these were grim decisions to make as a commander. Enders had been with them since last April and although quieter than most of the men, he did not take him for one of those, in fact, Otto preferred the quiet ones most of the time.

'There are plenty willing,' Kummer added, as if that helped.

'I see,' said Otto, his fingers stopped moving and he bit his lower lip. 'Well, it is what it is, we will take him to the woods.'

'Very well,' said Kummer, unable to keep a flicker of a smile off his face as he turned about, the moonlight glinting off the regimental badge on his helmet.

Otto stomped a boot hard into the wall of the trench, tightening his boot buckles and wiping away some of the mud off his toes. It was the law, not just a choice he reminded himself. Stupid Enders, everybody in the whole German army knew the rules, it was one of the first things they were taught at training, even since before that at school. There would be no backward steps, it was better to die than to surrender.

Otto hated killing deserters and cowards, and it could be easily avoided if they only sent men here who were willing to fight, there were plenty of them at home.

The moonlit march to the woods was silent, the jeers from the other men fading away as they rounded the final bend of the trench and stepped up into no-man's-land. A few had thrown stones, one catching Enders below the ear which left a trickle of blood spreading over his collar.

The British had been wiped out and silenced, certainly for a few days, there was no danger left out here now at night. They had pulled back to the reserve lines, the frontline now deserted. They didn't have the numbers to man it anyhow. They had watched a few British stragglers getting back to their trench at sunset, but they had not paused or even looked back, they just carried on limping and crawling back to the reserve lines and away from that place.

Otto noticed Enders the deserter said nothing on the walk, not a word, and if ever their eyes met, Enders quickly looked away as if looking into the face of his soon-to-be executioner made it too real. With the ceaseless lines of advancing British to kill that day, no one had noticed Enders slip away from the trench in the heat of battle. He had crawled in the opposite direction and taken refuge behind one of those undulating hillocks and he would not have been found if it wasn't for the ammunition resupply runners coming up from behind from the second trench line.

Usually, Otto's troop could make it through an engagement with the bullets they had on them, but they had run out of bullets on two of the machine guns. The barrels were red hot, smoke pouring from the carbines as the British just kept on coming, the gun crews had poured water on the barrels to stop them melting.

Enders, the traitor, had feigned all manner of reasons to Otto for his desertion, even trying to convince the men he had lost his marbles. Having just seen the mad British man in the field scratching at his face with a blunt stick, Otto knew what mad looked like.

A chill was spreading up Otto like a biting east wind, this was exactly how it had started the last time. That disastrous day in February last year, on Valentine's Day, and that realisation for Otto that if his men turned against him, there was little he could do against so many.

That episode had begun with cowardness, but there were a lot more of them opposed to the solitary figure Enders cut in the silhouette of the moonlight. On that February 14th, fifteen of his troops had refused to fight and had turned their rifles towards the officers and squared up to them just as the British blew their whistles and started running at them across the gap. He could still see their faces, that troop of betrayers had let the British come close to overwhelming them and if it hadn't been for Kummer dragging the ludicrously heavy machine gun forwards onto the lip they all would have been done for.

Otto reckoned Kummer had killed twenty, maybe even thirty men, including most of the men who stood opposite Otto from his own nation, the rest Australians from the other side. Once Kummer had dragged the gun and loaded it, he had started firing at the line of mutineers, then the attackers who were so close there had been nothing left of a few of them. The first Australian, within inches of their trench lip, had been sawn in half by bullets, his torso sliding off his legs sideways. With the angle of the gun slightly upwards, the second burst had removed the tops of the Australians' heads, almost scalping them. One man's headless running body continued on, falling into the trench and hitting the back wall with a smack.

Kummer's hands had been streaming blood by the end of the skirmish, the rattle of his fingers against the trigger guard causing the skin to fold back in layers almost to the bone. For his efforts he was a revered man at the front, and a highly decorated one. When told he had been promoted, he had refused it though, knowing this scaling of the ranks would take him away from Otto to lead his own command, and secondly away from the front on leave. Otto understood that some men were just born for this place, Kummer was one of them.

It had been a close-run thing though and the mutiny had nearly capsized them that soggy day, the minds of soldiers, once made up, were not easy to unwind. That corporal who had led the mutiny, named Muller, seemed so innocuous. A streak of a boy but even boys could have dangerous ideas.

It was a fine balance on the front, and it was getting finer, all were dissatisfied here, but the lessening of rations in that cold February had been their breaking point. Despite surely knowing in their hearts that rising in mutiny would not solve the problem, still they had met and schemed in the dead of night when officers slept.

The finale would be the same for Enders when they reached the approaching wood, it was now just left to see how he would act.

To the far east of the trenches on the edge of the untouched wood, a mine crater skirted the impenetrable line of the trees, the size of a submerged church. It was filled with water from the persistent rains and the jet-black surface reflected the moon above, the great white orb sitting mirrored in the centre.

Otto watched the line of men walk past who had come to watch, all heads bowed and hands on rifles, their outlines glowing in white.

It had been a black day when the mine that had caused the crater had detonated, the British had tunnelled almost to their forward trench without them knowing before some mishap on their part made the mine go off. What would have been utter catastrophe for him, and his men, was instead deadly for the both of them. British and German bodies were thrown up one hundred feet into the air, twisting together and overlapping before being buried again under the falling dirt. That was often the way in this place, tiny mistakes had enormous consequences. That wood represented the end of this part of the line, the trench line shot directly backwards from there, then went around to the south, they were one of the most forward points of the entire Western Front.

'Here will do,' Otto said, and the troop came to a stop.

The men had stopped on the edge of the wood on the far side of the crater, it made sense to shoot him here as opposed to in the woods as it was a shorter walk. Better still, if his body fell into the water, there was no need to dig a grave though whether traitors should have marked graves was an open and lively debate. Enders had refused any last words as they had stumbled along, Enders thinking the deep wood was where they were headed.

Enders was hustled to the edge of the crater, the toes of his boots stopping just short over the stinking water. His head jerked about, and his eyes went wide as he looked around behind him, not believing that they would do this here, that it would come to that bit sooner. For a moment he looked like he was about to speak but Otto stepped up quickly behind him and shot him through the back of the neck. It was slightly lower than he had planned which caused a jet of blood to spurt out making a scattering of drops on the surface of the water before Enders' body fell forward and hit the surface. Ripples spread out over the crater, the crests glittering in the light.

Otto heard a bottle uncorked whilst he just watched the body float face down unmoving; he could still smell the smoky discharge from the barrel of the pistol.

A memory took him back home, classical music was playing, and it had been evening. It was warm, the taste of sugar on his lips from a pastry and he was by the River Glan, his shotgun over his lap after a day of duck hunting.

They had come so far in miles from Reborn, but backwards in so many other ways. Was this what life was now? Shooting your countrymen in the dead of night as men around drunk toasting murder, Otto's hand spasmed and he let go of the trigger.

Secretly, silently, he said a word for Enders as the body began to succumb to the weight of water. As it sunk, the hole in the back of the neck slid beneath the surface with a sucking noise. Duty had carried Otto this far, but had something in him snapped? At this very moment, it all felt too much to bear, too much to expect him to do this all over again tomorrow when all he wanted was to be away from here, to be asleep and hope his daughter could one day forgive him for the things he had done in France.

Otto was about to order the men back to the trenches when one of his men coming back from the woods spoke up, 'Over there, a house.'

'Shut up,' the men jeered.

A private chorused, 'Full of naked women too?'

Kummer stepped forward, his face bathed in moonlight. 'Who would live here?'

'No,', the man said, 'I saw it. I got lost but I saw a house'.

Otto listened to the men jostle about the truth of this and turned to Kummer, 'What do you think?'

'Should we check it?'

Otto was tired, the last thing he wanted to do was tramp through the woods in the middle of the night on the promise of a tipsy soldier. Still though, his orders said he had to check and what if some little Frenchman was hiding away some British? Or better still, what if he had food?

'Fine,' Otto snapped. 'In formation.'

Some of the men looked surprised, a colour of dread crossed the face of the soldier who had announced this. Otto could tell he was instantly regretting his decision of informing the men, especially the feared Kummer, one did not waste the time of tired officers.

'I might have been mistaken,' the private said quietly, chewing on a loose piece of skin on the corner of his thumb nail.

'Did you see it or not?' Kummer said, his hands crossing

behind his back like he did when he was frustrated.

The man thought about his answer. 'Yes.'

'Let's move,' said Otto.

Kummer added, 'If there's a woman there, she's mine.'

The men laughed at this.

The house was there, they could see a dim light on in the upstairs room despite the efforts to mask the edges of the shutters with sheets. They stood on the other side of a river with steep banks, the roof of the farmhouse almost glowing white under the moonlight.

'What in hell's name are people doing here?' Otto said aside to Kummer.

'No idea,' Kummer replied, lighting a short brown cigar.

'How close are we to the front? Half a mile?'

'About, yes. No fighting here though, everything happens at the centre. The British haven't fired at it, neither have we. Makes a change from the mud. This wood is thick, do you think they know there is a war on?' Kummer smiled, tapping his index finger on the butt of his rifle pinned under his armpit.

'Still. This close to the front. Have the British been watching us?'

'It won't be them,' Kummer added confidently.

'How do you know that?' Otto retorted, almost challenging the man.

'Because they would have shot at us already,' Kummer said, slapping a hand onto Otto's shoulder, ash dropping from the end of the cigar.

He strode off as Otto checked the surrounds of the house once more and studied his trench map. It was banked on three sides, and it would be far more dangerous to go towards them or the front lines of the British once the war had started. Stay put, stay alive day by day and pray that all this passed, but the odds were miniscule.

To know a place like this existed so close to where he had fought, and murdered Enders, made Otto even more uncertain about what he was doing here. How could somewhere so beautiful and peaceful be this close to somewhere so destroyed and awful? He was not feeling like a soldier anymore, but more like a man who had made a lot of mistakes and needed to escape this place.

The men had circled the lawn of the house in quiet steps, the flat air smelt of men who had not washed in weeks, Otto was in his daze when he heard one of the men cock his rifle.

'Get that weapon down,' he said, almost surprising himself with the venom he had spat the phrase with.

Everybody turned. 'Sir...'

'But nothing,' said Otto.

Krupps' face hardened. 'You heard him, that was an order, get that rifle down before I come over there and beat you to death with your own helmet.'

The men all lowered their guns, all still looking at Otto.

'We don't know what's in there, or who. Best we try to signal that we mean no harm, they might know about the British troop movements. We don't want them hiding food if they have it.'

He said this with as much confidence as he could muster but he had been right in his musings, something was jarring, it was like he lacked the conviction to give orders and his men could sense it having shot Enders.

'Kummer, check it.'

Kummer nodded and stepped forward, his boots leaving footprints in the dew across the lawn. He was about to get to the door when it swung open and bathed all the men and the whole lawn in light. The man who stood there was young, in his hands, he held a load of bread and a pail of water.

'It is all I have,' he said in French.

Kummer nodded. 'Wise boy, opening the door. We would have had to burn it down.'

'There is no need, I want no part of this war,' the young Frenchman said.

'Too late,' Kummer sneered. 'We're here.'

'My friends...' the young man started.

Kummer snapped back. 'Do we look like friends?'

The Frenchman just stared up at him, his eyes flat and calm. 'You are welcome to all I have; I have never fought.'

'That I can tell,' said Kummer, shoving the man aside and striding into the house.

Otto walked quickly up to the Frenchman and tried to reassure him with a hand on his shoulder and a look he hoped promised they were not here for trouble.

'Answer me this friend,' Otto said. 'Do you know if any British came this way?'

The man nodded in the negative.

Otto felt relief wash over him, he could take no more killing today.

He was about to turn when Kummer gave a shout from the kitchen, Otto could hear his footsteps coming back towards the door, heavy determined steps, he had a hand behind his back.

'Tell me,' Kummer began. 'Are you injured?'

The Frenchman looked at Otto, then back at Kummer. 'No,' he said slowly.

'Then why the bandages,' and Kummer pulled a white cloth covered in blood from behind his back.

'I can explain,' said the Frenchman, but somehow Otto knew he was lying. He hoped that only he realised, otherwise, this young man was as good as dead.

'Go on then,' said Kummer giving him a rough shove.

The Frenchman didn't move when he was pushed. 'I can explain.'

Kummer was about to raise a fist, but Otto grabbed his arm. For a split second Kummer looked in disgust at his old friend, then he remembered his rank and disgust melted into confusion.

Otto had very little mask left to let slip and he knew the Frenchman's life, and probably his, depended on him holding it together until they could be free of this place.

'Let's talk,' said Otto quietly.

The Frenchman, Otto and Kummer walked towards the kitchen.

'Rest of you, keep watch,' Otto shouted as the door closed.

This Frenchman better have a good reason for the bloody rag, and he had better tell it fast as he did not know how long he could lie, or how long Kummer would keep his patience.

Chapter 11

Rider

William awoke with a start; his father Jolyon had been looking over him in his dreams with a hand on his chest, either pressing him down or checking him for wounds. He could not work out his father's expression, it had been disappointed but also relieved, William had reached out for him in his sleep, grasping at nothing.

'Dad,' he shouted which had jolted him awake.

Birdsong was echoing around the barn by the farmhouse they had slept in, he just lay still amongst it and let it surround him. He could hear the blackbirds on the roof, their little feet scratching, they would be watching out over the forest, scanning the horizon and the dew-soaked canopy, they would be hungry.

He was thirsty, the strains of the day before he felt in the stiffness along his forearms from clutching the reins and his throat was scratchy. The bandage around his ribs was still white which was good, but a dull ache ran up to the centre of his shoulder blades. The straw he had slept on crackled as he rolled to his right, and he dipped his canteen into the pail of water by his webbing. He drank greedily, the water rolling down his chin and dripping onto his hairless chest. The birds sang louder, and with a moment of piercing realisation, he remembered where he was, who he was with, and how they had gotten here.

The depth of his dream had allowed him those sweet few

moments of blissful ignorance, but calm was obliterated as memory clicked into gear. An unforgivable crime in the eyes of the system he was part of. His father had always said he was impetuous, bordering on rash, Jolyon had hoped the army might take that out of him, part of the reason he had made him join up.

Glumly he drank again, for now he longed to close his eyes and wake up somewhere else, in a different time, in another space and having made different choices. The tentacles of dread wound themselves around his neck until he found it hard to breathe.

The barn was empty except for him, the worn floorboards were made smooth with hundreds of hours of toiling, sawdust shavings were dotted around, it was sparse, but it had been safe.

Through the two small square windows, he could see the sun's fingers creeping over the top of the tree line, rays penetrating the yellow carpet of the dull sky. William knew he would have to sit at his own banquet of consequences one day, and it would be today. The promise of hope was replaced by the memories of the shots above their heads ricocheting off branches and the way the drunk British executioners had been thrown aside by the flank of the horse, he pulled on his shirt, buttoning it with trembling fingers.

The birds stopped chirping in an instant, the barn was in silence, just William's ragged breathing filled his head. There was a loud crack as a door from the floor below was nearly thrown off its hinges, the entire barn shuddering. Heavy footsteps thumped on the wooden stairs of the barn up to the annex where he lay.

William saw a giant hand grasp the top of the balustrade and a body swing round. William just sat there, immovable, a hint of recognition, but that was all.

A massive figure was heading towards him, the face he thought he knew but could not place it. The figure seemed to fill his vision entirely, the hand outstretched towards him. He knew that uniform, the one they had practiced sticking bayonets into at training, sandbags full of straw with painted faces on with downturned smiles.

The hand grabbed his shirt and William let out a whoosh of air from his open mouth.

'Get up,' Guy shouted, dragging him onto his feet. The man's face was strained, the creases under his eyes like an elastic band wrapped tightly around a blood-drained finger.

William hung there limply, his limbs bending and hopeless under his weight.

Guy shook him.

'They are here,' Guy said, his pupils widening.

William blinked, his mouth forming a large 'O'.

'The British. They are here. They are looking for you.'

William felt his head rock back from a slap across the face from Guy, next thing he knew he was soaked and could taste grass in his mouth as the pail of water was launched over him.

'William,' Guy urged.

'Yes...' William mumbled. 'Yes,' he said louder. Water rolled down him, and he tilted his head back, the coolness alerted him, and a spasm rippled through him.

'Where?' William snapped, flinging his webbing round him in one movement and balancing on the balls of his toes.

Guy pointed through one of the windows and even though William could not see them yet, the wood had taken on a more threatening tone. It hid an army coming for him, no longer his own.

Guy started to shove him. 'Downstairs.'

Guy swept up the two piles of straw in his arms, pushing them into a corner and ruffling them, ironing out the indents their slumbering bodies had made. He roughly kicked at the spot where they had slept, breaking up any loose straw. He spun, the bear emblem catching the light, flicked up the pail of water in one hand, grasped William with the other and started pressing him on.

'How long?' William said over his shoulder, his feet churning on the thin wooden steps so that he slipped down the last two on the soles of his boots, he fell to a knee but righted, smelling sawdust all around him in the haze.

'Two minutes, maybe three.'

William was forward again, busting onto the grass outside of the barn with the farmhouse lit up in dazzling white, the sun refracting the glare all around them. Somewhere far off he heard a distant shout, voices now of his own tongue and the crunching of branches and twigs under lots of boots.

Guy swooped down filling the pail of water from the trough and still held him tight all the way towards the white house.

'Faster, faster,' he kept saying, an urgent whisper that echoed round his head, he was close enough so William could smell the wine on his breath from the night before mixed with chewing tobacco.

Pierre Mulot the Frenchman stood there by the door, face dead set and heavy, Pierre's eyes narrowed as he saw the two escapees coming towards him. They had brought the war right here to his door and they had risked the life of his young daughter.

The British army were almost upon them, their voices now coming through the treeline, distinct words carrying over the steep banks of the Scarpe.

Pierre spat, 'Upstairs. Now.'

'Yes,' Guy said bluntly.

'Be silent,' was the last thing William heard before they shut the door of the farmhouse behind them, his eyes finding it hard to adjust to the light. It was colder in here than it had been the night before and he shivered.

He was still holding onto Guy, William whispered, 'The girl?'

'Shush,' Guy said whipping a finger to his lips. 'She's fine. They are ready.'

'Where are we?'

Guy released his grip on William, but no sooner had he done so, William jumped forward. There was a cellar door in front of him, a mouth of black ready to welcome them. William went for it, a good hiding place.

'First place they'd look,' said Guy dragging him backwards by his collar.

Instead, Guy pointed right and shoved him onto the stairs.

They were in the bedroom of Pierre, and it felt wrong to William, like this was Pierre's private space. Under the window sat a large oak chest with two black metal bands around it, Guy pointed, and William stalled.

'They'll look in here for Christ's sake,' William said.

'Shut up and get in. I have a plan.'

William felt Guy shove his legs onto the edge of the chest, he was quivering, and he swayed like he was about to collapse.

'Down,' Guy said, and William sunk to his haunches in submission.

They could hear shouts so close they felt like they were

already at the door, William watched Guy place the pail of water on the windowsill with the window wide open, tilting it so it hung half out. As he did, they saw the first of two British scouts come out from behind the trees, guns raised.

'My friends,' he heard Pierre say warmly like he was walking towards a long-lost brother.

'Hands up…' a British voice trailed off before Guy looked back at William and pointed to the floor of the chest.

The British began to filter out through the woods, and just as William sunk down, he caught a brief glimpse of the British commanding officer. The commander had found another horse and he pointed with his crop at the posse of men sent to find him, urging them onwards with thrusts of the crop.

Inside the chest, William watched Guy securing a knot in the handle of the pail, ensuring the pail kept balanced on the windowsill. He ran the string out of the window and fed it back through a crack in the wall towards the chest.

Guy looked down at him. 'Ready?

William nodded.

'Remember. Silence. I'm as dead as you if they catch me.'

He put a hand on William's shoulder and gently pressed him further down into the dank-smelling bottom of the chest.

Lying together, Guy threaded the string through the hinge of the chest and leaned over William, closing the top of the chest. The string was taught, running up through the chest, through the wall and holding the bucket on its angle.

William was fully pressed against Guy, they were face to face, and immediately he was pouring in sweat, the smell of their breaths mixing with the damp.

William watched Guy, gently, millimetre by millimetre pull the string until it was as taught as possible. Then Guy closed his eyes, he took long slow breaths, the air in the chest changing quickly.

William heard snippets of voices all around the house from below, and occasionally the calming tones of Pierre assuring the men he was hiding nothing.

'Please this is my home,' William heard Pierre say from the front of the house, the British must be right underneath them.

There was a clipped voice from below. 'We are looking for a man. Look at this photo. Do you know him? Have you seen him?'

William heard a piece of paper being passed around and knew it would have his own face on it which was an odd sensation.

The clipped voice was back, angrier this time. 'Do you know him?'

'No,' Pierre protested.

'He must have come this way.'

'Why would he come here? Do you think I like you people in my country?'

This seemed to satisfy the interrogator for a beat.

Pierre spoke quietly, like he was tired. 'This is my home, I will take this photo in case I see him, is that good enough?'

'Home or no home, we are going in.'

'There is nothing to see, just my daughter.'

William could sense a pause in the thoughts of the searchers, nobody liked children present in war.

'Sergeant,' a voice rang out from the front door. 'There's a cellar'.

Boots smacked down the stairs of the cellar and all the while Pierre assured the men, he had nothing to hide.

'Why would I lie? If I lied, you would kill me, no?'

'He has a point…'

The commanding officer cut him off. 'Silence. Check it.'

What felt like minutes passed as William heard the men call for flashlights. They were under the house, in its bowels, looking for him.

'Cellar's clear'.

'Dammit,' the commanding officer spat. 'One of you check upstairs.'

William jolted and Guy opened his eyes.

Footsteps began to come up the stairs.

William heard Pierre say, 'Very well,' as calmly as he could, but William now assumed it was only seconds until he was caught.

The footsteps got closer, there was the slap of a hand on the banister.

William was close to breaking, Guy put a hand on his forearm. The British soldier had reached the top of the stairs and looked in Lucy's room first, then there was a double bump as he opened the door with the barrel of his rifle, nudging it open muzzle first.

Any moment now the lid would fly open, and they would be done for, any second now a gun would be rammed into his face.

William sensed Guy twitch his hand, he held the string taught and higher as the boots approached the chest, centimetres away. There he and the man he had saved lay, the mismatched comrades bound together in life as they would be in death.

William was looking straight at Guy, Guy winked and let go of the string in his hands.

There was a zip of twine along the hinge of the chest, then the pail began to tumble downwards, it hit the edge of the water trough and made a shattering clang.

Shouts and gunfire broke out, William heard the bullets tear into the stone of the house. They heard the boots of the searching soldier turn and begin to sprint downstairs again.

Men were shouting. 'What the hell was that?'

'Don't know, something went bang.'

Pierre said simply, 'I think it came from over there.'

The British men kept asking what it was and one of them said, 'Hey, it was a bucket.'

'Well, where the hell did it come from?'

William could almost feel them looking up at the window, they would be coming back and more than one of them this time. Then another sound was carried to the chest, so softly at first William had to strain his ear against the top of the chest to make sure he had heard it right, Guy looked dumbfounded and didn't move. Then Guy's whole mouth creased downwards to a tight-lipped picture of sorrow, his eyes widened then narrowed to hatred, the grimace immovable on his lips.

The British had stopped yelling, quiet hushed chatter broke out amongst the search party, and he heard one of them say 'Oh, my god.'

'Silence,' hushed the commanding officer on the floor beneath them.

From inside the chest William was racked with nausea, as on the wind and rustling through the canopies of trees was carried the sound of loud singing from hundreds of voices, the singing of a marching song.

Chapter 12

Prisoner

Guy watched the British from where he was crouching in the open chest, William at his elbow was silent. The German singing rolled on across the wood, lifted over the waters of the River Scarpe and seemed to surround the farmhouse. The pleasant birdsong of the morning had been replaced with these gravelly voices drifting between the prey and the hunters.

Both ducked as the first tank shell hit the riverbank with a crack, sending a plume of water into the sky. When the sunlight hit the droplets, tiny rainbows flashed all around suspended in the air, a billowing black smoke ballooned up, drifting directly up in the flat morning.

The British soldiers, maybe thirty or forty of them were running in all directions as sporadic machine gun fire opened from the far side of the river from the treeline.

There were shouts to get to cover but panic was rife, a wall of noise came from opposite the house unmatched by the pitiful pops of British rifles firing at nothing but shadows.

Guy was on one knee, his eyes shielded by a flat hand. As soon as they had heard the singing the British soldiers had tried to get into formation, but the reputation of the enemy made them want to run which made them hesitate which determined their fate.

Guy watched as the undergrowth began to fold over under

the weight of wheels and boots. Small trees snapped in two and he caught the first glimpses of the German soldiers between branches. A relentless grind of metal thrummed which felt out of place here, in what had been their haven for the night, he could make out the distinctive helmets.

'They are here,' Guy said, slamming a hand onto the windowsill. 'There will be no escape for your countrymen,' Guy said, ducking as another tank round exploded. 'They are as good as dead already.'

The sharpshooters on top of the tanks began working away on the British formation, a British soldier folded over clutching his gut and fell forwards into the river.

'You cannot be caught here,' Guy added to William aside, pointing a finger at the oncoming soldiers. The ranks spread out from behind their tanks, it looked like a mouth getting wider.

There was a screech of metal on metal as the tanks stopped, one, then two, then three tank shells screamed into the British formation split seconds apart, sending geysers of mud skyward, the three walls of mud obliterated the sun for a moment and the whole house was frozen in darkness.

The British were thinning fast, some already lying still and some cowered down in balls. Guy felt William pop up next to him and take in the scene. 'Christ,' he said flatly.

Still looking ahead, Guy said, 'What?'

'That man, there. I know him. That's Hugh Cronk.' And he heard William's voice run out of air.

Guy looked at the man William had indicated, Cronk, who was looking for his own arm until a burst from the trees forced bullets through his face leaving nothing but a folded mouth and a fragment of jawline on his shoulders. A line of bullets screamed just under the windowsill and Guy ducked, pulling William down, the ping of the metal around the stone walls of the bedroom brought out a low cry from William.

William mumbled, 'Cronk?'

'Finished,' said Guy bluntly.

Guy watched the Germans surrounding the house on three sides, three fingers closing its grip. A few British troops made a dash for it, two reaching the edge of the woods and disappearing back the way they had come, the third falling, his hands outstretched. It reminded Guy of his own troops the day before and he wondered what had happened to the survivors, had they told the men where to find them? They now focused fire on the tiny remnants of the British forces, the British commanding officer was hit in the chest and almost jumped upwards off his horse. The horse sagged underneath him, its legs shattering under bullets, the bright bone poking out from beneath its knees. It lay there rolling over the top of the British commander, pulverising his corpse into the grass.

Guy was shaking William. 'Where did you put the horse?'

William just sat, shoulders slumped and head languishing to one side, a strand of dribble had escaped his lip and was hanging off his chin like a cut spider's web.

'William, please!'

Still, the boy did not move.

'Will. I beg you.'

A flicker of something from within.

Guy heard a word, he said it quietly, 'Hugh is dead.'

'Yes,' Guy responded.

William called more desperately. 'Dead?

'We will both die too if we stay here.'

'Okay.'

'Will, we must move. Can you follow me?'

'Uh-huh,' William said.

'You follow me, you live, okay?'

They crawled along the floor of the bedroom away from the chest that had saved them, the noise pitching as the tanks fired again at the riverbank where the last of the British soldiers stood against the onslaught behind the willow tree.

Guy rounded the corner of the bedroom door and there in the hallways was Pierre, his back pressed against the landing wall clutching his little girl to him.

He looked up, his eyes streaming, the tears making roads in his tanned flesh. His mouth opened and closed like a fish, his tongue white and covered in plaster dust from the crumbling ceiling of his house.

'Look at what you have done,' he said.

Guy tried to speak but no words came, just a feeling of annoyance that stepped down on the centre of his back. Machine gun bullets hit the inside hallway, rupturing the vase in the hall sending red petals shooting upwards and then floating down to the floor.

A volley hammered against the ceiling and sawdust and glass exploded everywhere. Through the haze, Guy could make out the shape of a figure in the front doorway, backing away from his executioners. It was a British soldier, he looked up and they met eyes. His face was one of fury but as he raised his rifle to his shoulder, he was shot from behind and sank to his knees, more bullets hit him as he spun down, lying amongst the red petals.

Guy shouted at Pierre, 'You have to get out.'

Pierre shook his head violently, clutching Lucy even tighter, her blonde hair was looped over his sinewy forearms, and he caressed the back of her neck with his hand. Guy could not see her face to check her, but he couldn't make out blood on her dress.

Pierre spat, 'Me? This is my home. We were safe until you and that man came here.' Pierre's bony finger was pointing at William making the boy groan gutturally.

'Advance,' echoed around the house.

'Get. Out.' Pierre screeched, wailing as he kissed the top of his daughter's head repeatedly, almost manically like he was trying to get as much love into her before the end.

'Where is the horse?'

Pierre did not answer.

'The one we brought, where is it?'

Pierre gestured towards the back of the farmhouse, towards the woods where he and William had climbed the night before.

Pierre buried his head into his daughter's shoulder and did not look up again, Guy knew he would die here.

Guy grabbed William by the webbing strap on his shoulder and hauled him to the window at the back of the farmhouse. It was a square of light in the gloom, the sawdust from the ceiling falling like ash. Heat from the burning grass, trees and bodies was making them both pour with sweat, there was a smell of roasting meat. The German soldiers were crossing the river, the last writhing bodies of the British shot at point-blank range.

'Will?'

William looked at him, just a fraction of him remained now.

'The horse, the one you saved me on, it is out there behind the house.'

'Anybody in there?' a German voice rang out.

'We will give you one chance,' said another.

Guy shook William. 'William. Do you understand?'

He nodded. He looked so young, he had been so brave, he

had saved his life.

Germans were now in the house, a floor away. They sent a volley of shots into the cellar, their barrel smoke drifting up to the landing, the cracking of the bullets on stone impossibly close.

Guy lifted William up, cradling him like a child towards the window through the raining sawdust.

'William, I have to let you go now.'

Their eyes met and both knew they would not meet again.

'You get yourself to the horse. Get out of here,' he said.

William's fingers grasped at Guy's jacket; he did not want to let go.

A voice rang out, 'I hear people up there, we just want to talk.'

Another said, 'We have food, drink, medicines if you need?'

Guy held William out of the back window overlooking the forest, leaning down as far as he could. His arm strained against the material of his jacket and William dangled there, his body limp, his boots swaying over the top of the long grass in the shade of the back of the farmhouse.

'Goodbye, my friend.'

Guy let him go and he fell straight down, his body rolling into the bracken behind the house, he lay still amongst the wildflowers and long summer grasses like he was sleeping.

'Please. Please,' Guy said, his back to the landing urging the boy to get up.

A hint of movement, a stirring, then he stood, shakily, uncertain of his own arms and touching his own face, he looked back up at the window.

Guy mouthed the word 'Run' and William stumbled off into the deep woods behind the house and then he was gone, the branches and leaves swallowing him into darkness.

Guy gripped the timber windowsill. 'I am up here,' he said.

The boots on the stairs below stopped, fearing a trap and a gun barrel wafted into view and the top of the metal helmet caught the light turning it a shimmering grey.

'Guy Schwarzbär.'

'What brings you here?' the soldier said, still not daring to turn the corner of the stairs.

'You will address me as sir,' said Guy before rounding the corner, flicking his Iron Cross out from behind his lapel and facing the man full on, his height and frame casting the entire staircase in shadow.

One of them stepped backwards for a second, the soldier's mouth opened in awe. 'Sir.'

The Black Bear stared them down, all the while he was wondering how far William was from the house by now.

Guy put his hands on his hips, the bear emblem now covered in sawdust. 'Nothing here but this man and his daughter. They were patching me up,' he said, pointing to his calf.

Both troopers nodded quickly.

'Where is your commanding officer?'

The soldier turned and yelled to the rest of the men to hold fire.

Guy looked down at Pierre. 'You should have run. There is nothing I can do to save you now; she will likely die too.'

Guy made his way down the stairs, the wood creaking under his bulk. The two scouts slammed their heels together and stood to attention, he had his story, now all he could hope was they believed him.

They had bought his story about escaping the clearing and

making his way to the farmhouse on foot, they had no reason to doubt him, the British that lay in parts around the riverbank were proof of their presence in the area. The major had taken one look at him, and the medals and waved him away like he was an irrelevance.

Pierre and the girl had been brought down to the front of the house, she had looked up at the men with a stoic grimace, her lips pursed together, and Pierre was shaking. The Mulots stood there in the Northern French sun, clothes torn, their house wrecked as the major looked over them, his face close to the Frenchman's. He had removed his hat and ran his fingers through his hair, sizing the father and daughter up.

The major tapped his watch, feeling the eyes of the men upon him, time slowed, and Guy closed his eyes, he heard a far-off call, a hunting bird.

'They live,' said the on-ground commander.

Guy opened his eyes, relief as cooling as the drink from the trough had been, the troops then moved quickly, assembling in three lines, and were heading back towards the tanks.

'You, the Bear,' the major commanded.

Guy turned.

'Stay close to me.'

As they walked away from the farmhouse, Guy did not look back; the Frenchman had been right, they had brought the war to them.

The major mounted his tank and looked down on the Black Bear. 'You, up here on the tank.'

The men loaded themselves up on tanks and carriers where they could, the rest ready to march, the engines started and a low rumble filled the valley, the smell of oil thick. Guy looked up and soaring high above was a buzzard, looking for its prey, it looked menacing and unstoppable.

Guy finally looked back at the Mulots, just as Pierre and the girl turned, the girl was clutching something in her hands, a piece of paper with a face on it the British had passed around. William in print stared back at Guy, the edges of the paper curling in the breeze.

Guy heard a ghastly clink from inside the tank, there was a sucking of air, then a boom that knocked the wind from the space around as a tank shell headed straight for the house. The tank jolted backwards, its wheels biting into the dry grass. Guy watched as the shell hit the front of the farmhouse shattering it entirely, a rumble roared around them, and the farmhouse exploded in a cloud of fire and smoke. The noise penetrated all, a screaming crack as the red-hot flames ate up all the air around it, the rubble tumbling down onto Pierre and Lucy.

Guy stood, yelling aloud in fury over the sound of the inferno, then he looked back, realising his mistake.

'Now we have you,' the major said to Guy staring straight at him, his eyes narrowed.

'Move on,' was the order the commander gave, so the tanks turned away from the grizzled scene where the farmhouse had been, just a wall of smoke and tumbling timber and brick in its place.

Guy peered at the wreckage as the tank headed into the trees but could not make out either the father or the daughter. The soldier within him did not leave a life of duty with a bang, but a sorrowful succumbing to the inevitability of this hell.

'Take him,' Guy heard somewhere distant, and he felt hands on him. For a second, he struggled, two men falling off the side of the tank and rolling into the bushes, his fist hit another square in the jaw, and he felt blood cover his own face.

He felt his hands being roughly yanked behind him and them being bound, thin wire being knotted over and over. The tanks all stopped again, now under the cover of the dense trees by a lake with a spit of land sticking out into it. This was the second time he had been a prisoner in as many days, the first time he had been saved, but this time he would not be, showing he did not want Pierre and Lucy murdered had been enough for the major to sentence him, something just didn't add up about Guy being there and suspicion alone was enough to seal his fate.

Guy could fight, he could plead, but it would do no good, he felt hands shove him roughly off the edge of the tank and for a split second he was falling then he hit the ground with a thump.

He had tried to save the boy who had saved him, he only hoped the boy would live, and that, Guy thought, might just be enough.

He did not even bother to stand; the days of the fighting Bear were over, exhausted, and hollowed out, the spirit of the bear floated up and away from this place for good. The body of Guy lay there, his eyes were blinking slowly and his mind blank, he looked down, arms bound and there on his chest was the proud bear emblem, still in fighting stance. He thought of his sons and shut his eyes as the tank turned and started rolling towards him. The tracks looked like a thousand sharp teeth inching closer over the roots and trees of the forest by the Scarpe; the boy he had saved had been worth it, he truly believed that above all else.

Chapter 13

Runner

A slither of light from the open doorway refracted off the gaps in the chest and covered Jolyon in a dull glow. It reminded him of the hues of a large church, he could see dust particles all around him. It smelt damp in here and he was excruciatingly thirsty, his wound throbbed in time with his heart and a crushing headache racked him. He must endure though; they were only a floor away.

His survival depended on the determination of the German searchers, his saviours lie, and him being quiet so let his mind go blank and started counting the particles swimming in his vision.

'One, two, three'.

They had heard the Germans coming, announcing themselves with the pistol shot by the crater on the edge of the wood and then the footsteps and voices getting closer having found the house. Jolyon had lurched up from where he lay, Daphne Mulot ramming a hand over his mouth to stop the scream.

His saviours had been calm in providing refuge for this fugitive knowing the stakes went no higher but by taking him in, if they were caught, they hadn't just signed his death warrant, but also their own.

They had dragged him spluttering from the river by his sopping wet jacket, strong hands had lifted him from the water and laid him down on the soft grass of the riverbank. He remembered being dragged by his feet, coughing, and then hazy memories of faces, he had felt no panic at hands undressing him, tending to him.

The Mulots had watched him tumble down the riverbank and could have left him, the value of life though was not lost on these people. They knew war better than most Jolyon assumed; it had surrounded them in this wood for long enough.

When they got him to the house, they had laid him flat on the kitchen table. 'You are wounded,' Pierre Mulot said softly, barely above a whisper.

He had looked down at his bare chest, the bullet hole now scabbing with caked blood.

He had nodded, and the man had brought a candle to look at it more closely.

'Daphne, some towels.'

The woman began filling a chipped metal dish with a faded blue rim with soapy water.

'Who... who are...?'

The man had silenced Jolyon with a gentle hand, the other raising a finger to his lips.

'Quiet now. You need strength.'

The man busied himself with cleaning Jolyon's clavicle, and then his shoulder blade where the bullet had come out.

'Not bad, not bad' he kept repeating over and over deep in thought.

The man put a beaker to his lips, and he drunk thirstily, the cold reminding him of being submerged in the icy Scarpe which made his queasy.

The man had applied some white powder from Jolyon's medical pack to his shoulder which made him wince. He had passed out for a while, lost somewhere between a gentle past in Edinburgh and a violent present in France.

The gunshot nearby had awoken him with a start and the look on the face of the man and woman assured him it was not some nightmare and was real and close.

They had strapped up his shoulder tightly and he could not move his arm away from his body, he looked at them squarely for the first time, the shock and intermittent blackouts of jumbled thoughts subsiding.

'I am Jolyon.'

'I am Pierre Mulot, and this is my wife, Daphne.'

'Thank yo—'

But the Frenchman cut him off. 'Not now. We need to hide you. They are coming.'

'No, I must leave, you cannot…'

'Quiet, follow Daphne, and don't say a word.'

Jolyon was helped to his feet and Daphne looped a firm arm through his free arm, grasping his hand in hers. Pierre watched him go, clearing away the bowl, powder, and rags, he had a thick black moustache which permanently made him look like he was growling. Deep-set eyes watched Jolyon leave and he nodded just once, a nod like they were in this together and all three of them had to hold up their end of the bargain if they were going to make it through.

She pointed up and Jolyon began to walk the stairs, it was a simple home, but a beautiful one. The banister was worn smooth under his hand, it smelt of oil like it had been freshly applied.

Daphne showed him into their room, and Jolyon almost backed away when he saw their marital bed, it felt wrong to be in here.

She dragged him on, a strength in her he had not expected, he felt dizzy as his eyes adjusted to the single candle burning but he allowed himself to be steered in front of a large wooden chest at the foot of their cast iron bed.

The chest was almost the width of the bed with two iron runners looping around it, it looked ancient, like it had been here longer than the house.

In this chest, Jolyon would roll the dice again, just like he had on the riverbank. To stay here and hide meant if he was caught it would be the end, the runner in him wanted to take to his heels on foot in the forest, but where would he go? Besides, despite the caring and practiced hands, a tiny spot of red was beginning to seep through the thick bandages that smelt of iodine.

Submerging himself in the chest was very final though, with the lid open and its innards shrouded in black it didn't look so much like a chest so much as it did a grave.

'I can't...'

Daphne let her head tilt to one side, just as the fox had done outside on the riverbank, her hair was tied tightly in a bun and there was a flush to her cheeks from the exertions of patching him up. Tiny innumerable freckles like stars mounted her nose and her eyes looked into him.

'We have already made our choice,' she said.

Jolyon let out a long expulsion of air, allowing himself to be helped into the chest. He noticed bloody rags, he assumed his, littering the bedspread but Daphne picked one up, the bright red still glistening under the candlelight. Her fingers ran down her body to the hem of her dress which she pulled at bringing it upwards with her laced petticoat, she started rubbing the bandage up her thighs. His blood covered her pale flesh, smearing in red like watercolour and Jolyon gasped, this felt shockingly intimate.

Daphne turned, hitching her skirt up over her narrow hips so he could see her buttocks which she also doused with his bloody rags. She carried on grabbing blood-soaked rags and dipping them in a bowl, then smearing her hamstrings, shins and down to her calves until the hems of her dress were smudged with his blood. Her hands scrubbed his blood into the fabric until her flesh and clothing were as bright red as the flare he had fired from the tank.

He was standing in the chest, open-mouthed and breathing rapidly unsure what he was watching.

She motioned for him to lie down in the chest which he did, all the while his mouth hanging open in shock and his fists clenched to drive away the waves of pain from his shoulder.

From outside came a shout, German voices, and lots of them, Pierre had been right; they were coming fast.

Daphne closed the lid and he sensed her lie down on the bed, the frame squeaking. He heard her collecting the bandages around her, they scrunched as she eased herself towards the head of the bed.

It was pitch black at first in the chest and claustrophobia had him by the throat, he had to find from deep within himself the need not to cry out or open the lid. It felt like a deep and terrible dream where he was under the earth in no-man's-land, alive and awake but forever submerged.

The front door opened below, and Jolyon held his breath, reminding himself firmly that these people had risked everything to save him and if he lost control, if he cracked, they were all dead.

'It is all I have,' he heard Pierre say below and then parts of the conversation drifted in and out, hidden by the thick wood of the chest and the flat air. The yellow light from the single candle had infiltrated the chest as his eyes became accustomed to the darkness. He could still see dust all around him and the muffled voices below felt further away, like he was looking down on this scene from above. Whatever Pierre was doing must be working as there had been no gunfire.

Then the tone of the voices changed becoming more urgent, there was an accusatory tone in the German voices, and he heard Daphne let out a small whimper over her lips.

He heard Pierre say clearly from below, 'I can explain the rag.'

They had found one of his bloody rags, the game was up, they would know they had a soldier here. He would be responsible for the death of this young married couple, and all because he had refused to die.

Footsteps began coming up the stairs and he lay flat against the cool base of the chest, gently sliding a hand over his mouth and exhaling through a gap in between index and middle finger.

When the footsteps were outside the door, Daphne began moaning, the noise built, gently at first, and then getting louder. Jolyon wondered what was going on and nearly opened the chest to check on her, her moans became more urgent like she was in pain as the footsteps grew closer and stopped outside the bedroom door. He could feel the edge of the chest bump as her body began writhing on the bed, one of her heels catching the top of it.

Pierre's voice was close now, he was up here too. 'You can see for yourself.'

The atmosphere in the room changed at once as soon as the Germans and Pierre entered, Jolyon let his breath out slowly through his fingers, and Daphne let out a short squeal of pain.

She was whimpering hopelessly; it was a pitiful sound like a rabbit maimed in a snare. He could feel the Germans taking in the scene, one of them was tapping on the doorframe with his finger.

Then Pierre spoke softly but clearly, cutting through the whimpering of his wife and surrounding Jolyon in the chest.

'A miscarriage. We have been trying for some time.'

Daphne gave a fresh set of sobs, and now Jolyon understood the need for the bloody rags.

There was tutting from a German in the room, he could sense that whoever it belonged to was annoyed at the sight that presented itself to them, he had clearly wanted to catch the Frenchman and his wife out.

'Now if you don't mind,' Pierre added.

Jolyon was inches away from the enemy, the eyes of the Germans would be scanning the room now, surely, they had seen the chest. He was within their grasp, they would look, he would if he was the German.

'Leave these people in peace,' a new German voice had entered the room.

'But, sir?'

'Get out of here, this woman is in distress, you fool.'

'Sir, I...'

'Look at the blood, she has lost a child!'

There was a series of grunts and almost as quickly as the enemy had entered the room, there was then the turning about of boots. Daphne continued moaning softly as the boots and men made their way downstairs and the voices became fainter.

Jolyon nearly wretched with the release of tension, he bit his palm covering his mouth. Minutes passed and there was nothing, until he heard Daphne's bare feet across the room.

There was a creak as the chest lid opened and Daphne looked down on him, her thin smile as warm as any sunlight in full summer. It was a smile like his mother used to give him when she'd missed him and behind Daphne was all light from the candle on the dresser, she was shrouded in it, the outline of her face perfectly illuminated in golden yellow.

Jolyon was shaking, his wounded body pressed into the soft wood of the chest feeling the rough timber against his cheek.

'I will write,' Jolyon said.

'I would rather you survived,' Daphne said laying a hand on his forearm.

'I don't know where to start.'

Pierre looked at Jolyon, checked his bandages one more time and gently patted his shoulder.

Jolyon was helped with his jacket, hanging limply off one shoulder with his other arm tightly strapped to his chest, his jacket felt heavy, and his regimental buttons were made dim in the light of the doorway of the farmhouse.

The Germans had believed their staggering act of bravery and deception, they said one of the Germans seemed a good man, and outside on the lawn he had castigated his men for pushing on with the search having seen Daphne prostate on the bed. Maybe he understood the pain of miscarriage, was there anything sadder than that, wondered Jolyon.

'It is best you go; the sun is coming up.'

Jolyon looked around towards the River Scarpe and the first hints of a new day were announcing themselves across the forest. He thought of the thousands of British soldiers who would also be beginning another arduous day at the front, those familiar smells and sounds. He wondered if anyone else had survived the massacre he had been wounded in, he would have been presumed dead already by now on the register, and he would have been, had it not been for the Mulots.

The pink sky of another hot day began to seep into the azure above and Jolyon knew which way he would head, there was not a breath of wind, just his own pained breathing and the soft running of water from the river past the farmhouse.

He was not sure how he should be feeling, he was wrung out and had said little as they had patched him up and overseen him eating some bread and drinking cool water from the river. His ready acceptance of what he thought was his end now felt an inherently selfish thing to have done and he hated that he had been that willing to give up.

'I will write.' He promised to them.

'I look forward to it,' said Daphne as if she really meant it.

Jolyon smiled gently. 'You will survive this?'

'We will find a way,' Pierre said, putting a hand around the shoulder of his wife.

'Thank you.'

'Goodbye, Jolyon.'

With a wave, he turned away from the farmhouse and the Mulots, the best of people in the worst of times. As he walked, small ebbs of pain made themselves known but everything felt lifted.

His breath rattled in his chest when he began to climb the hill behind the house, where the Mulots had said there was a place he could cross the narrowed river, from there he would follow it back to no-man's-land, back to war.

Two things repeated in his mind as he walked up, crossed the river, and then back down the other side, his pace slowing all the time. One was that he was certain his time as a soldier was over which upset him, not because he did not want to be, but a wound like this would see him sent home.

The second was for him to start a family, Evelyn he loved, and he had married with the intent of having children but the war, as it had done to so many millions had changed their plans. They had decided to wait, Jolyon and Evelyn, both having no idea whatsoever what awaited him over here in France and truly, none of them thought it would be this bad. Evelyn wanted to be a mother more than anything else, he had wanted to be a soldier and he had won that private war but wished he had lost, he wished he had been defeated one hundred times over.

He had reached the edge of the wood and in the flat light could make out the hillocks and craters left by the thousands of shells that had fallen here in the past few weeks. He could see the outline of the tank he had been shot in; it was like nothing had changed here but everything had.

He crouched down low, back in the space between life and death, his shoulder giving him a tug of agony against the bandages. He began to crawl amongst the bodies, noticing Leatherbrook's limp form, the crawl began to pain him, his strength was fading.

He wanted to get home to Evelyn, he wanted to be a father, and that would power him on for as long as his body held out, and as far as he had to travel.

Chapter 14

Gunner

Otto was in a state of bafflement, the day and night had been long, though all days out here marched on slowly, but a frantic slaughter dished out, drunken stupor, executing one of his own and then the scene at the farmhouse had left him spent.

No good could come of war, he believed that now, no good could come of the actions he was responsible for. It was not the killing that seemed to have driven this nail home either, it was the image of the Frenchwoman lying on the bed covered in blood. He could not have altered the course of the war, but he could have made different decisions, why had they interrupted such a private scene? He was the smallest chess piece on the world's most shattered board.

The finality of life had been reminded to him in that strange bedroom in the farmhouse and what really mattered most was not here in this place. He had been able to ignore that itch at the start when he had seen less horror, when there was still a faint belief, he would survive this and the repeated infractions on his conscience he could shift.

Seeing that farmhouse though, with the two young occupants had reminded him that this was not their land and it had been their choice to come here on the orders of a man he would never meet. He was now a soldier in a war he could no longer take part in, and that presented a grave problem.

Otto was boiling water, sitting on the fire step of the trench overlooking the battlefield of the day before, no one had moved on the British side, their trench was utterly deserted. As the sun rose over Arras in the distance, the piles of bodies that he could pretend were mounds of earth during the night now started to define themselves.

Before the farmhouse and his slide towards capitulation, he used to love these moments, the sun rising, hot coffee to come and no water round his ankles. This had been his favourite time of the war before, for it was still, and having just fought an engagement meant he was as far away in time from the next battle as it was possible to be.

Hours he had spent cumulatively in this hunched position, his eyes scanning the battlefield, not looking for anything, just marvelling at the feeling of being alive.

'That was long,' Kummer said.

Otto looked up at Kummer nodding, he lifted the coffee pot and poured the jet-black liquid into both their mugs.

'Where to from here?'

Otto sighed. 'Wait, I guess. No other plans, you?'

'Waiting again.' Kummer laughed running his fingers through his oily hair.

'Do you think we will win?'

Kummer took a sip of coffee. 'Of course.'

Otto felt Kummer look sideways as if he might have somehow spotted the change.

'Why?' Kummer asked.

'No reason really, just be an awful waste if all this was to lose.'

'Imagine how they are feeling then?'

Otto followed Kummer's pointing finger towards the abandoned trench lines of the British, still smoking and still. He was about to turn to Kummer and tell the truth, tell him he was done and tell him they should not be here when he saw a movement on the edge of the forest, he tried to hide what he had seen but Kummer stood straight upwards.

'You see?' Kummer said pointing.

'No. Nothing, I think.'

'You're crazy, there's someone there.'

Begrudgingly, Otto looked again and sure enough, walking very slowly with only one arm swinging limply was a soldier, a lone and wounded British soldier, the man from the tank.

Otto had a choice to make about the British man in no-man's-land whilst Kummer had dashed back to the trench to get his rifle. It being so early, they were the only ones awake apart from the lookouts at the far end of the next bend in the trench. They couldn't see the British soldier from there, only he and Kummer knew of him.

Otto watched the man through his binoculars, why in the hell did he have to arrive then? What was he doing? Looking closer, he saw that the man was injured, and badly. He was less walking, more stumbling towards his trenches, the last one left.

Bandages were wrapped around the man, clean and recently applied, he had come from the direction of the farmhouse from the woods, there was nothing that way but that one building. There had been a British soldier in there and the French couple had hidden him.

He could hear Kummer's footsteps coming closer, his short panting doing little to hide his excitement at starting the day with a kill. Kummer was built for war, built to endure until the end of this thing. The British soldier was coughing, he was weak, and his mouth was chalked in white with thirst.

Kummer landed with a jolt next to Otto, spilling his coffee up his arm.

'You want the shot?'

Otto answered over his teeth. 'No, no. You take it.'

'Excellent,' Kummer said, and he readied himself on the parapet, the butt of the rifle slipping easily into the crook of his neck. He lined the man up in the sights, steadying his breathing. With a faint click the safety catch came off as the British man, with the yellow morning sun on his face stumbled on, unaware he had been sentenced long after the battle.

Otto felt the dagger catch on the edge of Kummer's helmet, but it slid into his neck easily after that. He put a grubby hand over his friend's mouth watching the blood collect around the hilt of the knife and then begin to pour down its handle and through his hands. Kummer's eyes were wide, and he looked up in silent horror as his great friend, his commanding officer, extinguished his life right there on the edge of their own trench. Kummer's hand clasped over Otto's, his legs kicking and sending flicks of mud over the top of the parapet. Otto felt the breath begin to weaken on the palm over Kummer's mouth and the blood ejecting in rhythmic pumps soaked his grey sleeve.

Otto watched Kummer's right leg stop twitching, the eyes go dull then removed the blade in one motion, he wiped it on his coat and then slid it back into its worn leather sheath.

The British man was now climbing back into his trench and falling as he did. 'I am sorry,' Otto said to the corpse of his friend Kummer. 'Enough, though. Enough, now.'

Otto kept low as he crossed no-man's-land, time was against

159

him as the higher the sun got, the more of his countrymen would be waking up. Given their victory, the effects of the night before were being felt along the line and for once he praised the peach schnapps and its ability to comatose his troopers.

He had murdered his best friend, partly because of what he had seen, partly what he felt, but mostly he wanted the British soldier to live.

Silent and alone, no-man's-land seemed even more squalid, and without the bullets and bombs and his comrades with him it was devastatingly bleak. Bodies were everywhere, the stench appalling. Faces frozen in their death spasm looked at him as he scuttled past, rats skidded and scuttled over everything, disturbed by his trampling boots, one poked its sharp face out from inside the eye socket of a horse.

The broken wire littered with stuck bodies tore past as he approached the British line, there was no sign of the wounded man. Low enough to feel the water splashing up onto his chest from shell-holes, he reached the edge of their trench and looked down. Parts of men were stacked oddly at strange angles and a mass of uniforms utterly covered the bottom half of the trench, the ones on the bottom were submerged underwater.

Otto searched the faces and the forms until he saw his man and there, lying with his head curled up under the arm of one of his fellow brothers he lay. His form was pitiful, the bandages loose now off his waist exposing a ragged bloody patch on his shoulder and a hole at its centre.

'Friend?' Otto said quietly, all too aware of the panic his uniform would bring.

The man did not move.

'Hey?'

The man looked at him and fear filled his face, he began

scrabbling, his boots kicking dead men in their chests, faces, and necks.

'No, no,' Otto said, raising his hands in surrender, squatting on his haunches.

The man stopped wriggling, whether he had understood or had given up, Otto could not be sure.

Otto kept his hands raised and from behind his back pulled his pouch, he took out a canteen of water and rattled it, the water sloshing.

The young, wounded man was tall and lithe, his mousy brown hair filled with mud and dried blood. His eyes did not leave Otto as if this might be the beginning of some awful joke and he was falling for a trap.

'For you,' he said tossing the canteen to the British soldier. It landed a foot from him, nestled in between the heads of two dead soldiers.

He drank deeply, draining the canteen.

'Can you walk?'

The solider looked down at his wounds. 'Barely.'

'I can help.'

The British soldier still looked wary, but Otto slid down the side of the trench, noticing its appalling condition compared to their own. He had to step across a carpet of dead men that bobbed up and down in the water to reach the British man, his knees on someone's torso.

'You need to get out of here.'

The British man looked perplexed as if to say how.

'Will you let me look?' Otto said pointing at the wound.

The British man nodded; he was so vulnerable.

Otto set to work redressing the wounds.

When the two men were above the trench again, Otto handed Jolyon his pouch, it had water, biscuits, a compass, and more dressings.

Otto felt the heat of the sun on his back, their trench would be active now and at any moment a shot could ring out meaning the end of them both.

The British man looked back at the wood where he had come from and between the two men, somehow, was a bridge of understanding. Otto knew he had been at the farmhouse and Jolyon knew this was one of them men who had come looking.

'You should go,' Otto said turning Jolyon away from the German lines.

'I don't know... how...'

'No mind. We must try.'

Jolyon nodded and Otto saw him try to fill his broken lungs, they rattled unnervingly.

'Your men will not be that far.'

The British soldier, a firm expression on his face, took in the form of his once enemy. 'Will you make it back?'

'I will find a way,' Otto said letting his facial muscles relax.

'Go well.'

'And you.'

Jolyon began to walk away, the white bandages glowing, his shape cut clean against the rising sun.

Otto watched Jolyon limp off for some minutes until his shape started to disappear into the haze of the morning. As he turned, he took in the view of the battlefield from the other side, it was different, but also sickeningly similar.

The woods on the edge of the battlefield remained unchanged, perhaps the only thing that had. For he, Otto Zweck,

German soldier of the highest class was changed for good. Perhaps this small deed of mercy might atone for some of what he had done for his war was at an end. He pulled at the medals on his chest and let them tumble from his grasp down the edge of the British trench until they sank down into the watery mud below amongst the bodies of the fallen.

The sun was blissfully warm on his face, and he lit a cigarette hearing shouts from his lines, but he took no mind. With any luck, the British soldier was far from here by now and back with his men.

He began to walk towards his lines and the German forces where he was no longer a soldier, just a thing. A tiny thing who had tried to make a difference, and a thing that knew it would die over here, much sooner now he had given up hope of returning. Perhaps, he thought, as the voices of his comrades filled his ears, that was the whole point of it all.

Chapter 15

Rider

William was left on foot in the deep woods that reeked of smoke, it was no surprise the horse had scarpered as the cacophony of fire had been monumental. Occasionally he thought he saw a flash of it through breaks in the trees, but he put this down to blind hope, his eyes were playing tricks and at every new vista, he thought he spotted the bay horse. He was alone, lost, on the run and knew that whichever army caught him first, he was a dead man.

Having dropped from the window and escaped into the deep woods, he had climbed the hill behind the house where he and Guy had been the night before. They had both known that they had brought war to this place. Seeing it play out though, seeing British men tumbling, and Hugh Cronk killed, because of his direct actions, created a sense of such shame within him he knew he would never recover.

When he was on top of the hill with the green tops of trees stretching out beneath his eyeline, he had seen the explosion of the farmhouse volley up through the canopy. A cloud of orange light had blinded him before the dull boom echoed around him in tighter spirals making his ears pop. Tiny fragments of brick had landed in the bushes around him like hail drops, and a piece of white stone landed by his boot. Even in his darkest projections the night before, this was worse. He had been responsible for the death of his own countrymen, his friend, the kind Pierre, the little girl Lucy, and god knows what had happened to Guy.

He considered what few options he had and if he had had a weapon, he might have used it on himself. Countless bullets had flown past him in recent months, and he didn't even have one, one solitary piece of lead to blast through his temple. Had his deed been worth it? These tiny acts of kindness were so pointless compared to the ocean of bad deeds done over here. He had been naive to the point of idiocy to think this would have any consequence at all to the outcome and all it had done was shatter his own circumstances and anyone unlucky enough to be within his orbit.

He ambled onwards through the thick woods with no idea where he was, he was hungry and thirsty but in a masochistic way he enjoyed the feelings of discomfort as they reminded him of his errors, this was just the beginning of his atonement.

Hours passed and still no signs of life could be seen, even the birds and butterflies had vanished. He had walked by chance into his old camp, encountering the usual debris left behind after an evacuation. The British had left fast, or what was left of them after the battering from the enemy. Heavy tracks from trucks zig zagged away from the camp, and empty jerry cans littered the long grass from the hasty departure.

He scrambled through the remains he could find, picking at crusts abandoned for days in the grass and drinking cold coffee from a flask with a bullet mark in. He even sucked discarded tea bags and reattacked a chicken bone he found by the latrine pit that had already been stripped down clean. There was a surrealness to the scene, knowing the entire British army was on the move towards one place except him, Dunkirk would be their redemption or their end, there was only one way off that beach.

His father's voice was loud in his head as he dozed under a tree, feverish and overwhelmed. He had been at relative peace here the day before by the river with the Cronks. His father's voice lulled him towards sleep, the commanding monotone of his childhood and early manhood was not ashamed, and the words were unclear. In a way, his father looked almost happy with his boy in his features, but William knew that couldn't be the case, not after what he had done.

His father's face started to crumble, slowly at first, small pebbles like the ones thrown up from the exploding farmhouse started to fall off the features. The skin turned to fine dust like a creeping fog as the face was whittled down to a skull then replaced with a wheel, a circular gun carriage wheel painted in fading red. The wheel was being dragged by a hundred horses, all of them dying from exhaustion as they laboured on with bleeding shins.

Someone barked commands at them, a man in all black with a gas mask on his face. Another noise started to infect his dreams, climbing above the shouting man. As the wheel turned it started to shudder in protest, straining against the muscles and sinews of the ravaged horses. As the wheel spokes buckled under the pressure the horses chimed in unison with a low humming coming from the back of their throats, the horses stepped forward again in unison, as one, the wheel splintering into a thousand pieces and William lurched to avoid the splinters in his sleep.

The horses then rounded on William, all of them with their baggy reins and bleeding gums started to trot towards him, then to canter, their hooves in perfect time. None of them had eyes, just black holes where they used to be with the man in black as their commander, his feet astride two of them, the gasmask tied behind his head with barbed wire that dug into his cheeks and hair leaking red. All the while the screaming got louder from the horses' whiskered lips, the thundering horses' hooves were nearly on him, about to crush him.

He opened his eyes, delirious, sweating and panting, and he just had the time to see the tail wing of a plane, outlined in silver against the bright sun. He felt an enormous wave of heat then felt his body lifted straight up into the air as if he was being held aloft by burning hands. All his senses relapsed back into nothing and even the bleeding horses and their masked commander could not find him here, as no one could.

It was a full day until William regained consciousness and he was only aware of being alive by the tingling all over his flesh and a desperate thirst. He had no idea where he was, who had him under their watch and what lay ahead of him.

He remembered his dream of the hell horses with a spasm, he could picture every detail it had been so vivid. He could smell disinfectant and looked down on his body which was a tapestry of bandages. His skin prickled again, and he realised he was awfully burnt and where he could see patches of skin it was almost purple under the daylight, and scabs disappeared underneath folds of cloth.

Long white sheets had been hung from the ceiling to give him some privacy, and they rustled and curled in the wind from an open window. He knew he was in an infirmary but when one of the sheets blew back, he saw the window for the first time and across it were bars.

In panic, he tried to get out of bed, but his arms and legs would not move, his ankles and wrists were strapped to the bed, faded leather shackles dug into his limbs.

'Help,' he croaked, the thirst now manic and he heard a shuffling some way off.

'Hello. Anyone?'

In the doorway appeared a figure, a man in black with a gas mask was standing there, the man from his dreams. William thrashed against the bed, feeling his healing skin re-tear on his forearms and calves.

'Calm boy, calm,' shouted the voice but it was muffled behind the mask.

William saw the man approach and tried with all his strength to curl up, to get further away from the touch of the commander of the hellish horses.

'Please. No. I am sorry. I am sorry...' William shouted as the man reached out his hands for William.

The man in black pulled off his gas mask and threw it onto the floor.

'Be calm. I am here to help.'

William, eyes rolling and petrified saw the face behind the mask and it was a kind one, a calm one, a human one. Beneath the chin was a white band tucked into the black collar, he was a priest.

'Water...' William croaked.

The priest looked behind him and quickly held a mug to William's mouth which he drank gratefully, and it was so quenching he felt his eyes begin to prickle. The guilt, the fear, the dream, and the pain all combined and once tears begun, he could not stop them. They cascaded down his face silently, he did not have the breath to really sob, just to let the sadness roll.

From somewhere close he heard the singing of men, gravely British voices carried over the summer air and into his cell. With the voices came the smell of salt and the screech of a seagull. He knew the hymn; he knew it only too well and with the words came a sense of longing for his father the like of which he had never felt despite their private war.

"Breathe through the heats of our desire
Thy coolness and Thy balm;
Let sense be dumb, let flesh retire;
Speak through the earthquake, wind, and fire,
O still, small voice of calm."

William's eyes were scanning the room. 'Where are we?'

The priest bowed his head, his thick silver hair flopping over his black brows. 'We are in Dunkirk.'

'We made it.'

'Yes,' said the priest. 'But we have lost thousands.'

William dropped his chin, knowing he had been responsible for a score of them.

'Boats are coming for us though; our people have come to us to save us. Normal people, not soldiers.'

William felt a small surge of joy. 'That is good, no?'

'Yes,' said the priest and letting his eyes drift towards the window. 'The weather has saved us from the bombers, it was one of those that nearly killed you. A reserve patrol picked you up, they thought you were dead. The boats are here soon, all manner of small crafts to save an army, you will not be on them though. You, William Bremner, are a prisoner in your own army and you will be sent back as a such and sentenced on return. Your time as a soldier is done and what you do with the rest of your days is up to you.'

The matter-of-fact way this information was fired at William hit like short jabs in his solar plexus.

'I am breaking the law coming to you, William.'

William looked into the deep hazel eyes of the priest, with nothing else coming to mind, William whispered, 'Thank you, Father,' grateful even for this tiny concession.

'You are about to endure so much young man. You will be alone, utterly alone and I cannot protect you.'

'I see,' William said, his mind struggling to comprehend the gravity of the words steamrolling him, he was a pariah, a lone disgrace.

There was a crunching of gravel from outside as the singing ended and the priest stood, it would not do well to be caught here with the prisoner.

'Wish me luck, Father,' William said with a grimace, a phrase that reminded him of his father, his stoic ironclad Dad who did not leave the war as a disgrace, but a hero.

'I don't know why you did what you did, but in the eyes of the Lord it was the right thing to do, if not in the eyes of the people who will judge you. What they wanted to do in that wood was murder, and you stopped it. You will need to remember that if you are to survive. That is all I can offer you but do not let them take that from you, whatever they do to you, and I will remind you of this, it was no accident that bomb did not kill you, you have been spared.'

With that, the man in black turned, picked up his gasmask, slid it over his great thick grey hair and walked out of the room, his brogues clacking on the linoleum floor.

William could hear boots coming closer, men who would sentence him.

The breeze and the salt air filled the room, for months they had been running back this way to the sea, towards their homes and they were here, by some miracle they were here. He would not go back as he imagined though, not as a bitter soldier of war but as a sympathiser with the enemy.

The grey hull of the small craft slammed into the white-tipped waves causing the boat to roll as it fought forwards. William was at the mercy of the movement of the ship, chained to the outside of the cabin with his hips pressed forward against the ship's rail. Every bump brought agony, his incinerated skin stretched and pulled as the craft bobbed over the waves.

The captain had said nothing when he had escorted William aboard, his arms shackled and his feet dragging in the rough surf until they reached the gangplank. His legs had been limp, pulled through the breaking waves, the iron chains collecting seaweed in their wake. The captain's face had deep wrinkles burrowing from the corner of his eyes like a trench map. From the corner of his mouth hung a worn pipe, small puffs of wispy smoke reminding William of the trails of smoke in the woods from the farmhouse. William had said nothing as he was manhandled, hanging his head as the manacles were attached to the top of the cabin and the bottom of the rail where he would stay bound for the crossing back to Britain facing outwards.

Soldiers from all the regiments that had survived jeered from the beach as he was led aboard, the painted word on the back of his jacket in white reading 'PRISONER' enough to allow half of the British army to know who he was. They had all heard by now of the traitor who had saved a German commander and let him live. An act that had led to the death of forty-one British soldiers who had bravely gone to find this vile sympathiser by the River Scarpe.

William had known in the hills above the farmhouse he

171

would never recover from the actions of saving Guy, and the talk with the priest and the shackling to the side of a ship had only confirmed this.

Just before the ship had pushed off, a dreaded sight approached, it was John Cronk. He bent close to William's ear and spoke quietly so William had to lean forward. 'I'll find you.'

'John, please…'

Cronk cut him off. 'My brother died because of you. No matter how long it takes, I'll find you, and I'll make sure everyone knows exactly what you did, you will never find peace.'

The words were said with such venom William shrunk and Cronk gave him a last look of disgust. The below decks were filled with the wounded, leaving him the only soul visible from the beach on the foredeck. He had looked back only once at the direction of the wood and whilst he knew physically, he would never return, his mind and spirit had been left there. A large part of him, and one he had held close to his inner being since he was a boy had died over here. He had believed saving Guy was the right thing to do, but he had been proven wrong and more damaging than his incarceration was the excruciating sense that it would have been better to let Guy and his troopers die than face this.

The prison ship bumped along on the waves; the crucified shape of William being bounced around so hard his head had started to bleed from the rough edge of the cabin, the coastline of France begun disappearing in sea mist and gloom.

The captain and two wounded British soldiers were speaking inside the cabin, the captain was saying how brave the men were.

'Not bloody likely,' one said back.

'Cowards, the lot of us. Shameful.'

The captain tried to argue but it was no good, the two soldiers, wounded and covered in bedraggled blankets felt nothing but disgust about running away from France.

William could sense one of the men was about to launch into all the reasons the British were a spent force when he sat up. 'Lord above,' he said.

The other one followed his friend's pointed finger. 'Have you ever seen anything like that?'

The captain just said in a whisper, 'No, I have not.'

William opened his eyes at their exclamations, his lids burning from salt and saw the saviour's armada coming from the other direction. A myriad of crafts, some small, some big but all with one purpose, to save the British army. The people had sailed out to help, thousands of them all in a line of sail and colour passing his own ship going the other way.

As the smaller boats passed, on their way to do the greatest deed they would ever do in their lives, the captains, cooks, and mates looked up at the figure shackled and displayed on the side of the prison ship. Whilst they risked their lives, ordinary people, to do this great deed, what had this man done to warrant this? How disgusting an act had he committed to be treated as such? They would say it was because of men like this their boys never came home.

As the cliffs of Dover came into view in the distance, William knew this was not a home anymore, this was not a place he longed to come back to like every other soldier would.

On the day of the Dunkirk rescue, one man amongst the thousands would remember that day differently. A day when the very best of human endeavour was shown in the form of an armada, William Bremner would remember it for the opposite.

For it was the day he knew he would never be rid of his actions, he would never be free from war. Harder than any fight, harder than death in France, he would live on, damned by all and shamed by many.

Chapter 16

1924, Arras, France
Runner

Jolyon watched William run along the edge of the woodland, his little legs churning, occasionally looking back to check he had not gone too far with a mischievous look. William did not understand what had happened here, he never would, but it was important to Jolyon they had come together.

Jolyon had to steel his mind to return to the place where he had nearly died but bringing his son he saw as a rite of passage he was in the rarity to bestow on a keen mind, plenty of fathers had never gotten this chance. William was an astute boy, and a thoughtful one, and Jolyon wondered if this would stay with his son despite him only being five. What he would make of it, he couldn't know, how could anyone who hadn't been here ever truly understand it?

They had travelled across two days before, stopping in Albert where other pilgrims could be seen, coming back to where they lost sons, brothers, husbands, and fathers and trying to make sense of any part of it. Small groups, mainly silent, would gather under the shadow of the belfry, some looking over a map, some clutching medals sent home without the wearer. Lighting candles in the windows of home had been a national gesture, as had the general sense of pride mixed with unquantifiable loss, but for Jolyon he had to return.

The scars were still visible along the woodland, great craters now cleared of bodies but not metal and not memories. Jolyon fought off the nag of why he had survived when so many had not just as William returned saying he was hungry and Jolyon passed him the bread he had purchased from Albert, a tiny bakery open at dawn with a full moon hanging over the entire town. The silence of the morning had struck him, a place that for so long had been unused to anything but noise.

The belfry was to be repaired exactly as it had been before the war he had been told, the trees would be replanted, and they would do it all knowing that whatever the cost, much more had been given here than time. William took the bread and bit into it, and with a deep ache, Jolyon remembered the German who had found him in the water of the trench, fed him and sent him back to his own lines. As ever, when his mind came back here, and truly back here not hidden behind a haze of distraction, he asked who had really won and what it was to be human having seen both the very best and very worst of it. The enemy had nearly killed him, the Mulots had hidden him, and the enemy had then saved him. It was a lot to bare, but that was why he had come.

The farmhouse poked itself through the trees and Jolyon felt a sense of great relief it stood, and a nausea at why he had come back here again. Perhaps the Mulots were dead and new owners would stare out at him, wondering why on earth he had come, especially with a little boy who was too young to see this place. Maybe the Mulots would be there, but why would they want a reminder on their doorstep of what they had endured? He had said he would write, but to return in person felt so much more in keeping with his views of all pilgrims that returned, it was not a choice, but a duty.

'William, stay close.'

William ambled over to him having picked up a stick from the riverbank which he swished about his head through the still morning air.

William looked up at Jolyon. 'Where are we?'

Jolyon had known this question was coming ever since he had told Evelyn of his plans to come here, and she had agreed with a single nod. He had debated lying to his son, but what good would that do, there could be no secrets in his view of what had happened.

'I was saved here, during the war.'

William nodded, the stick now gently tapping against his calf.

'We were fighting close to here, and I was shot, you know the mark there?'

William nodded as Jolyon pointed towards his shoulder.

'These people in this house tended to me, saved my life. I wanted to return to thank them.'

'Is that the only reason we are here?'

'Yes,' Jolyon said, wondering if his son knew he was lying and pulled his son close to him against his leg.

They walked like that up to the front door, a lion's head knocker catching the sun, Jolyon feeling a rush of pride as William tucked in his shirt. Jolyon had wondered what this exact moment would be like, but now a sense of pervading calm spread over him like this was exactly the right thing to be doing at exactly the right time. He reached up and knocked, hearing footsteps from inside, pulling William that bit closer as the door opened. Pierre Mulot looked at him and without words, the two men stepped forward and embraced on the doorstep, William Bremner pressed between them.

Part 2

Saviour, Searcher, Rider, Lover

"All children have to be deceived if they are to grow up without trauma." – *Kazuo Ishiguro*

Chapter 17

Present Day, Arras
Saviour

The identical headstones caught the dawn light in a hundred yellow hues, the names, regiments, and ages staying in shade, the indented lettering blurring into black lines between rose bushes. All their stories and how they had come to fight here were different, their endings though remarkably similar.

These rigid white sentinels stood unchanging as Amélie passed them deep in her thoughts, the resting places of the war dead never judged, but they reminded her of a shocking time long passed that she felt the resonances of acutely. Her route through the war cemeteries of Arras was familiar by now, but every day brought a slightly different vista, the landscape altered constantly as the seasons bled by. Only nature whispered back with blowing branches, far-off birdsong, and the call of the past from a million voices silenced beneath her feet.

Every day this summer she had done this walk, going further and longer since meeting him in that café in Albert, little did she know then the ramifications that would have. A chance meeting it was, but they fell so quickly into each other's tread and being neither would recover from the piqued intimacy. In a state of deep ache and longing, these daily pilgrimages were as much a part of her now as her own reflection in the faded mirror above the sink in the Arras hospital where she worked. He had infiltrated her days, her dreams, her walks, and she was at a loss at what to do about it. The exhaustion of her pining left her close to catatonic at times and in the orange light of dawn she wondered if it was sunset the light was so similar, she was so tired.

Her six winter months she spent in Paris amongst the hubbub, tending to the infirm, six months were here in the summer calm where she worked still as a nurse, but also as an ear for the locals she had grown up with who fell ill. They had spoken about these people; he had been quietly impressed with her diligent care, no one before had shown even the slightest interest. She had met that sparkling man over a glass in The Hygee brasserie three months ago, he had come over to her and said he was writing a book on his family, he had that smile that could infatuate an entire room and the way he illuminated her through listening, just watching every minute movement of her mouth as she spoke. What walls she did have were quickly broken down, her attempts to keep them strong and immovable were hopeless.

She walked around the Arras salient, where the head of the river began spewing East from under the ancient star-shaped citadel. Her walk through the dead went along the Scarpe, before reaching her grandmother's farm and climbing into crisp white sheets on the single bed that had been hers since she was a little girl. The room was unchanged in years, the heavy hand-quilted blanket with faded pink tassels and the painting of the farmhouse above the headboard which had been there for decades. There was the gentle click of the boiler every fifteen minutes and a permanent smell of polish, streaks visible on the heavy brown furniture. She slept fitfully, no matter how far she walked attempting total exhaustion, his name would be on her lips, and each night she would send him love across the distance hoping he heard. She remembered the thrill at how close he was in that bed in Albert for that week of exploration, his arms enveloping her utterly, her legs intertwined with his. Him pulling her close against him, what he had believed then an unbreakable embrace in the dawn light, the windows wide open and his kisses fluttering along her neck, his fingertips brushing between her shoulder blades. How he had made her feel so wanted, like both of them had unknowingly been seeking a connection on a deeper plain but only now had their bodies reacted by unravelling.

In Paris, there was no time to walk, no time to look up or confront her error. There was always the noise of sirens and other people's private moments shouted across the rooftops, the flickering lights of bars, the high-pitched holler of sirens and the clatter of the bin lorries all night but that was winter, he had been summer, he was warmth.

Arras was home and where she had always felt most anchored. Her childhood friends from here had never asked why she walked so often now, and she ignored the whispers that in early summer she had succumbed to a broken heart. Her grandmother had told her the stories of these lands and as both her interest in the stories of the dead grew, and her search for peace continued, one walk a week had become twice, and twice soon became daily, she felt it almost like an atonement. He had walked with her that week he was here, until she had said she was not ready to leave Dubois and despite his brooding protests her mind had been made up and she told him to leave, the overwhelming reason a fear of falling too deep, trusting a man with her heart utterly. Dubois could be managed, kept, but not this man, there was something so angry and untameable it was a relish to fall for him. What a terrible mistake to have made, she had turned her back on what she had never realised she wanted until it was gone for good. Dubois and she had faded, as nothing could compare to him, not with how he made her soar, and she knew she did the same for him. A bond that had felt too good to be true, so unbelievable she had doubted its existence, questioned its grounding, and severed it.

These cemeteries of infinite peace and loss brought some calmness, but tied her to the past, a place she was not ready to leave yet as that was the only place, she could find him. It never felt like a duty to come here, and she could swear that sometimes, when tired, there were voices that urged her onwards with an invisible but gentle hand on the small of her back pressing her on.

She was not the only one who visited these places, they came with paper poppies, cornflowers, wreaths, and small wooden crosses that faded as the months went by after November. If she saw one askew or blown over, she would right it and ensure it stood tall. These temporary icons were for those who still felt the shockwaves of what had happened over a century before. How much longer would they keep coming?

This making right was a task she sought no praise for, and she felt the same about nursing. The surgeons got the credit, and the doctors were of course miracle workers, but nursing had its own satisfaction.

'Be nice if they said thanks to us,' Julie would always say as they watched patients exaggeratingly thanking the men in white coats. Amélie would just nod with a sideways smile, that would never happen as a nurse.

Nurses did a thousand good deeds a day, few were noticed, but all combined made a caring and safe place for the sick, dying and in need to be at ease. With her other colleagues, except Julie, they knew deep down this made up the heart of the hospital and that was a good thing and sometimes good was good enough.

She never sought praise, as a nurse, or as someone who righted wreaths and she felt a resonance with the bodies who lay in these places and what they had done for their freedoms. In a way, she was mourning too, and they encouraged her that only time would heal the wounds of old.

With her phone turned off to avoid the reams of messages from the night out, Amélie let her mind free, speeding and slowing like a maple leaf on a river. Her friends from work had asked her for a drink, but they knew about her walks and smiled gently, knowing this was her time. She would say she was tending to her grandmother but despite the puzzled look from Julie, always the most business-like about getting drunk, she did not bother to pry like she once used to.

When ambling, she thought of him and what he was doing now, a pang of despair colliding with a thrill of memory at his touch. She asked how her life might develop as the years accumulated and thought of her grandmother at the farm, old now, and wondered when that end would come. She hoped it would be met with a contented smile and an acceptance, unlike so many of the sadder cases she saw in the hospital. None of the men that lay in the immaculate cemeteries with the low brick white walls that were rough to the touch had met peaceful ends, how could they when the world was at war?

She was happy to let herself be led through life without too much thought of the future as so many of her old friends were doing. Her school friends seemed to always be rushing, her colleagues the same, dashing from shift to bar and to bed frantically, even their lovemaking sounded scheduled and a thing to be achieved not enjoyed. They sought validation in loud experiences, not quiet ones.

Life, they believed could be planned for, and when it did not work out, they were levelled with a crushing disappointment that was entirely of their own making. Amélie had fallen in love, truly, and let it slip between her palms despite him offering his heart on repeat, it was the unplanned nature of it all that had made her pause and made her physically stop it dead that night by the fountain and tell him which had killed them both in a sense.

The sun was making its steady downwards journey towards the horizon, the identical cut rows in the cornfield looked like Paris avenues off the Arc de Triomphe, and in between a hare darted from one to the other like it was delivering a message of great importance.

'Jacques,' she called as her boots marched along the dry white pebble path kicking up puffs of dust, leaving a line of chalk powder on her toecaps.

From the thick undergrowth, Jacques burst out, another stick in his mouth to add to the growing collection stacked by the front door of the farmhouse. He pinned his ears back and slunk towards her, great paws leaving indents in the chalk. Amélie bent and stoked the length of his soft red fur, smooth and hot, picking a burr from his coat and flicking it away which made a hoverfly change its flight path.

They stood next to Gourock Trench Cemetery where she always stopped for a moment to check the treeline. She passed here daily but she would not tell anyone why, this was her and Jacques' secret.

In the first days of summer, fresh from the Paris grind and

from saying goodbye to him, his last kiss still burning hot in her mind, she had been walking on the edge of Athies forest when she had seen a movement in the trees. Stopping still, Jacques had barked once which made the object obscured by leaves and branches stop. She scanned the treeline, until she saw a black mass coming from the forest, twigs snapping under its bulk. There, standing alone and watching her intently from the shadows was a bay horse. She had stepped forward, a hand outstretched, but it had skittered off immediately into the gloom.

Amélie had seen it again since, always in that wood, but with no discernible pattern to its arrival and only ever an outline. She had chuckled to herself in bed whether she was either going loopy or considered asking anyone else if they had seen the horse, but then decided against it.

Cumulatively now she had waited in vain for hours for the shadow horse by the edge of Gourock Trench Cemetery and only once had the sunlight caught it in full form between the trees and in that split second, she could make out a white diamond on its forehead.

With no sign of the horse today, she looked back at the cemetery to continue with her walk. She saw one of the graves was obscured by a branch that had fallen in the night from the oak trees that shaded half the scene. She opened the heavy black iron gate, closing it softly behind her, these were sacred places and she trod lightly on the balls of her feet. Jacques sniffed around the perimeter of the cemetery, checking the corners for any fruit that might have fallen from the pear trees that overhung the white-topped wall.

The pull to enter this place felt strong today, like these men who lay underneath were pleased with the company, a mistle-thrush chirped high up and out of sight. She had walked through cemeteries in the dark of night and not once had she felt alone, or lost, or scared. She felt comforted with just the patter of Jacques' paws and the moonlight to guide her, the great cross cast her body in the shade as she crossed the immaculately trimmed grass, the sword of sacrifice pointing downwards towards the earth.

There were about forty of the white headstones in here, not large by any stretch, some felt obscene in number, like looking up at the stars at night and finding the number simply incomprehensible in scale. Bending down she pulled at the branch, its twigs had wrapped themselves around the white Portland stone-like fingers. The leaves fell away, dry to a crisp and flaking into fragments in her palms.

'Private T.J. Smith

Cameron Highlanders, 7th Battalion.

12th April 1917'

Amélie cleared away the broken twigs and leaves from in front of the rectangular stone, making good the flowers that had bent but not broken under the weight of the snapped branch. She ran her hand over the curve of the headstone. 'Their Glory Shall Not be Blotted Out', it read at the bottom, the letters brushing against small clumps of heather.

Jacques bumped his head against her, nuzzling his way under the crook of her arm. She cleaned down the stone and took in the name for a moment. She wondered what it must have been like back then, had this man met a quick end? War had been all around, overwhelming and infinite, but where exactly had T.J. Smith fallen?

Standing and turning, squinting in the sun, she saw the bay horse with the diamond on its forehead, half hidden in the trees.

It flicked its tail lazily along its flanks and looked disinterested, turning towards the deep forest.

She bent down and ruffled the dogs' ears realising she had been holding her breath and stepped back out of the cemetery, nobody would have believed her, not even her loving grandmother.

Chapter 18

June 1984, Houndwood
Searcher

Isabel loved her father William dearly, but she ached to know the truth about her own history, she felt like a woman without a past. The secret he held at his core of which he had never spoken of had worn away at them both and had now become insurmountable. She had so many questions, and he had told so many white lies, but she needed to venture beyond what his imposed isolation permitted at Houndwood Farm. She had her own secrets; did he feel she was too naive to hear his?

She knew something terrible had happened to her father William, but he refused to speak of it, it was like he lived in grief. There had been jagged moments in her life when she had broached the subject, only to be met with a short rebuff and a streak of something approaching either disinterest or fury from him. She had stopped asking altogether after her early teenage years and they entered the great charade of never acknowledging something so pressing that would one day break them apart. Worse still, it was not a combustible series of battles where there was a clear winner each time, but a slow infecting silence that was killing them.

Without answers, she felt anchorless, destined to float without roots. She had been told by him once when he was drunk that her mother had been a lost soul and died young, shortly after she was born, so William had raised her alone. Perhaps because he was a single parent and had done everything himself, which couldn't have been easy, she had accepted this purgatory with the sacrifices he must have made. The veil though was slipping, and she found herself wanting immediate answers like time was running out to uncover the truth before she broke. Her mother had only ever been mentioned in passing like a ghost that haunted Houndwood, never truly visible except in splices. As to what her father had done with his life before he met her mother was a vortex.

'I don't understand why you can't just ask him,' Hugh said between inhales of the rolled cigarette.

Isabel stared out to sea; it was getting colder now the sun had shifted behind the cliffs to the west.

Hugh offered her the cigarette, but she waved it away with a flick of her hand. He inhaled deeply and lay back flat on the beach. 'I mean, how bad can it be?'

Isabel shrugged. 'Bad.'

Hugh rubbed his feet together, the scratching noise annoying Isabel. 'But, like, what happens? Does he get mad?'

Isabel shrugged again, more out of annoyance at the questioning, she had no answers on the topic. 'We just don't speak like that, okay?'

Three waves broke with rolling thumps before Hugh spoke again. 'Ah well, not like it will matter soon.'

Isabel looked down on him, pulling her hair up behind her and tying it. 'Why's that?'

'Do you not read the papers?'

'Not really, no, Dad doesn't like them.'

Hugh laughed, stubbing the cigarette out and flicking the

butt somewhere towards the inky line of seaweed nearer the breakers. An empty glass bottle of Coca-Cola rolled up the beach, then back away from them in the surf, perpetually rolling and always just out of reach.

'They say it will be war,' Hugh said.

'Who does?'

'The papers. Americans are back at the Russians, pissed they invaded Afghanistan.'

Isabel rubbed her hand along the sand looking down on it in the moonlight. 'Why is it their problem?'

'That's exactly it. It isn't really but if one moves the other must retaliate, same old story.'

'What's your point?' Isabel was bored. She cared little for the outside world having seen so little of it, so it frustrated her when Hugh spoke so grandiosely of the things he knew of and he had a way, just every now and then, of seeming disgustingly pompous when he spoke.

'I just mean if we all get nuked, which we will, better to ask him before it's too late, no?'

Isabel let her lips curl approaching a smile, if that happened, then nothing else really mattered.

Hugh began rolling again, Isabel watching the tip of his tongue gently flick at the paper. 'Afghanistan...' Hugh said softly, watching a gull hop amongst the sea debris. 'Why bother.'

'Maybe I will have that smoke,' Isabel said.

'Or maybe the cyborgs will get us,' Hugh said almost seriously.

'What are you talking about now?'

'Terminators. I mean it could be real. Have you not seen it?'

'What's a...' but Isabel gave up and bent to kiss Hugh, at least it would shut him up.

Not only was she alone here at Houndwood, but even people her own age were starting to notice how out of touch she was. Even Hugh, who she knew adored her utterly realised she was nothing like the rest of them. All of life was passing her by and all because William wouldn't let her leave this place, he hadn't said as much but he was hardly well enough to disappear one night.

Isabel knew William hoped she would one day take Houndwood over when he died, Hugh too had said as much.

'The past is your best preparation for the future, you have history here,' her father liked to say. How dare he? Nothing had ever been spoken of before the day she was born, it was like his life had started the day hers had. Hugh would never get it either despite his apparent willingness to please her with one eye on the grand old farmhouse. It was complicated further as in every other aspect of life, except the secrets, her father was her best friend.

Those worn hands that had cradled her since she was delivered to the world on a January morning nearly twenty years ago were her only family. All of Isabel's childhood memories were vividly coloured, the winter mornings when her father would wake her with hot chocolate before they walked the fields amongst the low-cut barley chaffing against scuffed jean legs. The dull yellow light of summer evenings when she sat on the bench by the back door, her father talking of bullfinches and dragonflies and counting them aloud.

The dogs would be in a manic scamper, but with a simple 'lay-up' they would stop stock still at her father's command with a click between rough fingers clotted with dirt from the garden and the smell of linseed oil. The dogs would trot back towards her father, ears pinned against coarse fur, slinking their hips, and curling around William's legs. Each one looked up at their master adoringly as Isabel had through those childish eyes.

Her solitude was not a prison when she was younger, her whole world was Houndwood and back then it was big enough. As she had not known her mother at all, she assumed she felt the pain of not having one less, it had never troubled her as a girl. Other adults had done the head tilts in her direction when she was little, but seeing her develop confidently, carefree and most of all happy, saw them subside by her teens until as with all death, people stopped asking altogether. Amongst the vast canvas of childhood memories at Houndwood Farm, one stood out more than any other and she held on to it when her anger threatened to spill over, or she had packed a bag secretly in her room to walk out again.

In her memory, she was standing on of the hill looking down on the farm, the hunting spring kestrels hovering below her eyeline swept the valley, and the reed grass shook in gusts. She knew that any moment the voice would ring out from below, the call of her father would echo off the outbuildings, rolling up the hills as the kestrel's wing-dipped back overhead like fighter planes.

Isabel would sprint down the hill, her legs churning to keep balance arms going like spinning tops and as she reached level ground stumbling and breathless, her father would wrap her in a tight embrace, the rough skin of his neck against her cheek.

'My girl,' he would whisper and swing her over his hip, carrying her off towards 'this new-fangled Kiev thing,' as he called it, enjoyed around the worn kitchen table always stacked with paint pots.

There had always been the painting. Did that provide some

clue as to what had happened when William was younger before she was born?

Isabel had only been four when she first knew of the room at the top of the farmhouse, she had no need or want to explore beyond her set parameters until then. During the day her father cared for Houndwood, a full-time task, but some dawns, and most evenings he would retire to the high room and close the door with finality, and she had never been in there, it was kept locked. The room had a magnetism to it precisely because if was forbidden and Isabel felt like the world's greatest secrets lay behind two inches of timber.

The room spilled into her daydreams as she tended to seedlings, repotting them gently into ever larger pots under her father's watch. Paintbrushes littered the sink, and her father was sometimes covered in a rogue streak of red or purple on his overalls when they ate but when she looked at one of the marks or asked, he would look away and say it was just a hobby and would change the subject.

She had seen flashes of the paintings when he opened or closed the door if she had hurt herself dashing about and needed his immediate attention. What she had seen through the crack in the door was a white farmhouse with trees surrounding it, the same house was painted over and over on all manner of canvasses, in all colours imaginable. The house was sometimes serene and perfect, other times in flames and burning. It was not her home he painted on repeat, but somewhere she didn't know. There was also a strange pattern on the floor, each corner with a different animal drawing on it, a compass in the centre and candles half burnt.

She asked herself before sleep, did she really want to know? Whatever it was, perhaps it was best left to him. People were allowed secrets, right? She had one of her own right now, and she had no way of knowing how to tell her father.

Walking up to Houndwood from the back, she cast her eyes back and watched Hugh disappear over the dunes towards his cottage around the bay at Endeavour Point. She might love him, but still wasn't sure if that was because there was no alternative.

The front door banged shut behind her, arms laden with eggs from the coop, a few rogue pieces of straw stuck between her fingers. She would ask her father about the past, tonight she promised she would do it. She would also tell him her news, maybe if he knew how she felt and how often she thought about leaving he would soften, maybe he would be happy for her?

The hallway was dark, just the familiar ticking of the grandfather clock in front of her in the high-ceilinged hallway. The distant crackle of logs, smoke, and home cooking lay heavy.

She shook her coat off and hung it up on the hooks by the door, balancing the eggs in one hand which the dogs looked hopefully at, the name 'Isabel' was still there in faded ink from when she had been little. Her father had never left this house, not since he had moved in decades ago and he had met her mother near here, and she had died here. They had been happy for a time, but something bad had happened. There were whispers in the village but whenever she heard them building, as only gossip can, she would walk away as if the words were a physical attack on her and her father. A part of her knew whatever secret he held was deadly, and she shied from its full force despite telling herself she wanted to know. Her father had no one else but the dogs, so if she moved away, it would kill him.

Isabel only admitted it at night to herself, but she was scared. William had moved here sometime in the 1940s and since then he and the house had grown into each other. They were intertwined deeply, man and nature and home all overlapped so that the edges of where one ended and one began were blurred.

The immaculate inside of the house was the opposite of the outside that was being lost to the elements. Ivy had claimed the front of the house for its own, declaring ownership with its impenetrable green tentacles. The gigantic oak tree with loose branches was now twice as tall as the house, like it was getting ready to swallow it, its branches pulling the house closer. All around the farm were piles of logs and fallen trees lying dead and forgotten, at night they looked like bodies. Her father was happy to let it be like this though, he had told her he was a guest of nature, passing through, and it could not be controlled.

Everything inside Houndwood had its place, every cupboard had a use, and every object in them worked, was well used, and was trusted. Trinkets were not to be found anywhere, nor were photographs, apart from one of Isabel and William that hung under a painting of a different farmhouse to Houndwood on the mantlepiece.

Isabel was thinking back to one of the first times she had kissed Hugh when he had kissed her on one cheek to say goodbye, but as he kissed the other side, his lips brushed the corner of her mouth. It was so deliberate, so subtle but also tender and incredibly intimate she had kissed him back. Just before he did, she had taken him in, looked at his full form, and tried as he might, he couldn't help the corner of his mouth rising in expectation and hope. Leaning in she felt his lips against hers, cautiously at first, then hungrily like all she had ever wanted could in that moment be ensnared and held onto forever as his arms tightened around her back and she felt his need against her.

Isabel stood there in the hall thinking of Hugh, a look of unease on her face. She wondered how to ask William about his days before she was born when she heard her father's footsteps above rounding the banister to the top of the stairs. She had to tell him her news as he would find out, the village had a hundred eyes and ears and combined it made up and animal that thirsted on gossip and thrived on the intrusion into the privacy of other people's lives to survive. William also had an almost sixth sense when it came to her, like he knew what she was thinking before she herself had ironed it out in her own mind.

She twizzled a lock of hair in her fingers, hair that only a few minutes before had been stroked by another man's touch. With no mother to ask, no one else here but him, she needed his counsel even if it was hard for him to face and it would be awkward.

Before she could speak though, her father had hit the bottom step in his faded blue slip-on shoes, crossed the gap to her sending the dogs spinning and picked her up like he had done when Isabel was a child.

'My girl,' he said close to her ear and somehow, despite Isabel wanting to hate him for his secrets and for being his warden, those thoughts, as they always did, faded away in his embrace.

Maybe she could work on him like he did on the paintings, and perhaps once they had eaten omelettes and drunk some wine, she would be braver and him more lucid, maybe she would find a way, maybe.

Chapter 19

June 1984, Houndwood
Rider

William tipped the easel over, sending brushes tumbling and paint spattering up the walls, the canvas toppled and fell face down onto the floor. Stumbling, his fingers found the window frame and he collapsed against it, his top half swinging out of the window. These spins did not come as often as they once did, but when they did, they hit hard and fast. His breathing rasped and rattled in his chest, and he put his hand to his chest feeling the small black book knotted in red and white twine.

Below him were trees, the dunes, and the wild sea beyond, the wind hummed in long blasts against the house. He could see no other house from up here on the top floor, no other that could look in. The gravel below was startling white, almost blinding and he was transfixed by it, it reminded him of the white stone of the farmhouse off the Scarpe which had been destroyed because of him. His eyes were mesmerised by it, and he felt himself lean a bit further out, his hips digging into the ledge, his fingers twitching, longing to touch it. He clung there, thinking of the words he had written in his diary, thinking of the years that had passed and asked if that much had really changed. He had not burnt the diary like he should have, a poison that had seeped into the walls of Houndwood but every time he went to do it, he realised it was the only place that knew the whole truth. No one would ever read it, especially Isabel, and he would destroy it before he died, he must spare her from the secrets and his grief.

The grasses in the dunes were bouncing under the wind, smashed down on repeat and then raising themselves up each day towards the sun. The churning ocean beyond looked black as a cloud crossed the sun, the white tops of chop surging with the swell and he stared at it, that small stretch of sea between nations.

Beyond the horizon, further than he could see was France where it had all happened so quickly, where that decision had been made to save Guy and his troopers. The Scarpe would still be flowing, that far-off ancient wood would still be standing, that war had passed. It still held the secrets of what had happened that day and only the trees, the Mulots and Guy Schwarzbär knew and all of them were gone.

He saw Isabel coming over the dunes and his heart lifted, it snapped him back into reality, away from the past of long ago. Isabel was running back towards the house clutching driftwood in her arms for the fire. Rhoda his wife used to do that before she too left him forever, and he thought of her often, another life drowned thanks to his actions. She had given him Isabel though, and when her eyes had first opened, he knew the vision of her face would be the last thing he pictured when he finally closed his for the last time. She was growing up quickly, and had so much to tell her, so much more he wanted to say. One more week, he would promise himself, before he told her the full story, but that week would roll into a month and here they were after nearly twenty years.

He stepped back from the window, pressing both hands into his face, and covered his eyes with the heel of his palms, holding them there and breathing deeply.

'Dad,' he heard from down below and the barking of the dogs soon followed.

He leaned out of the window and waved down.

William picked up the brushes, the pots, the pallet, the easel and the canvas. Today the house he had painted had been as it was when they had first seen it, when they had trotted onto that lawn in front of it and met Lucy, the horse had drunk by the water trough. His ribcage flinched at the memory of the shotgun pellets and Pierre cleaning the wound with antiseptic. They should have turned around then and run but the selfish pull of hunger, rest and to be away from war had drawn them in, its spidery tentacles of temptation impossible to resist. Then there had been the Cronks, Hugh who was killed trying to find him, and then John, the one who had then found him after the war forcing him to act before he lost everything again.

He placed the canvas with the rest, some showing the house just before the tank shell hit it, some showing it after, a pile of rubble and smoke. In every single one was the figure of a little girl who moved about the canvas depending on his state or mood. Sometimes she was in a top window, like she had been when they had first called up to her, the window shutter that had closed with a click. Sometimes she was by the river playing the shadow game, him pretending to chase her. Sometimes, just a face at the kitchen window, serving the rabbit stew the night before he had doomed them. Sometimes she lay dead at the foot of the house next to her father, that was the vision of the girl that found him during his seances, he had located her, but she had never spoken, just looked at him through a haze with dull eyes that showed both fury and a void of life that was taken away too young.

He noticed the mantlepiece top had come loose after he had tipped the easel into it, so he placed the diary in its usual place, and wobbled the structure back into place, covering the gap between wall and panel with the pots of brushes. Behind there lived his greatest secrets, it was the only proof left that he had been in the army, he had worked obsessively to remove any other trace. It was the only place he had tried to explain what had happened to him after he had rescued Guy. It had not hit the newspapers, the shame on the army would have been too great. People had found out though, John Cronk had told them all, and he had found him. William had thought himself safe here, where he had met Rhoda, Cronk had unearthed him though as he swore, he would on Dunkirk beach, and he had been left with little choice.

He could not risk Isabel finding the diary, but she never came up here. He had tried to be the very best father he could, and of all the freedoms he had allowed her, that was his one rule. Even as an adult, he forbade her from coming in here, for it was where he had endured his darkest moments as a young man just sentenced, a husband who was cursed then widowed, and a father who had no idea how to raise a child and found solace in the spirits of the gone and imagination on canvas.

Not once had he told Isabel to go to bed, brush her teeth, do her homework for he wanted her to be able to make her own decisions from the very first moment she had been able to do so. That was the freedom he had promised he would give her, never a life bound by any rules. His own family had forced him to go to war, so he had gone, and he broke the rules. Not the rules of man, but the rules of a system that did what was necessary and not necessarily what was right.

Turning the light out he looked at the mantlepiece again, behind which sat the diary. Maybe he should tell her, would that make it easier? No, she would run. She would leave him like everyone who had found out the truth had. He had told Rhoda at the start of their courtship when their love was at its zenith when she became pregnant, he had confessed to her one night on the dunes by the sea that he had saved a German and people had died, including a little girl, including lots of his own men. She had looked at him in horror, her face changing in an instant from the woman who fell for him when they met, to a woman estranged, a woman disgusted that the man who was to be the father of their child had been capable of doing something so treacherous. Her own brother had been killed in the war, she used to say he had died bravely whatever that meant, though William never asked. William tried to make her see his side from being a pacifist from the start and a sympathiser who had done a good deed, but such was her venom, such was her abominable loathing it had shattered them. Ten months later she was dead, almost the exact time it had taken to make a life in Isabel it had taken to break one.

He would die with this secret and Isabel would be free of it for good. As he left the room, a streak of red paint from his elbow caught the edge of the doorframe that looked like blood. There was a footprint too in red that followed him to the edge of the stairs where it ran dry, past the candle stubs and tarot cards scattered around.

As he descended the rounded staircase he thought of the last words of the priest on Dunkirk. 'I don't know why you did what you did. But in the eyes of the Lord, it was the right thing to do, if not in the eyes of the people who will judge you in this life.'

If only he had known then what had awaited him, he would not have tried so hard to stay alive, he would not have saved Guy.

Hitting the bottom step of the house he saw her, and whether she had been three, thirteen or thirty he felt the same as he always would.

In her eyes though, just for a moment, William saw something new for the first time and it troubled him. It was like a part of her innocence had changed, her features looked wary, her eyes darting, she looked suspicious. He batted that feeling away, but he knew the look, she was ashamed of something, and angry.

Holding her close, her hair on his cheek he wondered what would come next. As a father he should ask her for the truth, like all good fathers would, but how could he, William Bremner, great deceiver he was and the reason that so many had died ever speak to her about truth?

Chapter 20

Present Day, England
Lover

When James was still, which was rare, only then could he accept a part of him was missing and had been since he had said goodbye to her. On repeat he had begged to reverse time, to have said more, done more, but that was not the way with life as he was learning. The sweetest moment went by fast, the haunting ones dragged and pulled at his fabric until he was unsure what was left of a body and mind that once felt so whole.

He tried to tell himself that to have loved, truly, not for circumstance or whim should be enough, but in truth, it had left him wanting with a thirst no amount of water would ever quench and yet at the same time he was drowning from the inside. Why tell people to have loved and lost was better than to have never loved at all when it was plainly not the case? What galled him too was that his mind should not be on the love he had walked away from in France, but on his dying mother. Even that thought was irrelevant somehow, and despite castigating himself that he was evil or broken for feeling such things, his heart and mind offered so little rest away from the burning vision of her that it was all he could do to remain cohesive enough to form even the most basic of conversations. Hellos and goodbyes were hard to compute in his fractured mind, words, one of his greatest strengths, had taken leave. The one hello he sought he had no way to get to, he had no idea where she was, or if she wanted him. The one imminent goodbye to his mother he could not brace for was coming soon, and he had a sickening premonition that like that last look at the station in Albert to her, this too would slip by leaving a chasm of regret that was unfillable.

James took in the form of his mother like he had not seen her properly until now, scrabbling to hold onto every second despite a part of him wanting to be anywhere else. It was just so terribly sad, his mother, his closest bond, lay there with her hourglass almost empty and there was not a damn thing he could do about it. He was a fixer, a doer, resourceful and stoic but no amount of that could help now, he felt as useless as the gesture of fluffing pillows for the terminally ill. His longing look towards his mother he hoped would have been noticed; she was always so hard on herself. She was still graceful but looked wary and hollow. Even when closed, her eyelids would not settle, they flickered quickly about like a bird on a feeder.

She bobbed her head at him and spoke in a whisper. 'James, they are busy today. Please don't rush them.'

James rolled his eyes. 'Fine,' he said, drawing out the 'e' to show he had heard.

He bowed his head, interlocking his fingers and let his weight push through his elbows onto his knees, pressing until he felt a gnawing in his thighs. He stared down at his shoes, considered saying something else, then didn't, he wanted a drink but not more than one. A siren from outside rolled around the four white walls, but nobody looked up.

It was the smell he hated most of all in these places, linoleum freshly bleached and microwaved food. Hospitals saddened him, always had, and all hospitals had that 'smell', like the place he had eaten school meals. Not a pleasant smell, but part of the place, part of its fabric. Then there were the labyrinth-like maps at reception where not just colour and numbers were used to designate areas, but also letters and symbols. He had stood there after coming through the stuttering revolving door looking at the puzzle map, forgotten people shuffled past in gowns, and he hoped someone would visit them at least once this week.

Noise here in these places was disconcerting, mumbled for the most part but occasionally very sharp, very loud, and rhythmic. The bleep of a machine ticking down, always ticking down, the speed depended on the ward, time always the enemy.

Sitting watching his mother sleep, James resisted the urge to check his phone, everything else was on hold for the moment though the vibrations from emails were frequent and grating. James took a long pull on the bleach-filled air wishing he was outside and far away from her for a moment.

Privacy could never be found in a hospital and that grated, for a moment he was catapulted back to Albert and all the privacy that at the time seemed abundant, even eternal behind hotel doors. They could lock that door, drift away in nothing but each other, why hadn't he taken the chance to ask about the future? Perhaps the present had been so alluring, so overwhelmingly piqued he hadn't bothered, or didn't want to for fear of an answer. Here though, even behind a door that was closed, it could be opened at any moment to check vitals, take blood, or serve a meal wrapped in plastic on a plastic tray. Time of day was measured by medical administration and mealtimes; it was maddeningly regimented. The lights annoyed him here too, but that might have been the headache that had announced itself the moment he had woken up this morning, a sleep of forty-minute bursts, punctuated by thoughts of her on top of him, and clasped in his arms, and throttling his chest with such lust and loss.

James considered going to get paracetamol but something about complaining about a headache in a hospital where people were dying didn't seem quite right. There were a lot of lights though, great strips of them running along the walls like seeing the M25 motorway from above when you landed at Heathrow.

'It won't be long,' James said, gripping his mother's hand which felt cold.

He had felt people nodding with regret as he walked towards 'that' ward in the hospital. They had tried to brighten it with a large painting of a tree with bright red and green apples bobbing on its branches. It had faded though under the sunlight from the skylight above and all of it had taken on a yellowish hue.

'Mr Bremner,' the woman behind the white plastic desk had said looking up and taking in his form. 'You know the way?'

'Yes, thanks,' James said, trying to sound cheery but finding even the simplest greeting hard. His lolloping walk headed towards the room, his shoulders had sagged involuntarily, and he felt like the outline of his shadow on an overcast day when the sun didn't quite have the strength to break through the clouds. Nurses here were dead silent, business-like and nobody could escape the atmosphere that hung over the terminal cancer ward.

They tried all they could, they were marvels really. Even here, at life's terminus, they had made umpteen efforts to brighten it. Somewhere far-off strings played over the intercom in every room, just loud enough to be heard without offending. Flowers littered a lot of the surfaces, some given to the living who were still here, some leftover from those already gone.

Doors open even a crack were impossible not to look inside, and James castigated himself every time he did but was unable to resist. White bed, white sheets, white pillows, white faces staring straight up at white ceilings. Occasionally there would be a visitor at the foot or the head of one of the beds in the rooms, each one undertaking their own silent vigil until it was time to say goodbye, hoping for some last words of insight or love that rarely came.

It was strange for him, and for the rest of the well people here, knowing that the people they loved would not leave this place. In the hospice wing when they watched their loved ones slip away, he hoped it would be with good memories and having said all that was needed to be said.

For some that would not be the case, for some the troubling unanswered questions would be impossible to resolve with the secret keeper dead and James was one of them. He feared the future without his mother and with so many questions remaining about his own existence.

A breeze blew across them both, the windows were open as James had requested after the first few visits until they got the message. Churlishly, he had walked back to the room once when he heard the nurse close them and opened them again in front of her. Mum had always loved the open air, the outside. She was, as far as James knew, the person closest to nature he knew, and she would despise hot rooms filled with fake air and the smell of a soggy jacket potatoes left untouched on a tray in front of her.

'Morning,' he said again quietly, her eyes stayed shut though as they were most of the time now.

She didn't respond, the tubes and pipes spilling out of her looked like coils of barbed wire. The monotone beeps were only indicators that she was alive, that and the almost unnoticeable rising and falling of her frail chest.

James closed the door almost all the way, if only to try and stop passers-by feeling the same guilt he did when he looked in.

Private moments were so important at the end, but so very rarely possible when dying in the hands of professionals.

He picked up the orange plastic chair, its black metal legs scraping over the white floor. They were the same style of chairs he had sat on at Sunday School and appeared in all waiting rooms the world over.

He held her hand in his, a hint of warmth in there somewhere between the bones, muscle, and ligaments.

'James,' she croaked, a purple flicker of a tongue crossing dry lips.

He held up the beaker with the straw in and she sucked gently on it, her eyes closed.

'How are you?'

'I'm fine,' he lied.

Her face relaxed into a thin smile but a hint of a crease of a question remained on her forehead.

'That's good,' she said patting his hand.

'How are you today?'

'It's a lovely day out there.'

'Uh-huh,' James said, this all felt like wasted time, these trivialities. The impossibility of getting to the point, exacerbated by time slipping away in beeps, he had so many questions.

She nestled her head further into the pillow, her face turning towards him, but her eyes still closed. He looked down, picking at a loose bit of skin on his thumb. When he looked up, she was looking directly at him, her eyes taking him in. Her auburn hair still had some of its colour, it was just her skin that looked devoid of life and her teeth looked too big for her mouth, the jaw having receded with the skin collapsing.

'James,' she said again as if realising for good this time it was him.

'Hi, Mum,' James said, feeling the familiar pull knowing that as banal and small as these interchanges felt, they would be one of the last, he would miss calling someone mum.

A nurse was coming down the corridor and he cursed, he had been about to ask his mum point blank like he had practiced so many times in the car journey. The nurse bustled quickly though in bringing with her a smell of lemon disinfectant carrying a small paper pot full of pills.

'Oh, hi, James. How was your journey?'

'Fine,' James said sharply, as if he wanted the nurse to know this intrusion was badly timed, not that she could have known that.

The nurse looked down at the bed. 'And Isabel, how are you today?'

'Oh, I'm okay. Its lovely to have him here.'

'Yes, yes, it is.'

James watched the nurse tip the pills into his mother's mouth which she swallowed with some difficulty, he saw them carve their way down her gullet.

The nurse looked at Isabel, then up at James. 'I will be back in an hour to check on you, okay?'

James just nodded, his eyes flicking towards the door wanting her to leave quickly.

When she had gone and her squeaky shoes had receded, James stayed looking at the floor because it was easier that way. 'Mum, look, I need to ask about my family, before my father. I know he ran out, but what of your dad? You have never really talked about him; he is my grandfather after all. I want to know about all of you really. I don't know anything about where I'm from, not really. You have your reasons, I know, but I need to know.'

211

James looked up but Isabel was asleep, her rhythmic breathing short and sharp in her chest. The sun covered her face on the pillow surrounding her head in yellow gold.

'Mum?'

The pills had worked fast, and she just lay there, sleeping, unable to hear the burning questions. James would wait here until she woke up and then try again, like he always said he would.

Chapter 21

Saviour

Amélie felt the tiredness sit across her shoulders, pulling her towards the centre of the earth, the grass around her ankles tugged like fingers. The sun had disappeared behind the treeline half an hour before and her hunger was piqued, the double shift at the hospital meant she had forgotten lunch and no amount of coffee from her flask would beat the nag.

Somewhere far off the Arras to Amiens train departed with a whistle and began to rattle along and she pictured the passengers settling in seats and speeding to their destinations, the woods of Thiepval whipping by as they carved through the valleys of the Somme. That was the same train he had gotten on, that last vision of him through the window as he looked back at her, those blue eyes curving down slightly at the edges like he had finally accepted she was saying goodbye. He went away from her carrying the weight of five worlds on him.

Her feet caught on the cobbles of the main square, and she stumbled every now and then. It had been a frantic day at the hospital, a farmer had been wheeled in with serious injuries having driven over a rusted artillery shell. The iron harvest was underway, farmers crossing the old frontline with their heavy ploughs always brought problems, they had told her at school that ordinance would be churned up for another one hundred years. At her grandmother's farm, empty shell casings were used to store pencils or handpicked poesies of wildflowers.

Every year Amélie saw the piles of munitions caked in mud stacked up high in the corners of fields in autumn, waiting to be collected and defused in the dead of night. Visitors were warned not to touch anything but every year she would deal with two or three tourists who just couldn't resist picking up the weapons of old, assuming them as dead as the people that had fired them.

It had always been a rich farming belt here, that was why her grandparents never left, the soil was the best friend of the people that called it home but also dangerous. Like it had for her grandmother, farming brought them their means but all the time the threat of the past weaved through in those rusty brown cones. Reminders were everywhere for Amélie on her walks, the vistas punctuated innumerably with those little square plots with white crosses and headstones.

She watched tractors cut round them, farmers nodding in her general direction, they all always smiled brighter when they saw her. She liked to watch the gardeners at work too, tending to the plots. Tractors here were all supposed to be reinforced with iron plates under the cabin seats, it wasn't law, but it was foolish not to. This farmer had told them he was only ploughing lightly to prepare for the potato planting, he had taken the smaller older Massey Ferguson with no protection.

Amélie placed a caring hand on his shoulder as he spoke, the blade of the plough caught the top of the shell, exposed by millimetres, and detonated it, blowing the tractor forward. The machine was blasted upwards and twisted in the air. The calm was shattered with a flat boom, wildlife sent scurrying for cover and back acrid smoke poured upwards from the machine, another farmer had heard the crack and knew immediately what had happened. The doctor said the farmer was lucky the shell had hit the plough blade and not gone off under the wheel, otherwise, he would be dead.

The rusty hubcap had landed on his hip, shattering it, and one of the plough blades had looped over the back of the tractor, missed his head by inches but trapped his forearm under the sharp heavy metal pinning him there to the soil. According to the ambulance, blood had seeped into the earth all around the scene.

The ambulance drivers told Amélie it had reminded them of images from picture books they had thumbed at school, piles of twisted metal, a screaming man, and the smell of cordite thick in the air. He would lose the arm which made his future days somewhat of a problem, and he had cursed and shouted on the hospital bed, thrashing about, and complaining of a long-ago past.

He had looked at Amélie before the amputation as the anaesthetist was prepping. 'What am I to do?'

Amélie tried not to look away. 'Do you have insurance?'

'Pah,' he spat. 'Yes, yes, but what do I do with my days now?'

Amélie shrugged. 'Write a book on your family?'

He had grinned thinly. 'We have all read too many of those stories.'

'They are all different,' Amélie said, passing him a cup with a straw in.

'Maybe you are right. Was your family here in the wars?'

Amélie nodded. 'Very much so.'

'I could tell.' The farmer nodded.

Amélie had found common ground almost instantly with him, as she did with most she met. They spoke of the battlefields, the people that came to visit and the people that had died here.

With a sentimental 'indeed' he had accepted that as bad as it was, it was not as bad as what had been endured in the same place before.

'I was unlucky,' he said resigned.

'Half of everything is luck,' Amélie said aside.

'And the other half?'

'Fate,' she said looking at him.

Amélie respected the stoicism of these people in this part of France, her grandmother included, and their relationship with the past that was fractured. On the one hand it made them who they were, tough, sometimes immovable but friendly to anyone who came here to see the sights adorned with poppies and cornflowers and great monuments towering over the flat lands of the Pas-de-Calais. On the other hand, half of their lives were still back then, amongst the trenches and the shelling as everywhere they looked, they were reminded of it, her parents in Paris thought these people simple and stuck in their ways.

Onwards she walked through this landscape of past and present, thinking of the farmer who would now be out of surgery. Arras main square was busy, the late-night revellers sucking cigarettes down to the butt and finishing their glasses of wine, the edges long streaked. Laughter echoed off the bell tower of the town hall, as did the grind of chairs on stones as the young of Arras finally rose towards their beds. They would kiss farewell, some of them intertwined so closely that their shadows combined to make one mass. She missed the intimacy with him, that unique closeness. He had been at once both firm and gentle, his grip on her buttocks immovable, but his tongue soft.

She carried on, walking away from the town to the east, the buildings thinning out and the mass of illuminated windows left far behind. Past the shuttered shopping centre and around the bend past Gourock Trench Cemetery where the shadow horse lived. She thought of T.J. Smith but did not stop, her tiredness and fog of hunger were becoming constant and she felt sad at all she was missing.

Up ahead were the fields she needed to cross, now a flat dark grey against the horizon of night beyond. The rivets from the ploughs made walking tough and her shoes bent and twisted over the landscape, every step she checked for the peaked dome of explosives before pushing down. A hare bumped along the side of one of the fields, its orb-like black eyes reflecting the moon in them but after a quick scratch, it scampered off again in leaps.

This walk, maybe more than any other in recent times, felt longer, harder. The fields seemed to go on forever until she finally reached the edge of the Scarpe at the Moulins bridge. As only night-time can do, her problems felt more acute, more pointed, the ache of missing him more an open wound than a dull throb. She should cross the bridge, keep on the north side, and take the straight track home and sleep, rest would do her good.

Something though pulled at her to stay south of the river, to stay in the wild side of the woods. She let herself be guided by instinct, the going was tough, once or twice she felt brambles catch her and she let out short gasps of frustration as they did, and tears creased the corners of her eyes. The noise of the A1, the artery road to Paris boomed overhead in the underpass with a dull throb. HGVs sent tiny stones flying off the road, over the edge of the motorway that landed with soft plops in the lakes on either side of her. Her grandmother would be up still, waiting for her, she slept most of the afternoons now and did her crosswords late into the night.

Fampoux and Feuchy lay behind her now, their occasional

twinkling lights where families sat round tables fading into the black. Lights would be off soon, stories to children long finished. Even those from the town square who were making love would be done now, bodies lying next to each other in cramped beds, curled into each other, warm breath on the back of their necks, until drifting off as one.

Orion looked down from overhead, and it felt like she was walking into his belt, right inside of the central gleaming star. Orion the hunter, club and shield raised, had no doubt been a talisman for the men back then staring down on all their battles infinite in his knowledge and having seen it on repeat throughout history.

The ground dipped down a long slope and climbed back up the other side. She guessed she would be somewhere near the front line. She stopped in the silence, a large swamp to her right, there was a spit of land jutting out and she went towards it. Orion was reflected perfectly in the pool, two warriors now looked at her, one from above and one from below. The air was thick and close, and she was sticky with sweat, tiny crickets had begun their nightly orchestra.

On the spit she closed her eyes, nothing human made a noise, any din from roads or people was blocked here by the water, the reeds, and the trees. She felt like she might be the first person to have noticed this space in history, she felt alone but a small flame of something like hope, from somewhere unexpected had caught flame.

After her quiet reflection, and some words spoken aloud to him, wherever he was, she turned to leave. The edge of her foot caught on something hard by the outside of her toe, she ran her foot back the other way and it snagged so bending down her hands found an edge. Having seen the farmer earlier she thought for a moment before bending over to inspect it. It was too thin to be an explosive, but it was made of metal. Her fingers prized away and she wiggled it, it protested for a time. Out of the thick soil and cloying grass by the swamp it finally came loose.

She held it up to the moonlight, scrubbing at it with her fingers. In her hand she held the faded emblem of a bear, rotating it again there was no mistake, a black bear with Orion reflected in its eye.

The farmhouse looked serene, Orion was now hidden behind the treeline and the stars were dulled.

'Hello?'

Amélie climbed the worn steps of the farmhouse quietly, clutching the emblem in her hand, which now shimmered more brightly having scrubbed at it in the sink with a coarse brush.

No sound came from her grandmother's room, so she stopped at the crack in the door, peering in. There she was, sitting up and busy at her crossword with her focus absolute and for as long as Amélie could remember she had done this. She used to read constantly, novels mainly, but with her age she would say playfully she could not bear starting a good one and risk not making the end.

When Amélie was thirteen she had decided to leave her parents' house in Paris every year for the summer months. They were fond of each other of course, but with her grandmother she felt a bond that had been there since her childhood. They were similar people, in outlook and mentality, whilst her parents believed only real jobs happened in Paris and Amélie should go there if she was to make anything of herself.

Her grandmother had protested on her behalf, saying a young woman should be in the centre of her own destiny and free to choose. Her parents had baulked at the thought of their only child going to live with an eighty-something woman in the middle of nowhere for half the year. What would she do for friends? How would she find a husband amongst the trees?

The words had stung, but having her grandmother stand up for had only brought them closer. Amélie knew the main driver for her mother's fear was because that was exactly what she herself had done. She had been born here in the farmhouse, raised here, lived here for a time, and then quickly got married and found work in Paris fearing life was a bullet train and she was not on it. The soirees of Paris and the Metro made her feel like she had made something of herself, despite not having control over any of it. She said she wanted her daughter to be free whatever that meant, but she also wanted her to find a job better than a nurse and not to live where she was happiest.

The place was all important to her grandmother, as it was for most of her grandmother's generation. A home was more than a place for a family, it was the beating heart of every day's existence and that was as good for a twenty-year-old as it was for someone in their eighties thought Amélie.

'Nanna?' Amélie called again.

Her grandmother's eyes looked up, a gentle smile crossing her concentrated face.

'My darling,' her grandmother said, folding the newspaper neatly and putting the lid back on her pen.

They looked at each other for a second, both framed in the soft lighting from the bedside lamp with a blue and red ribbon tied around its base. They were unmistakably related, the likeness almost uncanny except for the years between them.

'You are late, long day?'

'Yes,' Amélie said. 'Another victim of the Iron Harvest.'

Her grandmother nodded, running a hand which jangled with bracelets over her quilt.

'I found something,' Amélie said excitedly, like a much younger version of herself would have.

Her grandmother patted the bed, just like she had done when Amélie was little. Amélie was always finding things, adventuring around the farmhouse and along the Scarpe for all sorts of trinkets, prizes, and things valuable to her. For years they had littered the windowsills of the farmhouse, documenting her many walks and adventures.

'Come sit,' her grandmother said again.

Amélie walked towards her, her feet squeaking on the wooden floorboards until they reached the thick red rug by the bed, she felt nervous but had no idea why.

'I was down by the marshes; I had not been that way before. There is a lake there.'

'I know it.'

'This was buried on the spit of land, right by the water.'

Amélie unclasped her hand, the bear emblem in its fighting stance looking up at them both.

Her grandmother gasped, and both her hands shot to her mouth.

'It... cannot... be,' her grandmother whispered through her fingers, gently taking the bear and holding it under the light.

Amélie did not say anything, but her grandmother was trembling all over.

'Nanna?'

'It cannot be...' she said again, breathless and turning the bear in her hand before holding it to her heart.

'Nanna, what is it?'

With her other hand, she clutched Amélie's hand in hers, the skin had gone cold all over.

'I know this bear,' her grandmother said.

'You do?'

'I do. It belonged to a soldier who came here.'

'When, in the war?'

'Yes. He came here. It was when...'

Amélie watched as her grandmother broke into gentle sobs. She dropped the bear and it clattered onto the bedside table, lying flat facing up at the bedside light.

Amélie reached forward and clutched her grandmother close, her whole body in cries that were muffled into her shoulder.

'Nanna. It's ok.'

She felt one of her grandmother's arms clutch her back, drawing Amélie even closer. The other gently reached out, and it rested on the bear. Under her hand the bear looked straight at Amélie, its silver eye staring at her. Who had this belonged to? And why was her grandmother so upset?

Amélie was intrigued. It was as if the past had forced its way back into their lives and right now, though Amélie, she could not work out if that was a good thing or a very bad one indeed.

Chapter 22

Searcher

His hands were assured as they held Isabel against his full length, he was more experienced yet more tentative than she would have liked. Under the stars over the beach, he kissed her, and she could sense his arousal. She felt lightheaded from wine, her torso rolling off the blanket into the cold sand which grated against her shoulders. His mouth closed around the soft skin of her neck, and she could have sworn he could taste her pulse in his lips it was beating so hard. One of his hands was stroking small circles on her stomach, tanned from hours toiling at Houndwood in a vest top which was now balled up a few feet away. Her back arched as she lifted her weight into him, stronger this time, pulling his thigh higher with the back of her calf. His hand circled her hips and pulled her into him again, the need becoming more raw, more desperate. The same hand began to flicker down her body, past her inner thigh. He pressed the length of his index finger and thumb against her and she let out a gasp.

'Maybe not here, Hugh.'

Despite saying this, she pressed his fingers further, her hand on top of his.

'Maybe more,' she breathed out.

His hands undid her denim shorts that caught only briefly on the second button. His fingers separated her legs, his hand spreading wider to push them apart, his fingertips ran over her.

'More,' she urged him on, looking up at him and biting the corner of her lip.

At the last moment of possible retraction, the final station before drowning in want she whispered in his ear, 'No.'

He stopped moving his fingers but left his hand there, it felt hot, and she almost told him to carry on.

He panted. 'No?'

Isabel shook her head.

His hand retracted slowly, and he looked flustered in the moonlight, making a low gurgling noise between breaths. Neither of them knew what to do but she saw his cheeks blush and he looked in deep thought, deep and angry contemplation, his profile a sharp cut out against the moonlight.

'I'm sorry,' he mumbled. 'It felt...'

Isabel kissed him lightly, but he felt further away. 'No, don't. It's me. I just...'

'No, no, me too. I think. I don't know, maybe?'

She ran a hand along his jaw feeling the day-old stubble scratching into her fingertips, the intensity fading and other thoughts coming back. Did she feel guilty? For stopping or for not continuing? His eyes looked intently down on her, the passion in his pupils still burning but his mouth in a grimace, almost a snarl, he looked like an animal.

'I need you,' he said bluntly, his hand retracing the line along her thigh.

'Don't,' she said firmly, and this time his hand stopped quickly and found its way to the sand.

She looked beyond him, past him.

He rattled a long sigh out over his teeth. 'Will you stay? Despite...'

'For a minute, yes,' said Isabel. She wanted to stay all night to see if that might break her resolve, but the passion had passed and with it the chance of abandon. She wanted to see what her father would say if she did not come back at all one night. She knew where this was leading and had a premonition of being caught in the act, it was not like she had many reasons to leave Houndwood after dark. Being caught with Hugh would teach her father a lesson, she was a grown-up and could make her own decisions but that felt too cruel, her inner war was at its height.

Hugh was on his knees, his erection still prominent against his loose shorts. His breath was shortened, and he put his weight on one hand, swinging himself round so he was lying next to Isabel.

'I'm sorry, Hugh.'

'God, no. Don't be. I just... anyway.'

She squeezed his hand, but it felt brittle. She closed her eyes, the soft lap of the swell against the beach breaking her stimulation.

Isabel worried the nail of her index finger with her thumb, her feet tapping into the amber blanket which still showed the creases where their bodies had lain. Aware she was nearly naked, her hand reached out for the vest top, but realising it was too far left her feeling exposed. When she left the house earlier with another flimsy excuse, she had intended to have sex with Hugh, one half based on desire, the other on spite.

Without knowing it, Hugh had provided Isabel with a way to kick out at her draconian isolation of no television, no newspapers, no radio, and the abnormality of her existence. Just books, dogs and toiling were not good enough. Her passion for him, like her frustration for her father, had washed over her, removing the consciousness of decisions but this time the maximum ramifications had been averted.

She had thought of little else but how she could use Hugh since they met, she wondered at night if that was why she had led him on. Despite this though, having sex on a cold beach felt wrong at the last minute. Nerves had pulled her up, she had felt out of control for a split second and had acted on instinct. Had she been right? Was it ever going to feel less significant? Should she just 'do it' like some of her friends had? Out of the three she could call friends, Claire had said it was good, Izzy and Serena had hated it, those were not good odds.

She had no one to ask about how the first time might be. Yes, she saw Claire, Izzy, and Serena once a month or so at the farmers market but how did she bring this up? They only ever spoke of periphery things like what they had been doing, not how they were feeling.

Her isolation at Houndwood was a barrier against knowing how to approach conversations like this and she revolted against her father for building it, walls that might seem invisible to some but not to her. She did not want to mention sex casually to her friends, dropping like a stone in a metal bucket. Maybe she would know more if she was allowed to connect with the outside world, Hugh said the films in the cinema were full of sex and adventure. She had borrowed The Camomile Lawn which had spoken about sex, but it always seemed rushed and with the man demanding and getting.

She and Hugh had spoken about their previous experiences, he said he had been with one other girl, but it didn't really work out as he put it. That bit had been easy, confessing to her virginity, the actual act of it felt much harder. They were both as willing but inexperienced as the other, both hoping the other would guide them but not knowing how to ask the other one to lead.

Hugh was rolling a cigarette. 'Are you okay?'

'Of course,' Isabel said pointedly.

He said nothing else, just stared out to sea, did he know how unhappy she was here? Had he worked out that he was just a distraction?

Hugh had come into her life when she had been least expecting it, collecting driftwood three weeks ago, but it felt longer now with how much time they had spent together. Kissing and touching on the beaches behind the dunes out of sight of Houndwood, similar every time, but never the same.

The beach had been her freedom, and her only own space for years. Her father never came here, never this near the water. She knew the sea here intimately and the rip tide that pulled from one end to the other, time it right and swimming was easy, time it wrong and it was lethal. She had noticed the bobbing head and thought at first it was driftwood, nobody from round here would be foolish enough to swim when the tide was as it was. No locals did, and no tourists came to this beach as there was no car park, no ice cream truck and no desire for the locals to have them there. The neighbouring farmer always found a fallen tree despite there being no wind to drag it across the road leading to the beach just in time for the summer holidays, to move it was to cross the picket line in the village.

In the churning water, it was no driftwood, it was Hugh. Isabel had waded in up to her hips, powerful and practiced having spent a life on this beach. His face looked white, and the dark blue waves bumped Isabel from one foot to the other. His body was being picked up by the current, the curling chop then submerging his head back with every set of waves. Her calves held firm against the rip, the sand rattling and sucking over her toes being dragged under. She had held out a stick from the beach and with each agonising second, he had coughed and strained his way towards it. She had gotten him ashore, his body blotchy with exhaustion, there was not a sound but his gurgling and no help coming. There was a horrible feeling in the air that something very bad had nearly happened.

When he had caught his breath, she had looked down on him, taking in the form of vomiting sea water onto the hard sand just up from the swell. His body was thin, the definition of his hip bones stuck out and his hands shook with the fright. He rolled onto his back and Isabel remained where she stood, arms crossed, and a disapproving look on her face.

Then he had laughed, great snorts of it which made him cough again so that he rolled back over onto his front, his back shaking with giggles. He hit his hand on the sand and apparently found the whole episode hysterical.

'What is so funny?' Isabel had said angrily and felt the tone of a little girl in there which she regretted later.

He tried to compose himself but began laughing again. 'It's just...' but he never finished.

Isabel, try and she might, could not help the corners of her mouth begin to lift and soon she too was laughing with him. She bent double, her hair falling all around her face as her hands gripped her knees. She cried tears of laughter that mixed with the sea salt still sticky on her cheeks.

That was how they met; she saved his life. Almost daily, he claimed he was fine and could have made it, but both knew if she had not happened to be there, he would have drowned. He had said he was cooling off which is why he went for the swim, but Isabel kindly reminded him of the dank flat day it had been, and he looked unsurprisingly nonplussed and just shrugged.

Their first kiss had come quickly, just like their first near-death experience and their first fit of joint hysterics. They had been walking a few days later, both pretending they had things to do but knowing neither of them wanted to be anywhere else. He had motioned up to the sky and asked what that bird was, she, foolishly, had looked and he had kissed her. At first, she had pulled back, then she had leaned forward as he did, their lips meeting and she remembered them being colder than she would have thought, but wetter. They explored each other with ease, with a familiarity that neither of them understood why they had but were grateful for.

Isabel had been ready to find someone or something different for a while, or so she told her mirror. As was the norm in her novels, she fell hard, fast, and fully into Hugh. He began to linger in her thoughts, there in dreams and even nightmares, the episode on the beach when she saved him went in her mind from being funny to a painful realisation of how close he had been to dying. The feelings were new, complex, and unchartered, the hand on the tiller of control loosening. Despite this, Isabel was determined not to be a tool that could be screwed, and the secret agenda of using him as a weapon for revenge had not been there at the start.

From the beginning she liked that he was the one more trepidatious around her, she knew and liked that she had the control. He was the one who had said 'I love you' after only two weeks, which she had replied she did too, but then spent the night awake knowing that she didn't. It had all taken her slightly aback, but she did not mind these new feelings, they were a good distraction and perhaps if her father knew what she now knew he would finally treat her like an adult.

Hugh had returned to the neighbouring family estate which bordered their land for the summer, so she had time to get what she needed from him. He was here to collect and plant pinecones for three months so as soon as they had met, they knew their romance had a time limit on it. His family were originally from around here, his father had lived here, Hugh though had spent most of his time at his grandparent's farm in Scotland. His father was not a nice man, he had said, but with his father dead he had returned.

Perhaps the nearing end was why the intensity boiled so hot, perhaps that was why she was wary of being hurt or perhaps she thought somewhat fatalistically that was why she had been destined to save him so she could free him from her shackles, and he was purely a mechanism to unlock a secret.

Her father presented an obstacle, though truthfully, she did not know how he would react, it would hurt him but that might shock him out of his coma. He had never failed to be kind, open and encouraging of her living her own life, this was different though. She was all he had, and now for the first time he would be sharing her with another man. Maybe if she told him openly, and honestly, he might tell her about his past? A trade of sorts.

It was getting colder; the sea had turned jet black and the waves were indistinguishable from the sky. She felt Hugh almost sense the goodbye coming, and they both loathed it.

'Until tomorrow?' Hugh said hopefully as he always did.

'I can't tomorrow, it's my father's birthday. We have this silly tradition of cooking together; I'm going to try and get him to the beach.'

'Maybe I could come?'

Isabel went quiet.

Hugh spluttered quickly, 'Just to say happy birthday. You know, introduce myself. Not as your lover...'

Isabel barked a laughed but it was not a normal-sounding laugh, it was trapped in her throat somewhere and it could not decide whether to go up or down.

'I don't know.' Isabel said, going to stand.

'I won't mention us, I promise. I will say I heard it was your birthday and wanted to drop some pinecones so he can plant his own trees, or something.'

Isabel thought about the ridiculous premise, nodded slowly at first then faster. 'That could work.'

'Ok, great.'

'Around eight? He is in the best mood then. Plus, I will have plied him with some wine.'

Hugh smirked, she had expected him to be nervous, or afraid but this news seemed to have swelled him, that made her feel good, he was proving useful.

They stood in unison, both helping each other up with no one taking the definitive lead off the other.

Isabel turned to go and felt Hugh catch her hand. 'One last kiss?'

She blushed. 'Okay,' she said like it was the biggest pain in the world when it wasn't.

They leaned into each other, a much softer more tender kiss than before, now the peak of where it had been leading had subsided. There was a lot in the kiss, thought Isabel, mostly that Hugh was prepared to face her father and so was she.

Isabel went to pull away but just before she stopped kissing him, she opened her eyes. Silhouetted against the light from Houndwood she thought she saw a figure standing on the dunes, it was dark, and she couldn't be sure. She leapt back from Hugh and wiped her mouth, her eyes wide in fear.

Hugh turned but saw nothing.

'Oh, god,' said Isabel.

'Isabel, wait…'

She had gone though, running up the beach.

When she reached the top of the dunes though there was no one there, the house was dark except for a single light in the painting room at the very top.

Chapter 23

Rider

It was William's birthday today, but it felt no different, he wanted no fuss. William was alone walking through the woods behind Houndwood in the dead of night, a man of two times, one day and one night, one in the past and one in the present. In the day he would tend to the farm, try to look after Isabel and be kind. At night though, after he painted and found the voices from the past if he could, and Isabel was asleep, he walked for hours. He never varied his route but kept to the same well-worn footpath that zig-zagged in and out of the woods across the seven bridges through near total darkness. The dogs would follow him, but not close, he let them roam.

Occasionally, he would utter a command if he hadn't heard them for a while and out of the gloom their shapes would come bounding up until they stopped dead at his heels, then they would be off again into the night like hunting wolves.

He had started walking here immediately after they had burnt the effigy of him all those years before, he would have tried anything to find peace. On these walks, he would think less about what he had done in France and saving Guy, and more about how people could act like they did towards him, and what had happened on the cliffs with John Cronk. He questioned the fragility of humans as beings, and the power of their views when they had a cause they believed in even if the cause was wrong. In

France, he thought he had seen that at its worst, but now he was not so sure, not after what had happened. He often asked himself about being a father, about Isabel and what future she had. Lastly, and most commonly he asked far higher powers what decisions he should take and whether the path he walked alone was the right one.

He talked aloud, and he tended to animals he rescued. He had realised that if he spent long enough in nature, particularly at night when the predators were roaming, he would see death and suffering on repeat. Violence was all around, most of it unnoticed as humans slept soundly inside their houses, out here though, in the wild woods behind Houndwood small battles between hunter and hunted took place constantly.

It had begun not long after the burning of the effigy when he had found the buzzard. It had gotten its claw stuck in a wire that had been left from an old phone line, it flapped powerfully but pitifully against the wire, the steel cutting into its talon. He had watched it for a time, meeting its eye before he approached. Hissing, it had gone for him but leaning back he had undone the wire with his fingers, and it had flown off. The next night he had seen it again, this time in one of the clearings pecking through the long grass for mice. It hopped on one leg and their eyes had met again. It chose not to fly off but stood there, its brown chest puffed out and spread its wings before he turned around and walked away.

There had been the fox in the snare, the drowning rabbits in the stream and the sheep with its head caught in the cattle grate. If he was too late and an animal was dead, he would dig a shallow grave and place it in there. He would collect some wildflowers, or if winter a sprig of holly or two and stick them where the animal's head was now lying, he wouldn't say anything out loud over their bodies, just thoughts.

He never spoke of what he did with the dead animals, not even in his diary. Whether he thought it was a way of atonement he had not asked, but deep down it brought him the only joy in his life aside from Isabel.

Tonight, he walked the banks of the small stream, the dogs further away than usual. Beyond the trauma and into the past he tried to remember a time before, what he had been like when had gone to war and was similar in age to Isabel. Memories were disjointed and fractured, his life felt like it only began after France, after the shaming at Dunkirk. Isabel could not stay here forever, as much as he had hoped she might, choices, and hard ones, were coming soon. John Cronk was dead which had lessened the fear of him telling her, but his family might, that cloud of suspicion that had dogged him since they met on the clifftops still lived in whispers. As he walked along the meandering water, he knew the truth would find a way as only truth can.

Despite Isabel not knowing his secrets and him forbidding television and newspapers, he did read the news. When she was asleep, he would unfold the paper the shopkeeper had hidden in its usual spot under the three-cornered rock by the long drive up to Houndwood. Every month he left cash in return for this gesture, every month his heart sunk a little further at the state of the world.

According to the print, the world was speeding up all the time, it was far broader with greater choice than the one he had grown up in. He saw what was happening with Russia, he knew war was on the lips of those who ordered it to happen, not the choice of the men who died at it. That filled him with a particular nagging dread that threatened to spin towards panic, similar only to his fear of the ocean. Both war and water had the ability to swallow people whole and never give second chances.

If war was coming, he was not sure he wanted to be here when it did, he couldn't fathom the idea of it, let alone the thought his daughter might be in danger. If the Cold War reached its zenith again like it had twenty years before, the United Kingdom was right in the middle of the aggressors, an entire island was itself no-man's-land.

These worries plagued him, and he knew they showed, and he tried not to think of what Rhoda his wife would have said. The truth was, she had not said much in their marriage after he had told her he had saved Guy her silence had been impregnable. When he was saving the animals and walking the night, he sometimes thought he saw her between the trees. He never acknowledged her, but more than once he thought he had seen a figure watching him.

Of all the things in William Bremner's life, Isabel was his pinnacle, and the burning of the effigy was his lowest, lower still than the trip back from Dunkirk. It was John Cronk who had started it all up again, and he thought it was Cronk at first who watched him walk at night, not Rhoda.

Cronk was the last person to address him on French soil, he had told him he would find him and reveal the truth. All those years ago when he had been soaking wet, injured, ashamed and in manacles and still it was Cronk's words that penetrated the most and had brought about the worst ramifications.

William had moved to Houndwood as soon as he was released, told he would receive no pay, would never work in any profession holding responsibility and have a criminal record for gross negligence for life, the tarred brush of sympathiser would follow him. His father, showing hints of guilt at sending his son to war had bought the house for him with the last of his savings. His father warned him this act in France would follow him, but William thought he could outrun it. And he had, for the first two years; in the first year after his return, his father died. Grief, strangely, had been a good distraction. William worried his father Jolyon died because of shame, but medically that didn't make sense. In that second blissful year, after a short period of reassessing what life would hold, he had met Rhoda, they had fallen in love and together they established Houndwood, a home, then Cronk had moved into the same village.

A horrible twist of chance had put one of the few people who knew the truth about him within striking distance, even here in the remote countryside where the sheep outnumbered people.

The truth was, as he found out later, Cronk had paid to find out where he lived, his quest for vengeance was unrelenting. Cronk had not taken long to spread the story and he had enjoyed doing it. Before in the village, it had been downcast looks at an outsider who was to them a young man of fighting age and should be over there. Cronk though told it all in the pub night after night to anyone that listened until their mass hatred combined and all the fears and dreads they had about the enemy and losing their sons were perfectly embodied in William's form.

It had been Cronk who had suggested the effigy, stuffed it with hay and even used his own British uniform on the figure. He could still see it now, the blazing body and the crackling fabric until the entire swinging torso dropped into ashes and embers onto the pavement beneath.

Cronk had spoken to Rhoda, whispering in her ear with passionate fury about how William had been responsible for killing his brother Hugh. At first, she stuck by her man, but over time, as the whole village turned, so did she. Cronk was the reason he was alone now, he had pushed Rhoda over the edge, he had brought war back to Britain when William was happy for it to stay in France.

William's anger boiled hot as he walked looking for an animal to save but there were none. The full moon meant even the stupidest creatures did not venture out into the open, like he wished he hadn't that night when he had met Cronk on the cliffs. William had gone looking for him, he wanted to apologise, to try one last time to make it right. It had not turned out like that though, they had come together, grappled and whether William had pushed, or Cronk had slipped, he would never know. Down the body tumbled though, shattering on the rocks below, the waves curling up and over the body. William could still remember the exhaustion of dragging the body back up the rocks, Cronk's limp arms trailing over the slimy rocks, his head making the occasional bump. He had buried him that night and never spoken a word to anyone, not even to his diary.

He walked on, the dogs now lost to sight and his own mind spinning with a mix of questions about Isabel, decisions taken that were wrong and why Cronk had done what he had done, and why Rhoda had too

A sense in him that something dark was coming settled on him, he had not had a feeling so strong since he was on the banks of the Scarpe before he stole the horse all that time ago.

Chapter 24

Lover

James said, 'So my grandfather was in the army?'

'Yes,' his mother Isabel had croaked.

'When?'

'Before the Dunkirk evacuation, he was near Arras.'

James was surprised, they did not seem that type of family. His mother Isabel had one true love, nature, not war, so his grandfather had clearly not passed it on by blood. When she had woken from her doze at the hospital, he had asked her as he had practiced, and she had conceded quite out of the blue.

She had told him her grandfather, William Bremner, had been in the Second World War but things had not worked out. He pushed her on that, and what that meant, but she declined to answer, and that left almost more questions than it answered. She just kept repeating that things had gone wrong, which is why she had not spoken of him, and James sensed a hint of guilt in her tone, a flash of remorse in her pallid face.

'He was so terribly broken by the whole thing,' she had said.

'Wounded?'

'No, far worse. He saved people, but he shouldn't have.'

His mother's eyes flickered, and she slipped into sleep. How had saving people broken him? Why shouldn't he have saved people? Pity for the man and a sense of guilt at his mother's state stopped him from shaking her awake, and he did concede that this was more than he had expected to find out that morning, so he let it be, for the moment.

Before a nurse informed him visiting hours were over, James, being who he was, immediately started researching on his phone. The Commonwealth War Graves site showed lots of William Bremners, but they had all been killed in action in both wars. Googling William Bremner led to nothing no matter how specific he tried to be given what little he knew. He tried all he could, typing, 'Dunkirk, rescue, saved' but nothing showed. How did you find out about someone who was in the army who had never spoken of it, and where it had clearly ended badly?

He could have waited to ask Isabel again, but he was acutely aware there might not be any more from her, she was fading fast, and she could well rebuild her walls that had taken him so long to scale. He was dogged, he had always been and when it came to finding out about his own past, he would be determined to the point of obsession. An idea came to him, and once locked it was impossible to shift, he knew where to go. It was his style to be bold, and now he had this precious nugget of information he wanted to prize open the secrets for good, the story of his own life felt like it was just being written. A small part of his racing mind did realise this was also a perfect distraction from his troubled heart, he had been looking for one. By burying himself in this, perhaps the acute pain of being apart from her would lessen, or at least dull to the point of allowing him to rest for even a night.

James stood stock still, his arms held behind his back, hands clasped like those he was copying all around him. There were drips of water going down the back of his neck, the droplets working their way over the skin and trickling down the inside of his jacket, but he chose to ignore them.

James said nothing but looked around taking in his surroundings, marvelling at the order that things were being done, like it had been done like this since time began. There was an old man opposite in front of the railings who stepped forward a pace from his line of friends and fixed James with a stare, the rain being absorbed by his purple beret. He wore a double-breasted blazer, the entire left side covered in medals. Above the medals was a paper poppy, the raindrops making small dark circles on it and his eyes never left James.

Police horses were trotting down the deserted main road, a road usually throbbing with traffic and men and women were starting to amass in small groups, greeting each other and shaking hands. There was an atmosphere in the air of tension, of expectancy, of respect and the distant rattling of drums.

An old woman had come and stood next to the man in medals opposite, she put a hand over his forearm, and he looked back at her then they both stepped forward carrying a wreath which they laid with precision, two small steps back then a curt nod at the Cenotaph.

James missed nothing, taking in all the soldiers and all the families around him, a lot of them wore the same expression. With an anticipation covering the entire scene, the bugler played and London fell silent, an entire city stopping. Those two minutes seemed to go on for James, they always felt longer, and his mind flashed from past to present. He recalled the images and videos from school of men slipping up muddy trenches, of the places he had visited when he had gone to Albert and Arras the first time to write and had met her. The serendipity made him stumble internally, he had gone to the battlefields to write a story about them, the whole time not realising his own flesh and blood had been in the army and near to where he himself had slept, eaten, walked, and fallen in love. He had been drawn there to write on war, on his family and on what it must have been like but everything he had read to date missed the point, he wanted something else, for others to read an alternative. Actions, tactics, and engagements were the currency of the war story, but what he wanted was to understand the people, were they changed for good? Stories and places matter. That week in Albert, he had passed through the cemeteries, walked with her too, and they spoke of what he wanted to write, and how he would bring something different, something altogether more personal, something about his own blood. She had said her own family were involved but when he had pressed, she had gone quiet, it had been the only time he had come close to upsetting her and he did not want to do that again, so he left it.

When the bugle sounded again and the crowds increased in tension his mind was made up, he stepped forward towards the old man in the beret when people began to disperse.

The man looked up at him. 'Hello,' he said sternly but not cruelly.

'Good morning, a beautiful service.'

The man nodded and inclined that he would rather this stranger got on with it.

'This is an odd question to ask, but I found out my grandfather was in the army recently, early in World War Two. He wasn't killed, and the usual websites don't have anything on him. All I know is it was before Dunkirk and near Arras, he saved people but shouldn't have. Do you know where I might look?'

The man took him in, weighing him up. 'Strange.'

James tilted his head.

The old man thought for a moment. 'And there's no

records?'

'Not that I can find, I don't really know where to go.'

The old man said having checked with his wife, 'I could say try archives, or museums, but they don't usually turn up much, especially not here. There's only one way I would do it.'

James looked expectantly.

'You must go over there,' the man said.

'Go over there?'

'Yes, to Arras, if that's where he was based. The people there still remember, they know far more than books. You will just have to start asking.' The old man turned to leave.

James looked a bit confused. 'Sorry, just to be clear, go over to Arras and just start asking about my grandfather? He was one man.'

'Go to the museums, talk to people, ask around, someone might know. Even if you don't find everything out, you'll know more than you do now.'

James hadn't thought of it like that. 'I guess.'

'Don't guess, just go.'

James watched the old man turn, feeling guilty he hadn't asked the man a single question about himself, but he didn't seem the type that would have minded. If that's what it took, he would go to Arras then and start asking, he had no other option. He would leave soon; it would be a pilgrimage.

The prospect of excitement at an adventure did comfort his questions, long held questions, but it also reminded him of who lived near Arras. She might be near, though she had said she was moving to Paris for good. Had she lied to protect him? To stop his returning? For the first time, he wondered if perhaps fate was involved in what was becoming a seemingly immovable path he was on. What would he say to her? Would he see her at all? No, she would have surely moved on, she would be in Paris, maybe it was just him who still felt the licks of lost love so acutely. Again, more questions began to rumble, but as the old man had said, he was never going to have them answered in London, so to Arras he would go.

Chapter 25

Saviour

The bear emblem was wrapped in a linen handkerchief in her coat pocket, she kept checking it was there. It was cold, so Amélie was walking quickly to keep warm, and she did not want to be late for her meeting. The Place des Héros square was deserted on a Sunday morning, Arras remained asleep, stacks of chairs surrounding folded tables lay cluttered like cairns.

Pigeons circled the bell tower of the town hall high above, darting and weaving like war planes. Crisp yellow light reflected off the golden dome where the Marseilles hung limply. Amélie checked again on the emblem with her fingertips, and she thought briefly on him, what he would have said about her discovery. He might have put it in his novel, he had such big dreams, dreams she would never know now how they turned out.

When her grandmother had recovered from the shock of seeing the metal bear after its discovery, she had told Amélie the name of the owner, Guy Schwarzbär. She said she wanted Amélie to find out what happened to him, and when she had, she would tell her how she knew the German soldier and all that had happened in that summer in 1940.

Until her grandmother knew the fate of Guy though, she would not speak of it, it felt wrong to. It was not for Amélie to ask, merely to do such had been the longing for answers in her grandmother's face. The war was a part of her grandmother, but she had never spoken of her time in it, or the people she had met during such times, and this was Amélie's chance to know.

She had set to work online but to no avail, nothing came back. She had started by typing all that could relate to a bear in the German army but nothing specific narrowed her search. She checked regiments too to see if any had that emblem, it was on the flag of Berlin. She researched the surname next, there were a lot of Schwarzbärs in the German army. Eventually, she found two Guy Schwarzbärs, one who had survived the war, and one who had not. She wrote emails to the Federal Archives in Berlin and then called, but without anything but a name, not even a rank or a number she had heard nothing concrete back, just hold music and a curt 'We need the serial number.' Not everyone wanted to be hounded for information about the past, so it was not as easy as just asking and getting, she hadn't given up though.

A friend of hers at the hospital, Nancy, said there might be a way when Amélie spoke of her quest and its failure to launch and why it was so important to her.

'My father works at The Carrière Wellington,' she had said over a coffee in their break between shifts.

'The tunnels?'

'Yes, New Zealanders were there during the war, he's something of a resource on the war, especially what happened here.'

Amélie had nodded. 'How would he find a German though?'

Nancy smiled. 'Oh, he thinks himself quite the detective. He is always asked when they dig one of them up during the harvest to repatriate them, buried all sorts over the years. He likes it I think, I don't think nation really matters to him, just that they can be at rest.'

'If you think it is worth a try.'

Nancy nodded. 'Of course, he's always loved all that war stuff. Besides, not much better to do and a visit from you might make his day. When will you meet someone?'

Nancy jabbed Amélie's arm, and she smirked. 'Soon. Maybe.' She thought of him and wondered if he had met someone new, thinking what it would be like to see him again, to kiss him.

'You know it would help if you lived in the centre and not in the middle of the woods. I have a room coming up. It's yours if you want it.'

Amélie did want it in a way, would her habits soon be unable to be broken? Maybe doing this for her grandmother would feel like a proper thanks and begin the long process of goodbye, no goodbyes were easy. She would always love the farmhouse, and always go there, but maybe Nancy had a point.

Nancy was typing into her phone between bites of an apple. 'My father says he will meet you. Who are you looking for?'

Amélie said all she knew. 'A German soldier called Guy Schwarzbär, wore a bear emblem, possibly late thirties, fought in Arras in the Second World War. My grandmother said he was famous.' Even she knew it was thin.

Nancy raised her eyebrows. 'That's it?'

Amélie nodded, slightly embarrassed.

'Dad says he will see what he can do. He says to meet him on Sunday morning, you know where the Carrière Wellington is and the citadel?'

'I do.'

'There is a spot beneath it by the barracks, black plaques on the walls, they shot resistance fighters there.'

Amélie said, 'I'll find it'.

Nancy stood, grabbing her tray, and looking serious for a second. 'You know, it doesn't do anything for you clinging on like this to the past.'

'It's not for me,' Amélie said, slightly pointedly.

'No, I know, it's for your granny. She can't expect you to care like she does though. My mother was always plagued by the war until she died.'

'It's good of your dad to help me out.'

'He's like you Amélie, thinks the war is still going on and it matters.'

Amélie bit her lip and pretended to laugh. For people like her grandmother and Nancy's father, maybe in a way it still was.

Walking slower now, Amélie saw Nancy's father at the bottom of the slope by the black square stones pressed into the walls, their names were not all French, they came from all over and were murdered here. The ground was hard underfoot, the edges of the bark chippings holding onto the morning frost. She waved from the top of the hill, and he raised a hand to his temple in greeting. He had one of those faces that looked stern even when happy, his thick eyebrows permanently in a frown.

When she walked up next to him, he had looked away from her and was looking back at the black marble stones.

He said without looking at her, 'Know what these are?'

Amélie looked at the names on the stones, a blend of nationalities and ages inscribed in gold.

'I haven't been here before, but I knew it existed, sir.

'You can call me Andre. These people were shot. Resistance fighters.'

Amélie looked at the names. French, Spanish, Algerian, even a British name or two.

'The man I am looking for was not like that according to my grandmother.'

'I know, I know. But it's important to remember not all the dead are glorious. They were bad times, and people did bad things.'

Amélie nodded, not sure what to do. 'I have some breakfast, Nancy said you liked chouquettes.'

'I do,' Andre said, his face finally warming. 'Let's walk, there is a nice spot beneath the barrack walls.'

They walked in silence, all the time Amélie desperate to know if he knew any more about Guy Schwarzbär. If Andre hadn't found anything she was not sure where to turn next, maybe the farmers would know something. Her grandmother had been so eager to know more about the fate of the German, what would she tell her if she failed?

They sat on a faded bench; the cold abated a bit as they ate the small pastries and Amélie poured out black coffee from her flask.

Andre wiped his mouth with the edge of a napkin, his voice sounded darker almost. 'Do you have the emblem?'

Amélie already had her hand round it and pulled it out in one motion, the white cloth bending back as she handed it over revealing the eyes of the bear. Andre held it gently, unwrapping it from the centre corner by corner, he held it up to the light.

'Fascinating,' he said softly, almost a whisper.

Amélie couldn't hold back anymore. 'Did you find him?'

For the first time he looked directly at her, hazel eyes with flecks of gold round the pupil took her in. It was like he was looking into her, through her, checking her motives maybe, checking she was worthy of both his time and what he had to say.

One corner of his lips lifted. 'I did.'

Amélie felt a surge of relief.

'Strange case,' Andre began.

Amélie noticed the silence all around them at the bottom of this place beneath the barracks. She thought of the cemeteries that surrounded the farmhouse, the emblem on the spit of land and now this meeting with Andre, they all felt connected.

Andre coughed gently into his napkin. 'Guy Schwarzbär was a hell of a soldier, but he did not meet the end he deserved. Few did back then, but he was regarded as one of the finest in the entire German army. He fought in both wars, highly decorated in both too.'

Amélie wondered why this soldier had been at her grandparents' farm.

'He survived the first with honour, made it home and started a family. That's when he got harder to find. I went through the German records from then, and I found him at last. I lost the trail when the second war started. See, he did belong originally to the Berlin-Reinickendorf when war broke out, but he wasn't a Nazi. He was Wehrmacht and all their officers' files were moved. I made some calls, Nancy told you I like this kind of thing?'

Amélie nodded. 'She said you did, yes.'

'We all have stories; all have a past but his was more tragic than most I have read. His family were wiped out after he died, they were sent to a camp to die. Bastards even went after their own, even the families of veterans. Before the second war, it seems when he joined up, like so many of them he wanted to be a soldier again, it was what he knew and what he was good at. Things changed though, and fast. Some of them really had no idea what was coming, I truly believe that. All the officers from the first war, from the Wehrmacht, were reassessed to see if they were suitable, awful,' Andre spat.

He took a pause, rubbing his hands around the emblem again. 'If any of them knew what it was like in the first, people like this Schwarzbär would have seen the problems earlier than most. Maybe he should have led them all and not been shoved around, but I guess there was little he could do. His files, as were other veterans, were moved to the Department of Military Archives, which is why it took some digging. Only the Wehrmacht officers from the first war went to those archives, but he is there. Guy Schwarzbär, the black bear.'

'My grandmother will be delighted.'

Andre thought about this. 'Just remember, not everyone wants to remember the past so much as her.'

Amélie was aware she was watching the lips of Andre taking in every word and memorising it for her grandmother.

She said, 'Did he live?'

Andre held the emblem up to the yellow morning sky. 'No, he didn't. Something happened and that I could not find, but I don't understand why such a man, such a soldier was suddenly turned on. Usually that happened at home after rotation, maybe a comment in a bar in Berlin got you killed, but not at the front. Men said all kinds of things, but he was killed by his own. And you know the funniest thing?'

She shook her head.

'Last record of him was here in Arras. Well, if I am being honest, his last record was just outside of Arras by your grandparents' farm, that's where he was killed. Not a stone's throw from the river and your home.'

Amélie was almost jogging, under her arm she held the bunch of flowers, some wine and the emblem was back in her pocket. Her and Andre had spoken more, but not for long, and he could tell this news needed to be delivered fast. They had promised to meet again after Amélie knew her grandmother's tale. Andre made her swear but insisted the next time the pastries would be on him.

She wasn't sure why but on her walk to the farm she had picked up the flowers from the only open florist at that time on a Sunday, and the wine was more for her and her grandmother in case they needed it. Despite the pressing news she had for her grandmother she had walked due north away from Arras towards Neuville-St-Vaast, there was a German cemetery there from the first war. She knew Schwarzbär wasn't here, no one was from the second war was, but she felt the urge to do something good. Maybe she felt sorry for Schwarzbär and for his family.

She reached the cemetery in just over an hour and a half having said farewell to Andre, leaving him to go to church as he did every Sunday morning. It had turned into a bright day, a hint of warmth behind a blanket of cloud. The German cemetery on the crest of the hill was deserted, as were the roads, it was like she was the only person here in this part of France.

The black crosses were too many to count, hundreds and hundreds of rows ran backwards. Beyond the point, her eye could see they curled on over hillocks, underneath all the men buried in pairs. It was not as bright as the French or British cemeteries she thought, more sombre, almost sadder, there was little hope here amongst the black crucifixes, just a wish from the men there to be occasionally remembered.

Huge oak trees, almost as old as the cemetery judging by their size reached up towards the sky. Their branches did not move, nothing was moving here apart from Amélie, she walked between the first and second row, the names calling out at her.

The flowers with the band of pinecones still tucked under her arm, she stopped at one of the crosses. There was no reason why, she just stopped here at another that looked like all the rest. She knelt and placed the flowers at the foot of the black cross, the petals nestling into the thick green grass. A bird in one of the trees began singing cautiously and she ran a finger along the name on the cross and said the name aloud.

'Otto Zweck, Musketier, June 6th, 1917'.

Chapter 26

Searcher

William had taken the bait and Isabel had been cooking all afternoon as her father painted upstairs. She had been dropping hints all day about her plan to make this a birthday for him to remember. The sweet smell of onions with white wine and butter filled the house, behind it the tang of tarragon vinegar from a homemade béarnaise sauce trying its best to split.

The barbeque on the beach seemed more informal, and a more spontaneous way for them all to meet. Hugh would arrive after William had relaxed, and Isabel had given him wine, she would steer clear of any conversation likely to irk. Together they would try and force the past from William, hoping the introduction of someone new and clearly important to his daughter might jar him into action. At the very least, they would tell him of their courtship, it would prove she was grown up and the fear of losing her was the final play to get him to talk. Speak now or face the consequences.

Isabel was making his favourites, the beef felt sticky in her hands and was covered in oil, rosemary, and garlic. She would braise it in here, charring the skin, then slow cook it on the embers of the fire pit.

'Smells good,' William had said close behind her, Isabel had not heard him enter.

'Sticky slow beef.'

'Must be a big day for someone?'

She was on edge but replied, 'Just be ready for sundowner, okay, Dad?'

He had nodded once before going upstairs to paint, he held a glass filled with white wine which Isabel had insisted he pour early being his birthday. A streak of watercolour in purple had come off his hand and onto the glass which slid down the side through the condensation.

As well as the beef, she had boiled potatoes and wrapped them in foil with knobs of butter poking up from between them. There was asparagus, freshly picked, to char at the last minute before serving on the plates she had packed up into the picnic hamper that was so unused she had to take it outside to wash the dust off.

Hugh was arriving at the beach at just after eight, and it was now five. Leaving the beef to marinade, she walked down to the beach, collecting driftwood on her way to add to the pile Hugh had been making throughout the day without William knowing. He had dug a hole in the sand and layered the edges of the sand with rocks. Over the top he had begun to build a pyramid of faded driftwood which Isabel now added to, forcing the sticks upwards into a wigwam shape. At the foot, she scrunched up some hay, twisting it into little balls ready to light.

The sea was calm, not a wave could be seen, and it looked almost oily black. Visibility was good and she swore that once or twice she saw a tiny boat bobbing miles out nearer to France than Britain.

She was nervous about all that was to unfold in the coming few hours, to find out the truth, perhaps, but also to introduce Hugh to her father. She had no idea which way either would go, but as she sparked the lighter and saw the hay begin to curl and smoke, she closed her eyes and pleaded for it to go her way. The flames curled up like open palms, reaching upwards to the sky.

The fire caught William's face in mid-smile. 'You really didn't have to do all this.'

'It's your birthday,' Isabel said kindly, rubbing the backs of her hands in agitation that she passed off as cold.

The beef had been perfect, it had torn away in their fingers, and they forgot the knives and forks now buried under empty bottles and napkins with red blotches on. Their plates were left discarded next to them on the sand, the wine making them both relaxed as they sat back against the dunes, the long reed grass scratching at Isabel's bare legs.

'Dad?'

William looked across at her, she felt those intense eyes searching for an expression on her face, half covered by the orange glow from the fire. She had topped it up with driftwood a few minutes before and it popped and crackled. The flames were above the pyramid of wood again and it was licking towards the bright moon above.

'We need to talk.'

William shuffled in the sand, one hand on his knee tapping out a slow rhythm like a dripping tap.

'What happened to Mum?'

Isabel was shocked at how quickly she had gotten to the point, maybe it was the wine, or maybe it was because she had been denied this for so long.

William took a long sip of wine, almost draining his glass. 'She died too young.'

Isabel nodded. 'I know Dad, but how?'

'She was not happy. Not for a long time.'

'Because of you?'

A flash of fury crossed his face, made more severe by the firelight. 'Not just me, Isabel. But I was part of it.'

Isabel nodded; she was gripping the wine glass so tightly it might shatter.

She spoke more quietly but deliberately, a hiss from the flames making the end of the sentence come out more violently than she had intended. 'Did she kill herself? Is that why you haven't told me?'

William looked out towards sea, his fury evaporating in his features like the smoke drifting away from the beach.

Eventually, he spoke. 'In a way she did, yes.'

Isabel felt a chill run through her, was it anger? She had guessed this was always the case, that her mother had taken her own life, hearing it from him though, made it real.

Isabel tried to look closer at her father who was still staring towards France. 'Was it me, was it because of me?'

He yelped, or what sounded like it. It was a guttural sound of such sadness that she instinctively reached out a hand for him.

'God, no, Isabel. Not that. It was something I should not have told her, well, that's how it started. But also, there was a man who lived here who made it worse, he pushed us.'

'Who was he?'

'Someone from my past.'

Isabel knew what she wanted to ask, but one step at a time. The last few minutes had been astounding and the pieces, of which there were far more to find, were at least making themselves shown.

Isabel spoke again, topping up her father's wine as she did, hoping to keep him in this exact state. 'What did this man do?'

'He tormented us. And I did nothing. I did not fight back; all the fight was taken from me a long time ago.'

Isabel urged him on. 'What was this man's name?'

William half barked, and she heard his teeth click together. 'John Cronk.'

Isabel repeated the name in her head, she had only heard it once but already she hated him. Now she could ask more, now she could go back in time with her father. She felt now that she knew what had happened to her mother, though there were still swathes missing, he was more susceptible. She felt like she had opened a diary and was only just beginning to read the first few chapters.

She was about to speak, about to ask her father if he had been at war and that was how it started when she heard a crack of wood that had not come from the fire.

Her father stood. 'What was that?'

Isabel froze, Hugh was coming. This was the worst possible time; she had her father where she wanted him. She could feel his window of openness, a window that had been unopened for twenty years begin to shut.

She heard Hugh moving closer, he had stuck to the plan. Isabel had never expected her father to speak like this, with all her heart she wanted Hugh to silently understand, turn around and be gone.

William stood to his full height, his face twisting in the smattered light. 'Whose there?'

Hugh stepped into the orange glow.

'Hugh,' Isabel said without thinking.

Her father looked at her, then back at Hugh, his face changing, the anger was melting away, and in its place was horror.

Hugh just stood there, and Isabel guessed he was sensing his timing could not have been worse.

Hugh said, 'Mr Bremner… I'm…'

'It cannot be,' William said, raising a hand to his mouth and looking pale.

Isabel went to reach out a hand for him. 'Dad?'

She was worried, he was teetering from foot to foot looking ghostly, he was pulling hard at his hair and strands of it were left bunched in his fist.

William stuttered, 'You died, you took her from me. I watched you fall.' He then walked backwards from the fire, his shape and features being swallowed by the black and the dunes.

Isabel was in between Hugh and her father, a hand outstretched to each one. Her father was sliding away, just as the truth of all that had happened was, she would never get this chance again.

Hugh looked baffled. 'What's going on?'

'I don't know, it's Dad. He was telling me about how someone that lived here. He pushed my Mum over the edge. She killed herself, Hugh.'

Hugh went to embrace her, but she pushed him away, the pieces were starting to make themselves clear and she felt sick. As she heard the front door of Houndwood slam in the distance a sickening realisation swept over her. Hugh had said his father was not a nice man, that was why he lived with his grandparents and he only came back here for the first time this summer.

A howl from William cut the air as he climbed the stairs to the painting room, Isabel knew she should go to him.

'Hugh. What's your surname?'

Hugh looked down at his feet. 'Why?'

'Just tell me, for fuck's sake.'

'Cronk.'

Isabel's spirit dropped and she emitted a low breath.

She said softly, 'Was your father John Cronk?'

Hugh nodded.

Isabel started walking backwards like her father had done, looking at the figure of Hugh by the fire he had built with her, the one who had helped her concoct the plan to get her father to talk.

William thought it was John Cronk reborn and not Cronk's estranged son. The son of the man who had made her mother kill herself she was now in love with.

Hugh said, 'Isabel, wait…'

She did not though, she slipped into the black gloom and the dunes, the dogs following, and started to run back towards Houndwood and whatever was left of her father.

Chapter 27

Sufferer

She had finally stopped knocking on his door and gone somewhere else in the house. He had ignored her pleading to talk to him, he did not know what to say, he never knew what to say.

It was dawn, or nearly dawn and a flat light filled the room with an almost indistinguishable yellow that caught the colours of the innumerable canvasses. The sea was booming against the beach and William felt a shiver run through him. He thought back to that crossing, how cold he had been lashed to the side of the prison ship. The fever that had taken hold of him, intermixed with the repeated soakings by the freezing waves, that cold had never truly left him.

It was not that he disliked the idea of his daughter meeting someone, he knew it was bound to happen but of all the people in all the world why did it have to be Cronk's son? He had known she was up to something for the past fortnight, it was not like their life allowed for changes in routine that could go easily unnoticed. He imagined she thought she was being subtle, disappearing every day and night to collect driftwood, how much did two people really need? The pile by the backdoor had kept growing, until even she realised that it must have looked ridiculous, so she had started tossing them into the woods behind the house. When he found them there on his night-time walks trying to save animals, he knew.

He assumed it was a boy, it was only natural. The problem was what that boy Cronk could tell his daughter, of the past and the rumours of murder which were almost the truth. Rhoda, the only woman he had ever loved had killed herself through drink because of Cronk. Despite his pleading, despite his apologies, and despite the birth of a little girl, it had not stopped Rhoda in her quest to numb the shame. If Isabel had questions, how could he give answers without revealing the truth, about what had happened in France and about what had happened on the cliffs that night?

His daughter would have questions, of that he was certain for it was at times of change and new experience she would need him as her only consort, times had never changed so quickly. He had seen them kissing on the beach, but he knew he was outlined against the shaded hillocks and long grasses, and she couldn't be sure he was watching.

It was like Hugh Cronk had been sent to him as a final spite, the burden of his trauma had been so great. He could still feel Rhoda's limp body in his hands, the sand scratching at the skin around his lips as he tried to resuscitate her that morning. He could still taste the alcohol on her breath when he breathed his air into her hopeless lungs. Whether she went to the beach to kill herself or just to walk and be away from Houndwood and who lived there and drank too much, he would never know, but the empty bottles nearby suggested she had sat inebriated, toppled backwards, tried to get up and failed. Her knees were raw and cut suggesting she had struggled when realising she was dying in the surf.

Standing, William walked towards the fireplace in the painting room, he moved the pots and brushes and pulled loose the mantlepiece revealing the diary. He held it in his hands, its edges dog-eared and dark yellow from time. He ruffled its pages, his brow creasing, it was, he told himself, just a diary, it was just a deed from a long time ago.

A flicker of hope, a feeling he was unused to fluttered within him, he had tried his best to be a good father, and maybe his reward would be her confidence. For right now there were two clear choices and consequences ahead, front up and tell her and risk abandonment again, or keep this secret bolted to his heart where it had always lived and risk losing her forever.

He looked at the paintings showing that fateful day on repeat from so long ago and he thought of Guy Schwarzbär and wondered what had happened to him. Had the Black Bear died over there and been spared a life half-lived under the cloud of shame that followed him? He had saved both people and animals, was that enough? Perhaps it was time to say goodbye, goodbye to them all from so long ago, goodbye to the Scarpe and the farmhouse that had sat within his waking moments for over forty years.

'Isabel?'

From the open doorway, his voice sounded hollow and weak, he was lacking conviction in his words.

He would take her to the spot where her mother had died that evening and tell her all. He would build a campfire as she had, he would cook her favourite, this time of mussels in white wine with shallots. He would open a special bottle of wine, the one he had been saving. He would sit there, he William Bremner, and tell her exactly what happened. He would explain about France, about Guy, about the horse, he would tell of the girl and the Frenchman who had saved them, the ones whose lives he had taken, and the British soldiers he was responsible for killing.

What happened here in the village with the burning of the figure, and why he painted the same house repeatedly, what had happened that night on the cliffs and how he was still not sure if Cronk had fallen, or he had pushed him. Lastly, he would tell Isabel why he had remained silent until now. Why, he was ready, if she was, to finally put the past behind them. Why, by doing this, he was in effect giving her the freedom he had never had, a future away from war, secrets and from the past.

'Isabel?' His voice sounded stronger now, he felt his breathing loosen.

There was no answer, just the house and the dogs padding about downstairs, he should have answered her earlier. He felt lifted, dreamlike almost like he was gliding above the staircase as he went down.

'Isabel?' He called again, but nothing was there but the empty house.

Had she gone to the boy? His last chance to save face, when he had seen his great enemy in younger form, and he walked away again.

William stepped quickly along the path, drizzle turning to rain, his cheque shirt was stuck to his body, and he called her name over and over.

The dogs bounded along beside him, sensing his unease at not finding his daughter. They sprinted ahead like lookouts for him, he was waiting to see their heads bow and ears pin back when they saw her. They did not though, all four disappeared over the dunes, their tails cutting through the long reed grasses. William was out of breath and panting, the rain getting heavier making it harder to see. His calling volleyed back at him with the offshore breeze, the tide was whipping away from the beach sucking the churning water back into the sea.

Across that stretch of water, those waves would hit France, the seawater meeting the mouths of hundreds of rivers and tributaries, one of which would be the Scarpe. His eyes began to flick from place to place never settling until he could locate her form.

He walked down to the sea edge to look along the bay. Would she be out on the rocks where they fished during calm seas together? Had she built a shelter for herself like she did that time when they had a particularly bad fight about her drinking a whole bottle of wine before she was twelve? She had vomited all night as he held her hair back and stroked her face.

The wind pushed William forward, edging him towards the sea. He felt tired, not from a bad night's sleep or even a month of bad sleep but like a whole life spent beaten down. He was exhausted, trying to control the fracturing state of a mind one half locked in the past, one in the present.

'Isabel?'

Nothing came back and even the dogs now started to worry, looping around in small circles chasing their tails. They howled as the wind grew, and William felt himself lifted almost by the battering, his shirt clacking against his torso. In the distance, he thought he heard a voice, but he was not sure if it was coming from behind him or from out at sea. He scanned the horizon but could see no boat, no figure in peril. He turned, the wind making him shield his eyes from the whipping sand pummelling his face.

That voice again, ghostly, and far away.

'Isabel? He called again but knew not even the dogs could hear him now. The sand was swirling around him, he put his knuckles to his eyes and rubbed which made it worse.

He scanned along the dunes through the blur, looking for the voice. Two outlines became clearer walking down the dunes towards him. For a moment he thought it was soldiers, coming to take him away, the way their knees moved was like marching as they scaled the dunes.

Then he saw Isabel, and the boy Cronk, and his heart lifted. They had found him; they had not gone, he reached out his arms and she did the same though still so far away, a chasm between them ready to be crossed.

William noticed her hands, becoming defined against the rain and the sand hitting him horizontally. Its familiar edges became clear, its small black shape with faded twine. In her hand, she held his diary, his secret place, his greatest shame.

Something dropped from within him, like a last stone thrown into the sea. He was all there in that diary, a catalogue of sins laid bare. There was no pretence to his words, no build up and no way for him to explain why he had done what he had done, just action and consequence, no chance to tell his version of it. It was not meant to be read but to be spoken aloud by a sorrowful father to a hopeful daughter, it was supposed to happen that night. How would she ever understand? She would leave him just like they all had, just like his wife, just like his soldiers, just like Guy, just like everyone.

'No,' he said softly to the wind, unsure if he made a sound or his mouth just moved.

He turned his back on them both, their shouts now audible and clear. The dogs began to bump his legs as if they knew what he was thinking, one of them tried to block his path but he shoved it aside, its fur wet from the thumping sea. He started walking, his feet soon submerged in the water.

'Dad?' He heard but it sounded far away like it had come from the water, not from behind him.

He carried on, the sea freezing against his knees and thighs. He felt breathless, the cold stabbing at him but weightless too as the current began to pull at him. The voices were further away now but he heard splashing, he just looked straight ahead, his feet leaving the bottom of the sand and the rip pulling at him, beckoning him deeper. The tide had him and he knew then, his choice was made.

Beyond the horizon lay France, the farmhouse and the Scarpe. He was heading back to where it all changed, she would never have understood, she was better off never knowing. Let her make of it what she thought, but without him there it would be easier. He had not been to his own father's funeral; Jolyon had been buried without his son there, this would be the same.

His breath got shorter, and the first full mouthful of salty water made him cough, he felt the water cover his ears, all the time the splashing and the voices and the barking getting weaker from behind. He did not even look back at Houndwood, not at the one place that had offered him something of a sanctuary, he did not look back at Isabel either, for this was his end.

Heading back towards a point in time he had never faced, he felt himself sink, the rip still tugging his chest forward and away from the beach.

William Bremner sunk beneath the water, and a last hope sprung up to be rescued, to be pulled clear. He even reached out a hand above the surface and skyward, but no one came, he was alone out here all the while drifting towards the Scarpe. As his head went under for the last time, his last thought was of Isabel. She was free of his past, free of the shame and could live as she intended to.

Under the cold water and now far out at sea, the last of his breaths was given to the waves. He knew it was his last and peace found him in the black water, a peace he believed that would never have been found any other way.

Chapter 28

Lover

James' mother had decided she wanted to die at home, he understood why, he would too. They had set up her bed in the downstairs front room, the vast bay windows looking down on the dunes, beach, and sea beyond. They had moved her from the hospital the day before knowing she was reaching the end of her road. The faces of the nurses were a giveaway, they didn't quite say it was over, but they had stepped up their efforts in making her comfortable. James saw no difference in her, but the nurses and doctors clearly had a code or could see something he could not as they had agreed, almost too quickly at their plan to ship her home.

The ambulance ride was odd, strange to be in one without sirens and driving away from the place that can save people. It had bumped its way along the tracks and potholes, James continuing his silent vigil over the frail form of Isabel.

'Keep going,' he had said a few times from the front seat, but he wasn't sure if that was to himself or to his mother.

At Houndwood, his mother lay with her eyes closed, reminding him of one of the tombs in Westminster Abbey carved in marble of long-dead Queens. Her hands were crossed over her chest, the veins blue and bulging but not really pumping. Her tiny lungs moved up and down, the only sign of life within her, the skin had discoloured, it looked waxy.

To make the move home, the doctors had upped the morphine, now saturating her blood, she no longer looked or felt like her. There were vague hints, but the house felt cold, a spectre had slipped into her feeble frame and in doing so sucked out all the light.

Houndwood was as he remembered it for the most part. The outside storm battered and fading, the wind always blew here and inside was simple but charmingly so, everything had its place. There was a painting of a farmhouse above the fireplace that had always fascinated him, it had a little girl in the top window dressed in blue. He had always liked it, always felt drawn to it. He had asked his mother about it, but she had brushed it away, her eyes glassy, saying she had bought it in a shop years ago and it meant nothing. 'It was just a house,' she had said.

Houndwood had been his grandfather's home first, but his mother had not said much of his presence, but with what James had found out about him being in the army, he wondered if he had come straight here after the war. Throughout his life, James had been told his grandfather had died in his sleep but when she told the story she was lying, and she always looked lost and away when she lied. Her eyes flicked far out to the sea and the waves breaking on the soft sand. She had never left here, she did not like the modern world and was determined to cling to the past.

'I have always been happier with the world close around me,' she used to say. That was possible here in part, it was cut off and lonely. She said she had all she needed from the beaches and the woods that went on for miles around, besides, she did not want for much.

James had not argued, everyone had their own right to live how they wished. Now though, she would enter the abyss thanks to the cancer churning its way through her, chomping at all the light and the spark that was left and he had more to ask.

'We made it,' he had said only once when she looked comfortable in a nest of pillows.

His mother nodded, a rare flash of conscience came over her, she looked at him.

'I'm sorry,' she croaked.

James looked crestfallen. 'For what?'

'The painting,' she said pointing at the one above the mantlepiece that had always fascinated James. 'You need to go there. It was painted by your grandfather, a farmhouse by the Scarpe.'

James clung onto the words; his fingers worked together. Isabel fell into a deep sleep, and he stood, walking over to the painting, taking it in fully. Looking back towards his sleeping mother he wondered if the little girl was her when she had been younger. He didn't know this house though, and the Scarpe was in France, and of all places by Arras exactly where the old man at the cenotaph had told him to go.

James walked along the beach and thought of that week in Albert with her and for a reason he didn't quite know he longed for her rabidly. She was the first person he had gotten close to, certainly to that degree of love and he wanted to tell her about his grandfather and about the quest he was soon to embark on.

He walked for a while, wondering if he would see her again, in many ways the fact he had decided to go so soon to Arras was not just because of the imminent death of his mother, but to find her.

Tomorrow would see a stream of people coming and going, a blend of healthcare workers, doctors and some of his mother's friends who wanted to say goodbye. They were not really friends, just some of the few souls who had ever encountered Isabel Bremner in sixty years of never leaving one place. She knew the postman as well as anyone but at least he was kind. James was annoyed at the thought of these forthcoming interruptions, why should they get the chance? Nobody got to say goodbye in an accident. He wanted and needed all the time with her, even if to ask her one last time what had happened to his grandfather before he was born, maybe she would realise she was nearly dead and concede.

He looked up at the sea, a desire to cry but no tears coming, he was numb, his actions and thoughts coming from another place. His mother had been ill for what the doctors had said a remarkably short time which did not make anyone feel better, but James would rather have been told straight so he did not dislike them for this.

'Cancer does what it wants,' James had said to the doctor after the diagnosis over a cool coffee from a Styrofoam cup when she was given weeks, not months. For a split second, it made James think he should live every day to the fullest, make a difference, but he soon slipped back to living his usual life, with the added knowledge that his mother was soon to die. The nuggets of information she had given him though had lit a fire, and in a shatteringly dark way, he wondered if he was willing his mother to die quickly not just to ease her suffering, but so he could begin his own quest. The past had never provided answers when he had asked others, so he would have to find them himself. He had been raised alone at Houndwood until he was sent off to school at thirteen in Kent, he became aware, he guessed, at about three or four that half of his parental sphere was missing. He had begun to ask in the only way a child would, his mother said he had left and that, whilst saddening had quelled the inquisitiveness until his teens. Then he had started to ask how, why, where, when and the details of this mysterious figure. His mother had said it was sudden, tragic and she did not want to go back there. His twenties had been fraught with flashes of rage, bitter words and accusations all met with his mother's impenetrable stare and him storming out again. Once she had said a name, 'Hugh', but flat denied it the day after and had never mentioned it again. Windows had smashed, a lot of plates and glasses too, but her ignorance of his pain nullified his rage to hopelessness until they both gave up.

She would not relent; he would not break, if she was the sea, he was the shore. Of all the traits he admired in her, he loathed her stubbornness most of all. In truth, and until now, he had never really investigated the past, just assumed one day his mother would crack and be forced to tell her son the truth. Was that arrogance? Was it not in her interests, was that not the principle role of a parent? To prepare and protect, not confuse, and expose his failings by her blinding inability to give him what he needed most.

As the memories and self-loathing bubbled, James felt the beach whip cold, his silent brooding had reached its zenith and now he just felt overwhelmed that time had run out.

He nodded one last time to the sea, folding into himself like wet playing cards. His throat was raw but not from crying, and Houndwood had taken on a different form with his mother's death so imminent. Even from here, his favourite view of the high house on the hill, any joy for the place felt snuffed out. The lights from the windows now punctuated against the gloom of the evening unnerved him slightly, the shape of the stones by the dunes looked like a giant fist whose fingers he could never unclasp.

Maybe with one last effort, one last pleading to his mother and her knowing that when dead she could not affect the future, she would talk. Whatever it was, and however bad she would not be here to see the fallout.

The flashing blue lights flickered off the sides of the house and there was the rumble of an engine, James began to run.

The dunes pulled at his feet, slowing him enough for the ambulance crew to get there first. James ran up the pathway, peppered each side with lavender bushes filling the air. The door was open, the bland hallway staring back at him, and he could swear the console table was mocking him, its draws and handles like eyes and a mouth upturned.

He rounded the hall, his foot slipping on the rug that read home with the 'h' and 'o' badly faded.

She had died without him here, her only son and child. Her only light was him, and with her death so too had some of his light faded forever.

The ambulance crew tried their best, but it was hopeless, James had put a firm grip on one of their forearms after watching them relentlessly pump his mother's chest for over a minute.

'Stop,' he said once, they looked at him, his veneer slipping, real anger was to the fore, and they conceded.

Then they just stood sentinel-like near him like a headstone, his mother looked sad even in death, no hint of a peaceful sleep crossed her face. He had braced himself for anger, for tears, for anything really but nothing came at all.

He touched her only once, stroking the back of her hand as he felt he might regret it if he did not at some point in the future.

He looked up, a weight beginning to tighten in his chest. Ahead of him, all he could see was the painting above the fireplace looking back at him, it almost mocked him, an alternate version of a house just like this with a happy little girl in the window. Even its colours were the opposite of the greys here, it was bright, light, and sunny. Here all it felt was dark, wet and like it would last forever. The full scale of answers had died with his mother, and so it was up to him, he would leave the moment the funeral was done.

Chapter 29

Saviour

Amélie clasped her hands round the chipped metal coffee mug, it had gone cold. Her grandmother was speaking still, her story one that did not seem possible, the bear emblem had been just the beginning. When she had returned from meeting Andre, her grandmother had been waiting on the steps of the farmhouse and she read Amélie's expression, her light step giving away that she had news.

Amélie called out, the bear held out in front of her, 'Andre found him, Nancy's father found him.'

From the distance, it looked like her grandmother conceded something and Jacques did not come bounding towards Amélie for once, but stayed on the porch, alert under the faded Marseilles.

Amélie was speaking quickly, 'Guy Schwarzbär. He was killed near here.'

Her grandmother nodded like she had been expecting to hear that and had tapped her knuckles twice on the doorframe and held her arms open.

They embraced, both nestling into each other's shoulders.

'My darling. I think we could do with a coffee. But first, can you get the chest from the barn?'

'The chest? What chest?'

'The one you used to hide in.'

Amélie looked put out, she wanted to hear the rest of the story. 'Oh, why do you want it now?'

'Amélie, go and get the chest,' her grandmother said finally.

It was heavier than she remembered, and she had to drag it across the open space caught in the sun between the barn and the house. She clunked it over the doorstep, and it slid more easily on the red-tiled hallway, sweat glistening on her forehead, Amélie gave it a final push into the kitchen.

'This better be the right chest!'

Her grandmother laughed. 'There is only the one. Now, shall we begin?'

They had sat opposite each other around the faded wooden kitchen table, a tapestry of coffee rings and the same placemats with pheasants and partridges on that had been there all Amélie's life. Her grandmother had spent a few minutes staring out of the window over the Scarpe, past the gently blowing willow tree to the treeline beyond, she had stroked Jacques rhythmically on the top of his head.

Amélie had sat patiently, waiting like she used to all those summers nights long ago when her grandmother would read her a bedtime story. Her foot tapped on the floor, occasionally bumping the edge of the huge oak chest which took up what felt like half the floor.

Her grandmother's nightgown had flowers embroidered on it that all came together when she moved, folding in on themselves. The poppies and cornflowers, the daisies and forget-me-nots all overlapped and intertwined.

Her eyes met Amélie's, her features hardened. 'The war, Amélie, was not all what you will have heard or read.'

Amélie was fixated on her grandmother and leaning forward

on her elbows.

'There were terrible things done, unforgivable things. But there were also good things, and strange things. There was a lot of luck, and sadly, what I remember most of all from that time is that there were unlucky people.'

Amélie imagined this idea of luck, she had always viewed war as clinical, decided, and final, that was how it was described in books.

Her grandmother rubbed the back of her hand. 'Sometimes in war, things were done that were not normal. I don't mean the good or the bad of soldiers, more the good and bad of people themselves.'

Amélie leaned back in her chair, her eyes never leaving her grandmother's face as she spoke and she rested a foot on the chest.

'As you know, I was born here in this house, just before the beginning of the Second World War. I was five when the Germans came through here, just five when the British were going back the other way. They had been beaten and they were on the run to Dunkirk, a desperate army. We did not like them much, the British, this was our home, but they were better than what followed. There was an evil, a curse that spread everywhere. I could feel it in the water, in the woods and see it on the faces of the men that came here that May afternoon. Your great-grandfather and great-grandmother lived here during the First World War. Vile things were done, but there was morality then but not in the second, and not that day.'

Amélie did not move, and she barely breathed as her grandmother spoke of the British and German soldiers who had arrived on horseback, the British one had saved the German from an execution and the many men that had died because of it. She told her this is what she meant by war being 'odd'. It was not normal to save the enemy but would be normal in a time when there was no war, it would have been the right thing to do. She said she had always tried to teach Amélie what was right and what was wrong but those in war had to suspend everything they had learnt at a moment's notice; decisions were made on a whim.

Amélie had heard how her great-grandfather had offered them shelter, broken bread with them, knowing the position he was putting them all in, her grandmother could remember that after eating rabbit stew. The consequences of taking these men in had been disastrous but the creeping inevitability that it would end like this had been impossible to avoid and yet they did nothing to stop it.

Amélie watched her grandmothers hard veneer crack for a moment when she spoke of the events that led up to what would form her most poignant memory from childhood. How this one action on a horse by people they did not know had led to another, then another until everything came crumbling down. The chain reaction, she said, especially in war had its own energy and its own devastating force and it had come to bear down upon all of them so quickly.

Amélie felt herself begin to weaken and her throat began to tighten as her grandmother explained more about that day. Why the bear she had found was important and what finding it there meant for the person who had so proudly worn it. It meant he was dead; he never would have taken it off any other way.

After the attack by the Germans, how she was alone in the woods with no home left. An orphan who did not give up, and how she had rebuilt the farmhouse with the help of locals. How a little girl had slept there amongst the ruins and smouldering bricks determined to rebuild her home. She had slept in the chest as it had survived the explosion, the chest had provided her shelter, just as the men in both wars had used it for.

Her grandmother told Amélie with a strong voice how scared she was they would come back, sometimes still she thought she heard the boots. How she could have sworn at night she could hear men with wolves' faces coming down the hills towards her but knowing they did not exist. How she had survived on water from the river and scavenging from the woods until the people of Arras had heard of what had happened to the family in the farmhouse. How those good people, a large group of them of all ages had convinced the Germans they meant no harm and let them pass. They had risked their lives to walk out there with tools, with supplies and with an iron will determined to see if the story of the little girl who had survived and lived alone was true.

The war had raged on for years but that part of France, she had said clutching her breast, had seen its worst fighting of the whole war that year. It moved all over the world, touched every square mile, but did not come back there to Athies forest or to the Scarpe. Yes, the bombers flew over, first all heading to London and then years later back the other way to Berlin. The fear and the suffering were in the air for years, but she had survived. She and the people of Arras had built a shed of sorts to house her and her things, then they had taken turns working on the house. Amélie's grandmother worked like the adults with a saw, hammer, and nails. By the time the war had passed, her grandmother had rebuilt the place brick for brick, stone for stone.

Her grandmother pointed at Amélie's foot which still rested on the chest. 'I nearly burnt that.'

Amélie took her foot off the wooden chest, it had taken on a new life.

'I thought it would remind me too much of what I had lost.

Actually, it started to ensure I never forgot what I survived.'

Amélie stroked the back of her grandmother's hand. 'I'm pleased you kept it.'

'Me too.'

In her teens, she told Amélie she did what her family had always done, tended the land and woods around the farmhouse meeting her grandfather, the son of one of the men who had rebuilt the water tank.

All the while she said the war never left her, but with what she had seen she was not sure she wanted it to. It was so much part of her, burying it away and would have done no good. It was a part of her existence, a huge part, and with it had come so much bad, but also so much good in the end for it had made her strong. She belonged to this place, these woods, and this house. She honoured the memory of her own family by rebuilding this place and living in it just as they would have had the SS battalion not come calling.

Amélie felt this was a good time to pour something stronger. Her grandmother had reached something of a conclusion, and she had returned to staring out of the window and stroking Jacques. A darkness had crossed her face and she looked pained, a chill had come into the room, it was late and even the stars were sleeping behind thin clouds.

'Grandma?'

She looked at Amélie.

'What you did... is amazing. You are so strong. You...'

'The story does not end there, Amélie.' The sharpness in the tone made Amélie stop pouring the cognac.

Her grandmother sighed and Amélie finished pouring out two glasses.

'Sit down,' her grandmother said gently.

Amélie did, making sure to keep her feet away from the chest.

'I thought I was fine, of course I did. Yes, I accepted the war was part of me, those of us who wanted a future all did, but something happened when I was older.'

Amélie held the crystal glass and took a slow sip feeling the liquid warm her.

'You were not even born when it happened, but your mother was. She must have been about your age or close now, very young.'

Amélie felt like the entire of her past was being unlocked for her in front of her eyes, and all thanks to the silver bear she had found.

'Someone came here.'

Amélie nodded.

'It was long after the war, but she was in pain. She too had a connection to this place. I thought I was fine, I really did. I thought I had accepted what happened to my father but...'

She stopped and took a long pull of her glass, Amélie watched her hands shake as they did.

'She came and I threw her out, I could not accept what had happened, I did not hear her reasons. I failed and all the lessons I thought I had learnt were a sham.'

'Grandma, who was this?'

She signed.

'Look, Amélie, I have never asked anything of you. I have been good, yes?'

'The best.' Amélie meant it. She loved her parents, of course, but here was where she felt at peace. The house had always drawn her towards it, as had the woods, the river and the cemeteries running through this part of France.

'Good, because I want you to do something for me.'

'Anything,' Amélie said, sliding the glass aside.

'I need you to find someone for me, I need you to track down a family. I need you to explain what I am about to tell you to them, and why I did what I did. I was wrong, but this must be made right. For the good of us all.'

Amélie nodded.

'You have to swear to me,' her grandmother said locking her hands with Amélie's.

'I do.'

The next morning Amélie walked high up into the woods above the farmhouse looking down on the forest below. She thought of what she had been told, and where she would start. She understood why it mattered, why it all mattered even now despite being eighty years ago.

High above a buzzard circled and screeched once, she would fulfil her grandmother's wish, of course she would. Were there really people alive out there still suffering because of it? According to her grandmother, there might be, and it was up to her to fix this.

She arrived at the farmhouse after her walk, and it felt calm. What had been said the night before had made her the key to resolution, her work as a nurse would have to wait today, she had work to do in Arras, where she would begin.

'Grandma?'

There was no answer back from the house, Amélie wanted to get going. The sooner she began, the sooner she could fulfil the wish of the person she cared about most. Her grandmother had carried the truth alone with her for over thirty-five years.

Amélie climbed the stairs quickly. She knocked on the door

but there was no answer which was unusual.

'Hello?'

The door opened with a creak and her grandmother lay there, propped up with her crossword open on her blanket. Amélie knew she was dead before she felt her.

Lucy Mulot, who had survived the war here, who had rebuilt this house, had slipped peacefully away. Amélie cried but not bitterly, just with sadness, a melancholy sadness that was made sweeter by what they had shared the night before. It was as if handing on the baton of the past and giving Amélie this quest had been her final act, she had known she did not have the strength herself to finish.

Now she had to fulfil the last wish of Lucy, the last wish of someone she had loved more than anyone. Lucy would sleep forever knowing she had demanded the past finally, after all these years, be confronted and healed.

For they were out there still, Amélie knew she held the key to it all, and perhaps, she mused as she picked up the silver bear from the bedside table, that was exactly the way her grandmother Lucy had wanted it all along.

Chapter 30

Searcher

William Bremner was buried by Houndwood in the same plot where the animals he had rescued lay, there too were the dogs long dead, Pippin, Whisky, Ranger, and Foxtrot. It was a bright day at least, a hot day that sounded like the days from France he had described in the diary Isabel had now read more times than she could count.

Isabel watched silently as his dogs had circled the space where he lay underneath as if they were not ready to come to terms with the fact he was not coming back.

Watching her father walk out to sea and drown was an ending to a story she now understood a little more about, she did not know it all though. As angry as she was, she could understand why he had taken his own life when she was lying awake at night staring at the ceiling, trauma had finally won out.

It had been a life that came down to one moment in time that changed everything. A life that had been endured and she his only lasting sense of joy. There was fury yes, at his passing, but disgust at herself and she blamed herself, not just for the death of him but the way she had behaved that led to it. She knew a lot of people did blame themselves after the suicide of someone close, but this was a direct action on her part after finding the diary and the consequences would be everlasting, she had in a sense, she felt, killed them both.

When she, her father and Hugh had been by the fire on the beach and her father had walked away into the dunes, tears in his eyes, she had feared his retribution. The worry of recrimination though did not meet the facts. He had always been kind up until his dying day, but she had not trusted this. She assumed that he would be furious, uncompromising, and vile, she thought he would ban her from seeing Hugh and her enforced isolation would increase.

After calling him over and over and banging the door of the painting room after the fire she had walked away from the house which she blamed for a lot of this. How could she be expected to confide in someone about modern feelings when that person had never left this house? What did he know of love and fear? When she read the diary, a lot more than she gave him credit for.

When she had left Houndwood after trying to rouse him from the panting room, Hugh had been walking too in the distance, but she did not want to see him right now. He had come towards her though, his arms held out in surrender, and they had kissed briefly.

Hugh had run a hand through his hair. 'He won't answer?'

'No. I don't know what he will do.' She had fought back tears of frustration, of loathing and a new sense washed over her looking at Hugh, she was choosing him and not her father. That led to an even darker rising sensation, she wanted to cause hurt to her father. He had kept her locked up here like a prisoner and she wanted to punish him for it, she wanted to break into his stupid painting room and see what he hid in there.

'I'm going back to the house', she said coolly.

Hugh did not argue, he dropped his hands off her shoulders which had gone rigid. She told Hugh to leave her be, she had something to do. He had looked taken aback at the ferocity in her voice and walked away into the dunes and the dunes swallowed him, and Isabel smiled cruelly at her idea.

She had hidden and watched the house, seeing who would crack first. Would she succumb as always and go to him like she had since she was a little girl? He would scold her, shame her for her choice of man and tell her the rest of her life she could never leave.

After an hour, she had heard him calling her name, firstly from the top of the house. Feeling the long grass stab into her stomach, she watched. She had lain flat against the dunes staring and saw him peering out of the top window looking for her.

She heard her name again, calling louder and closer now as he descended the worn stairs covered in paint. Past the familiar table and chairs, past the bench where they used to sit and count dragonflies.

'Isabel.' It sounded hollow now, like it had lost some of its weight, or some of its feeling.

Then he was there, all of him, in the porch where he always greeted her, where he used to call her name and she would run down to supper.

It had started to rain, and he called her name repeatedly and a pull of all the good he had done for her made her want to stand up, to shout, to embrace him and to talk about Hugh and face the consequences. She did not though, she stayed rooted there watching as the worry on his face deepened, and the great sense that he had done something unforgivable began to dawn on his face.

'Isabel.' It was so close and near, she ducked. He passed almost over her, feet scuffing, and for a second, she thought he must see her. She buried herself deeper into the sand and the grasses as his faded shoes went by. He called her name from just above her, shockingly loud and it was in these moments she would think back that she had been given more than one chance to act and to save him.

With his back to her and heading down the dunes she had run to the house and up the stairs. She knew she was breaking the rules, in fact the one ironclad rule he had, and the wind started battering the windows as if to alert her father to what she was doing.

Up the stairs she moved, beyond the second floor, a place she had rarely been. The door to the painting room was open, for the first time in her entire life, she could go in as she pleased, and she stopped just short of the threshold. The black metal key, the handle of which was a knotted tree was in the lock, the string from where he kept it round his neck swaying like he had just released it. Looking again from the window at the top of the house, her father and the dogs were now walking along the beach, just figures in the distance, black spots on the horizon, she could have sworn he looked back and saw her.

The door opened with a long creak and her hands went to her mouth. She knew there were canvasses here, she had seen glimpses throughout her life, but there were hundreds. The walls, the floors and even the ceilings had different-sized paintings on. All of them showed the same farmhouse in different states of destruction. In some, the building was untouched, in some it was on fire and others just a pile of rubble, still smoking and burning. In all of them there was the little girl, always wearing blue, the little blonde girl staring back with a hateful look directly at her.

There were candle stubs and a star in wax on the floor, marks where lines had been traced in charcoal which made a map of somewhere she did not know, in it was a river and a house. Isabel shivered and turned to the door expecting to see him there, she could feel him almost watching but there was nothing but the howl of the wind and the rain on the windowpanes. A long solitary cry from one of the dogs was carried to her from the beaches. She took in the room, all of it, the kaleidoscope of colours and brushstrokes, it was a palace of madness, a palace of secrets.

Isabel only said one word out loud, 'Why?'

Her eyes were torn from the paintings, looking for anything that wasn't the malevolent little girl. Her hand instinctively twitched and on the mantlepiece behind pots and brushes was a black diary, the hollow slot where it had been hidden away for years was exposed.

She knew this diary contained the truth and she edged towards it, her hand outstretched, knowing within its pages held what her father had tried to keep hidden for all these years. One last chance to turn back was not taken, one fleeting doubt that this was a forbidden act. Carried on the wind she heard him bellow her name all the way from the beach, panic in his voice now, like a final warning that she should turn about, leave the room and leave this be.

She flicked the pages back and forth trying to compute the words quickly, he had been a frontline soldier. She had only ever thought him home guard, a coward or something that was not willing to die for his country, all men were involved in that thing somehow but all of them that were there she had assumed would speak of it, especially to their children. He had endured what that must have been like, lived in the crucible of war. Here it was, an entry that was almost a conversational account of his days by Arras and the River Scarpe. Was this where this house was he painted? I suppose it did look French in a way, but didn't all places look like what you wanted them to if you needed them to enough? Her fingers shook as a few blank pages, some slightly charred, others with what looked like blood but might be red paint flicked past. Then she had read the entry about his shame, him strapped to a ship during Dunkirk to be sentenced. Then there was more, an effigy, John Cronk, and the few parts of him left.

What the hell had happened over there? Was this why her mother had killed herself? He saved men, wasn't that a good thing?

A lightness had flooded her just then, she remembered that. Now she knew this, now she had at least part of the secret it would be that much easier to talk to him, she could tell him that whatever had happened, she would understand. Times had changed, the war was gone, and he had done a brave thing, a good thing.

She had set off for the beach at once, the diary in her hand. Coming over the dunes with the diary, the rain now thumping down all around her, drops making mini craters in the soft sand like explosions. Hugh stood up, never able to truly go away and started running next to her and as they ran, she held the diary out in front of her, as it was the first thing, she wanted her father to see, they could cross the bridge together.

He had turned and that look she would never forget, a man had fallen away in a second, his being had slipped into an abyss of disappointment and shame.

Isabel screamed into the wind as she ran, saying it was fine, that she did not blame him and that they could talk. He did not seem to hear though and inexplicably started walking out towards the sea. She had been hysterical, calling for her father to stop but he never looked back, not once. She rammed the diary into her pocket and hit the water running, the sea was churning, and seeing anything was almost impossible with the rain beating her face. He was far out now, the rip had him, the white chops crashing on his back and pummelling him. She watched him drifting out, always out of reach, and knew if she swam out too, she would drown. Hugh caught up with her and pulled at her legs, she thrashed for a bit but then the figure of her father bobbed underwater for longer each time until it did not come up. A final set of waves, seven of them, slammed him down and then he was gone.

Screaming and shaking, Hugh had pulled her from the water, in her pocket she could feel the diary digging into her. If she had left it there, in its natural place, they might have resolved it. She carried it forward to show she understood, but he had seen it differently.

A swift flapped overhead, fighting against the heavy rain and heading out to sea. Its tiny frame was being battered and tossed about by the wind. Isabel looked up at it, a bird she knew would not land until it reached its end. Her father too had floated, never finding land again after what had happened to him in France.

*

The farmhouse had looked exactly like it had in the paintings. Two months had passed since he drowned, and Isabel had only recently decided to come back to where it began and ended for him. The first six weeks had been a blend of numbness, organising the house then reorganising it and trying to convince herself she was in love with Hugh.

Her grief made her passionate, but also unpredictable and

when she and Hugh made love, it was with a ferocity that felt untamed and beyond her years. Her need to feel something, anything but coldness was absolute, and they had lived a nomadic life for those first few weeks, the only conversations were about what they would eat, or words spoken at the height of lust. Her body was now a vessel, those moments of ecstasy its only rest.

Any trace of her father had almost vanished from downstairs, she moved all his things to the shed by the dunes. She had not been upstairs yet and slept on the sofa, she could feel him just beyond that top step with his hand on the banister, his immaculately made bed and the painting room.

Hugh had tried to help how he could, brining newspapers now they were allowed, filling the fridge, and even suggesting they bought a television. She had declined the last offer, it felt too soon.

'I need to go there,' Isabel said one night, entwined in each other's limbs.

'Where?'

'To the farmhouse he painted. To where whatever happened that made him a prisoner, whatever that means.'

Hugh had nodded and stayed silent, gently rubbing the curve of her shoulder. Of all the things they had shared, she loved him for this act the most but was still not in love with him. He had not challenged, had not asked to come and just silently understood she had to and that it would be goodbye forever.

He had gotten up. 'So is that it, then? You just leave?'

'No, Hugh,' Isabel said with venom. 'It's you who leaves, this is my home.'

Little did she know then a part of him would live forever within her and was growing already.

The trip to Arras had been disturbing, memories of her father from her childhood right up to the point of his suicide came at random. Strange sights set her off; a family catching a train at the Gare Du Nord, a field full of barley waiting for its cut, a lone tree standing strong in the flat lands of Northern France.

The local tourist office had given her a map of the area, but it was asking at the tabac off the main square where a kind elderly man behind the counter had shown her the way. She had cut away one of the canvasses from the painting room, one when the house was not destroyed, and rolled it up along with the diary, her newly arrived passport and her overnight bag. The stocky alert looking man had unrolled the canvas and said at once he knew where it was, walking out onto the street with her.

'Up the Rue des Rosati, until you reach the Scarpe. Chemin de Halage will take you right there. Be careful in that forest, it is easy to get lost.'

Isabel noted he looked excited for her as if he could sense her quest was important, but how often did women come into his shop with rolled-up paintings asking for directions?

Remembering she had nowhere to stay she asked if he knew of anywhere.

'Of course,' he had replied. 'You come back here after, and we will get you sorted.'

Isabel had felt sadness creep up on her instantly, as the kindness of the older man reminded her too much of home. She had turned, thanking him over her shoulder and set off before he saw her break.

She was walking faster as she got closer, the river narrowing as she got deeper into the forest. She had no idea what she would say, or who was there, but it did feel right to be doing this. Her father had never returned here, but by doing something he never had felt brighter, more hopeful.

The house was an exact replica of the rolled canvas in her hand, it revealed itself by a clearing that ran down to the river's edge. There was a peace here by the banks of the Scarpe and she felt more confident as she approached the house and with still no idea what to expect, she knocked on the door.

Footsteps came from inside the house, bare feet on a stone floor, they were assured steps.

Isabel looked up as the door opened and took in the figure, a woman of about forty, strong and slim. Her blonde hair was fading to grey, her cheeks and nose scattered with freckles on tanned skin.

The woman spoke. 'Can I help you?'

Isabel realised she should really have worked out at least this introduction. 'I don't know,' she stuttered.

The woman did not move, she stood crossing her arms with a pinched look of approaching annoyance and Isabel felt uneasy, she decided just to start talking and it came out in a rambling string of words.

'My father was here. I think. In the war. He died recently. He never really came to terms with… I have never known what happened. But he was here. He was here, I think?'

'I don't know what you are talking about,' the woman said flatly.

'He was here, he saved Germans.'

The woman remained unmoving, her lips still a tight line but Isabel saw a flash of recognition in the eyes, and something else there too. She could have sworn she saw the grip the woman had of her own crossed arms get tighter.

Isabel continued, now feeling clammy and running out of a reason to keep talking. 'He wrote a diary. He painted this, hundreds of times, I think he felt guilty.'

She unfurled the painting and thrust it towards the woman, in her other hand she held the diary out like an offering.

The woman looked at Isabel, then at the diary and finally at the painting. She uncrossed her arms. 'Wait here,' was all she said, and she walked back into the house. Isabel saw her go into the hallway where a large oak chest was pressed against one wall. The woman had taken on a different tone than Isabel had been expecting, she had assumed that this private quest would end well. The old man in Arras had filled her sails with hope that this would all work out for the good.

The woman opened the chest and looked back at Isabel with distain. The look again, there was hatred in her eyes as if it was narrowing and fast. It was building as the seconds ticked by as she reached into the chest and pulled out a piece of paper, cursing as she did and slamming the lid.

In three long strides she walked back towards Isabel and shoved the paper into her face.

'Is this your father?'

Isabel looked; it was. But not the father she had known, he was much younger here, no older that twenty, on the paper it had his service number and a regimental badge.

Isabel stuttered a few noises, 'Err…'

The woman spat the word out, 'Well?'

Isabel nodded and said quietly, 'Yes…'

'The people that came looking for him had this, and I have kept it all this time waiting to see if anyone would come.'

A last shred of hope fluttered in Isabel and she went to speak.

The woman cut in. 'His own men came looking for him, they were killed. He saved the enemy and this man, your father, was why my father died. Get out of her and never come back.'

Panic was swirling inside Isabel, had her father murdered someone? She went to speak but the woman cut her again.

'I wasn't asking, leave. And don't you or anyone from your family ever come here again.'

With that, she slammed the door and left Isabel standing there as the first tears began to fall. She was distraught, alone and had no idea what to do next, this was why her father had never come, it was why he had buried his secrets.

Crying freely now, her vision blurred, she bundled the diary up inside the canvas and shoved it through the letterbox and she heard those dreaded strides coming back towards the door, but she had already fled towards the woods.

'I will burn it all,' the woman yelled.

She could feel the woman looking at her back, but Isabel would not turn back. She sprinted through the trees along the Scarpe to get back to Houndwood and her isolation.

She wished she had never come, she wished William was not dead and finally, she wished she had never found out her father's secret and knew that it must die with her, whatever the cost.

Chapter 31

Lover

The funeral had been a blur and the church had been almost empty, James spent most of the service looking at the refracting colours in the stained-glass window. He had sat alone in the front pew, the only family Isabel had left, and he remembered Lord of All Hopefulness sounding pitifully sad with only a few quiet voices muttering the words. The vicar was tired, too tired to make a single point of difference between this service and the next and his words were hollow and general. Her coffin was tiny, he knew he would think about that for years.

The eulogy James gave was short, he had struggled to know what to say as he knew so little of her life before he was born. A tiny part of him wanted a long-unknown father to make an appearance but that was not going to happen. The passing of the funeral meant he was closer to leaving for Arras, the city had taken on an oasis-like quality in his mind, he hoped for too much from it.

He could think of no words of his own, so he borrowed some from *Birdsong*. He had read it annually since his mother had recommended it, and he had believed in his naïve youth it held clues as it was the only book she read aloud, she had practically forced it onto him.

He felt himself lurch awake; his face pressed against the

train window. The dream had been getting stronger each night, the same dream on repeat but filling with more detail each time. There were horses, hundreds of them, riding towards him where he was bound to a solitary tree in a field. All of them were emaciated and dying from exhaustion as they laboured on towards him with bleeding and shattered shins.

Someone barked commands at them, a man in all black with a gasmask for a face. He would struggle against the knots that held him but could never be free. Each night this week he had woken up before the horses churned him down, but each night they got closer. As he dreamt now, they were almost on him, he could nearly make out the features of the man that commanded them. Hooves reared up to crush his skull, the underside of their bellies covered in words he couldn't read. The train rattled on, the valleys thinning out on either side revealing the flat lands of the Somme on both sides, huge wind turbines arched upwards, and he could see the towers of Arras in the distance.

Arras was a city of two different hopes for James. The past one he had hoped for his mother to be better, for him to find inspiration for writing and when he departed to see his lost love again despite the finality of her rebuke. The present city he pulled into he hoped to find out about his past, it was all he wanted now. He couldn't help but feel that if he could solve this, the past hopes he had harboured would all be closer to resolution.

Arras was not how he remembered it, it was even more serene and beautiful in structure, its allure though had faded in time and there was a nag of dread in him. He felt, for some unknown reason like he was at home here but there was darkness in this home, one he had come here to clear out.

All those months ago he had started here to begin to write and by chance gone to Albert one afternoon having been told that was where the real impact of what was given here could be most keenly felt. It was not in the cities that the great sacrifice was most acute, but in the quiet places and in the open fields. In Albert, he had met her, she could be close even now. He was certain he wanted to see her but when he pictured the actual moment of taking her in his stomach flipped like only unrequited love can make it do. Here in Arras, so close to where they had spent that week of bliss, he missed her. He had expected his feelings to abate with trying to find out about his grandfather and the death of his mother, but this was her home, and he should have known memories would come quickly and hard.

He took a seat in the Place des Héros and ordered a coffee, the city was at full tilt, rushed and busy with brisk clips of heels on the cobbles. They had walked here, across those same cobbles one evening at the very end of that week, the goodbye looming heavy over them both. He had stopped dead and asked her plainly if she thought they had a future, he believed they did, she did not. The pain was not such a stab now, more of a dull ache that covered him. The words he had feared he could not quite remember exactly, but he did remember how he felt. He did not plead, and he did not break until he was out of her sight and touch.

The clipped waitress took his payment for the coffee, and he unpacked his bag and laid it out on the table. He had a notebook, a list of places to ask about his grandfather written up in neat blue scrawl, and the rolled-up canvas of the farmhouse he had taken from Houndwood.

It was thin, but he had to start. The words of the old man stuck to him, as did his mother pointing towards the painting with her last breath. The answers were here and starting was never going to be easier so he best get on with it.

He began in the tourist office, feeling preposterous unrolling a painting and asking if they knew it. They hid their smirks well but said, no, they did not. His day was spent like that, moving from place to place asking about the house in the painting and hoping each time there would be a flash of recognition, but he had no luck.

James was tired and starting to get the sense this was a colossal waste of time. Eating a ham and cheese baguette as he walked, he saw signs to the Carrière Wellington with a poppy on and thought he would go. He didn't go with the purpose of finding the house from the painting, but he wanted to see a museum, something different than the flat looks of hotel and restaurant owners when he had unfurled the canvas.

Either side of the ramp leading down to the entrance were images of the young men and women who had been here in the First World War, he was always struck by the optimism in their faces, their eyes always ablaze. There were mine carts to the right of the ramp, the ones used during the war, and he reached the glass doors just as rain started to fall.

'Excuse me,' he said to the receptionist who looked up with a smile.

'Hello, the next tour has just left. Sorry, you will have to wait.'

'Oh, I wasn't here for that. Is there anyone here that might know about the Second World War?'

The woman looked a little pained, this being a First World War Museum. 'There's Andre, I'll ask. Can I ask your name?'

'James Bremner.'

She smiled and offered him to look round the gift shop with a hand.

James waited, looking at the images from back then of Arras

wondering if his grandfather had been near any of them. Andre announced himself in front of James with a hand out in greeting. 'Hello, I believe you wanted to know some things?'

James stood taking in the man with golden flecks in his eyes, his kind face.

'Yes…' James stumbled.

'Come, let's go to my office.'

James felt warmed by Andre, maybe because of all the impersonal looks he had gotten with his ridiculous efforts to find the farmhouse by Arras.

When seated Andre said, 'How can I help?'

'My grandfather was here, in the Second World War. I only just found out and my mother died telling me not much more, I am so desperate to know.'

'I'm sorry to hear that,' Andre said genuinely. 'His regiment? Name?'

'William Bremner, I don't know anything else.'

Andre looked sad. 'Ah, that will be very hard to do.'

James felt a wave of disappointment and nearly got up but thought he might as well try one more time. 'I do have this.'

He unfurled the canvas, and for a long moment, there was silence.

Andre looked straight at James intently. 'How did you get this?'

'My grandfather painted it, apparently it's where his life changed.'

'I know this place.' Andre said in a whisper.

James felt his heart click. 'You do?'

'Yes, it is by the banks of the Scarpe, due east. But something worries me.'

'What?

300

'You are the second person in a week to ask me about that time, and this place.'

James let his mouth fall open. 'Someone else is looking?'

'Not exactly,' Andre said. 'A girl I know, she too wanted information. Does the name Guy Schwarzbär mean anything to you?'

'No,' James said.

'And your grandfather was William Bremner?'

'Yes.'

Andre let a gentle smile cross his lips. 'I think its best we get you to this farmhouse, you two will have a lot to talk about.'

James was in such a daze he let himself be led to the man's car which started with a groan. Arras began to whip by and not for a second did he question the man, where he was going or what might be there. He let himself be taken back to the past, and crucially towards its resolution.

Chapter 32

Saviour

My name is Amélie Mulot and this is our story, and it concerns both our families.

My great-grandparents were Pierre and Daphne Mulot and they lived in a farmhouse by the banks of the River Scarpe, where I am writing from, it is my home.

They lived there during the First World War when the armies were on either side of them and they survived by being deep in the forest that surrounded the house. One night, in 1917, they found a wounded British soldier and saved him from the river. He was your great-grandfather, Jolyon Bremner. German men came looking for him, but they hid him in a large oak chest, and he survived. He came back to my great grandparents after the war, thanking them, with your grandfather William when he was a boy.

Your grandfather was William Bremner, and he came to the same place in the Second World War by chance, the same farmhouse as Jolyon, his own father had come to. He arrived on a horse having saved a German soldier, he had tried to do the right thing in a time when so much around him was wrong. My great-grandfather Pierre and his daughter, my grandmother Lucy, were there when they arrived. Your grandfather spent the night there with the German, and they were friends. The next day, British men came looking for your grandfather with a photo of him, but he escaped when the Germans arrived after hiding from them in the same chest. The Germans killed my great-grandfather Pierre and left my grandmother Lucy for dead, destroying our house. Guy the German was murdered, I found this out for myself recently. He was known as the Black Bear.

My grandmother Lucy blamed your grandfather for her father's death, and she kept the photo of William the British search party had, she hated him. She said he had brought war to them, but he did not mean to. He had, after all, been saving a life.

Recently my grandmother asked me to do something, and it was to find you and tell you this story.

In 1984, my grandmother Lucy had a visitor. It was your mother, Isabel. She said she had used her father William's diary to track down the farmhouse. She had a painting of the farmhouse that your grandfather had done. When she arrived, she tried to explain who she was, but my grandmother was not kind. She blamed your family still, she blamed William still. She showed your mother the picture of her father and threw her out saying she never wanted to hear from her again. Your mother left, and we never heard of her again.

I tell you this as Lucy, my grandmother died recently, and she asked me to find you, it was her last wish. She wanted me to explain what happened. She felt a terrible sorrow and guilt for what she had done to your mother. She should not have blamed your mother for what had happened so long ago. She told me that in war, normal things do not happen and what your grandfather did, despite leading to the death of her father, was the right thing to do.

I have so much more to tell you, you will have so many questions. I have the diary of William Bremner; it is next to me.

I have always felt tied to this part of France, to what

happened here, maybe you will too.

Amélie reread the letter which laid out the facts, but she still had no idea who to send it to or where to send it. There were thousands of Bremners and despite hours of trawling nothing could narrow down her search.

To distract herself from the futility she busied herself making the house look as immaculate as it could, though in truth that had never been its charm. As she went from room to room, she let her hand run over the cool walls, the house Pierre and Daphne had saved Jolyon in, the house that was destroyed and then rebuilt brick for brick by her grandmother. Some places deserve to be stayed at forever and continue beyond the bounds of a mortal life for they are homes.

She opened the chest and checked it again. In it, she kept the letters, the diary, the bear emblem, the painting, and the photo of William. Trauma had wound its way into these people, secrets had broken them, and it was a time to forgive, but she did not know how where else to look.

She went downstairs to make lunch and heard the noise of an engine coming along the track by the Scarpe. She peered out of the window but did not know the car through the flashes in the trees.

She heard the doors of the car open and close and quick steps make their way to the front doorstep.

She opened the door and her heart fell, standing there was James, the man she had loved in Albert and Arras, the man she had said goodbye to and thought she would never see again.

She whispered, 'James?'

He too looked in utter shock at what he was seeing, he had clearly not planned on seeing her.

'Amélie,' he said.

She looked down at his hands and he held the painting, the edge of the canvas blowing in the breeze.

'Oh, my god...' she said.

'My grandfather was William Bremner...' he stuttered.

'My darling,' she said and crossed the gap between them and pulled him into her embrace.

Chapter 33

Lover

James washed his face in the large white basin in the bathroom at the end of the hall. Gripping the edges he took in his reflection, gaunt from the past few weeks. Freezing water dripped off his chin and made small plops on the porcelain. He wondered if his great-grandfather and grandfather had used this basin, he hoped they had, he could feel them here all around.

He picked up his shoulder bag and made his way to the stairs. He let his hand run along the wall, cool to the touch.

Amélie looked up from the doorway of the farmhouse below, her hand wrapped around the faded timber. 'Are you ready?'

James nodded. 'Yes,' he said, and his feet marched towards the light from the doorway.

They began the walk through the woods, away from the farmhouse with the square lawn in the bright sun, their arms full of all they would need. The white farmhouse was left behind, as was the swaying willow and the gentle Scarpe.

Wildflowers laced their walk, the stems of poppies, daisies and cornflowers bending back when they passed but not breaking. Through the sycamores they strolled, Amélie looking back occasionally, a smile of contentment on her lips. A song thrush was singing from the top of a high tree, but James could not see it. Jacques, her dog, skittered back and forth across the path sending reams of butterflies into the air which surrounded them.

James thought of Amélie as they walked, he thought of chance and both their families and of fate. She was the one who had been driving the past to be confronted at last, without her there would not have been resolution.

They continued walking up an incline, past a bend of the Scarpe in the deep woods until they came to the clearing. It was strange, a place where trees had refused to grow even though they should have. Nothing had changed here for years thought James, not since that day when the rider had left on his horse. Not since the day his grandfather had saved someone and was then judged for eternity.

Silence was surrounding them in the space, nothing else watched this illuminated scene, this scene that had wanted to be played out for a long time. He felt like finally he was coming home, and he knew Amélie would be feeling the same.

James and Amélie stood side by side, his arms still wrapped around the shoulder bag. Amélie was first to approach the hole in the ground they had dug the night before, in the hole was the chest from the farmhouse.

She unfurled her hands, took one step forward on the grass and laid the bear emblem that had begun the resolution inside the chest. James walked up next and silently he dropped in his grandfather's diary which landed on the chest with a thump. Amélie dropped in the photograph of William, held for all this time in the chest where Lucy had kept her secrets.

James looked at the photo of William, the eyes of the then young man in the photo looked back, eyes that had no idea of what was coming. They continued like this, one after the other.

James laid an urn in the hole, his mother Isabel's ashes pressed up next to the picture of her father William. Amélie put the ashes of Lucy down, next to the silver bear emblem of Guy. Lastly, both Amélie and James put the painting from Houndwood of the farmhouse, over the top covering everything else in shade. The little girl in paint from the paintings looked back at them.

James wanted to say something, but nothing felt right. In that clearing, the same clearing where William had made his choice, they buried it all and James began to fill the hole. His arms worked methodically as the black soil covered the painting first, then the silver bear was obscured until all was underneath them. He smoothed the soil over back and forth with the spade, Amélie looking on unmoving.

James walked with the spade in one hand, Amélie's hand in the other as they began the walk back towards the house.

'I think we will start with a soup,' Amélie said, James laughed.

The laughter filled the wood as they fervently began talking about how many courses they would eat and what their favourite foods were. It felt like he was just beginning to understand, and he did not want to leave this place ever again.

James looked at Amélie, straight at her eyes, and wondered if she was feeling the same as he was. Of course, it was to be here; of course, it was to be now given what they had just done. For in all the world, and all that had happened in it, there was nowhere else it could be. Nowhere else they or the ones before would want it to be than here. The burying finally of a secret past would give way to new hope.

'I love you,' James said.

'I love you too,' Amélie replied.

As new love blossomed on the banks of the Scarpe, James thought that of all the millions of bodies from both sides laying under the earth in France and Belgium, not even one would pull them back towards the past with clawing fingers. Instead, in the cavernous darkness and soil beneath their feet where the chest now lay, these men would shake hands with each other and embrace at last.

With open palms and greetings, they would whisper of lasting peace and hail the resolution of this fracture in time at last. As they kissed, James could feel the sun on his face unlike the ones who were left there and remained there still, they had long forgotten the feeling of a sunrise on their skin. Those things were for the living, and for the living these buried souls had given it all, including his own ancestors. They had done this for the people who walked above them, for those who remained after it was over and for love. They asked for little, but that at the going down of the sun James and Amélie would always remember them.

THE END